Moore

—

Castle of the Wolf

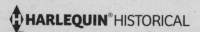
HARLEQUIN® HISTORICAL

Recycling programs
for this product may
not exist in your area.

ISBN-13: 978-0-373-29794-8

CASTLE OF THE WOLF

Copyright © 2014 by Margaret Wilkins

Printed in U.S.A.

HARLEQUIN®
™ www.Harlequin.com

***Rheged took hold of her shoulders
and regarded her sternly.***

"There is doing a thing because honor demands it and there is being honorable to the point of madness. I tell you, it's madness to marry Blane."

"Do you truly want me to marry Sir Algar, Rheged? Would that make you happy?"

"God, no!" he said through clenched teeth. "I would rather—"

"What?" she pressed, his manner and the look in his eyes making her heart race and her breathing quicken. "What would you rather?"

"What I want does not matter, except that I would see you safe. You won't be safe with Blane."

"I would be safe with Sir Algar, though," she replied, "and cherished, no doubt, as well as given whatever material goods my heart desires."

"Yes," he snapped.

"That would be enough, do you think? And I should be content to be the substitute for the woman he loved and lost?"

"No!" he said, his voice husky with need as he tugged her into his embrace and captured her lips with his own.

* * *

Castle of the Wolf
Harlequin® Historical #1194—July 2014

With thanks to Nalini Akolekar,
everyone at Spencerhill and my writing buddies
for their advice and support, and to my family
for all the love and laughter.

MARGARET MOORE

Award-winning author Margaret Moore actually began her career at the age of eight, when she and a friend concocted stories featuring a lovely, spirited damsel and a handsome, misunderstood thief. Years later and unknowingly pursuing her destiny, Margaret graduated with distinction from the University of Toronto with a bachelor of arts degree in English literature.

Margaret began writing while a stay-at-home mom and sold her first historical romance to Harlequin® Historical in 1991. Since then she's written over forty historical romance novels and novellas for Harlequin® and Avon Books, as well as a young adult historical romance for HarperCollins Children's Books. Her books have been published in France, Italy, Germany, Great Britain, Australia, Belgium, Switzerland, Brazil, Korea, Japan, Sweden, the Netherlands, Russia, Poland and India.

Margaret currently lives in Toronto with her husband and two cats. She also has a cottage on the north shore of Lake Erie in an area that first became home to her great-great-grandfather.

Chapter One

ENGLAND, 1214

The flickering light of the torches and beeswax candles in the great hall of Castle DeLac threw huge, moving shadows on the tapestries depicting hunts and battles hanging on the walls. A fire blazed in the long central hearth, warming the chill of the September evening. On either side of the hearth, knights and their ladies sat at the tables closest to the dais where Lord DeLac, his daughter and the most important guests dined on a sumptuous repast. Hounds wandered among the tables, snatching at the bits of food that fell into the rushes covering the flagstone floor, while a weak-chinned minstrel, dressed in blue, warbled a ballad about a knight on a quest to save his lost love.

Sir Rheged of Cwm Bron didn't care about the feast, or the ballad, or the other guests. Let the nobles spend the rest of the evening amusing themselves with banter and drink, dancing and music. He would rather be well rested for the tournament on the morrow.

As he rose from his place, straightened his black tunic and started for the door leading to the courtyard, he ran another measuring gaze over the knights who would compete with him in the melee, a contest more like a true battle than a tilt in the lists. Some of them, like the excited young fellow dressed in bright green velvet, or the old knight already dozing over his wine, could be dismissed outright, being either too young to have much experience or too old to move swiftly. Others had clearly come more to enjoy the feasting and entertainment than to win the prize.

Rheged glanced again at the prize resting on the high table, a golden box embossed with jewels. That was what had brought him here, as well as ransoms for arms and horses from those he defeated in the melee. Since he was a veteran of many a real battle, a melee was more familiar to him and, he thought, a better test of true skill.

While he strode down the side of the hall, whispers of the other knights and nobles followed him like the wake after a ship at sea.

"Isn't that the Wolf of Wales?" one drunken Norman nobleman slurred.

"By God, it is!" another muttered.

A woman's voice rose above the minstrel's music. "Why doesn't he cut his hair? He looks like a savage."

"My dear, he's Welsh," another nobleman drawled in equally disdainful reply. "They're all savages."

There had been a time those whispers and insults would have infuriated Rheged. Now it didn't matter what they thought of him, as long as he triumphed on the field. And if his long hair made them think he would fight with all the fierce determination of a savage, all the better.

Taking a deep breath of the fresher air, Rheged stepped into the courtyard and looked up at the cloudless sky. The full moon lit the yard as bright as day, yet there was a hint of rain on the wind. It would be a light rain, though. Likely not enough to postpone the melee.

A door opened in a long, low building to his left that was attached to the hall, sending a shaft of golden light onto the cobblestones. The noise of clattering wooden bowls, chopping and the querulous demands and orders of a harried cook told him it was the kitchen.

A slender, shapely woman in a dark gown and lighter over-tunic, carrying a large basket, slipped out of the kitchen into the courtyard. As she nudged the door shut with her hip, he recognized Lady Thomasina, his host's niece, dressed in nunlike garments, her long, dark braid swishing down her back like a living thing. When he was introduced to her upon his arrival, he'd been impressed by the bright intelligence gleaming in her brown eyes. Later it became clear that she ran the well-regulated household, and not Lord DeLac's beautiful daughter, Mavis, although that should have been her responsibility.

Rheged watched as Lady Thomasina crossed the yard to the wicket gate, the smaller door inside the huge double gate. Despite her relatively plain attire, Lady Thomasina had a dignity and a graceful carriage that no garment, however costly and well made, could enhance.

She spoke a few quiet words to the guards, who opened the wicket. Then he heard voices that sent his mind racing back to his childhood—the grateful words of the poor and hungry who would receive the remains of the feast.

"Thank you, my lady!"

"Bless you, my lady!"

"God save you, my lady."

"There is plenty for all," she replied. "Come closer, Bob, and take something for your mother, too."

There would be no bruises or black eyes from scrambling for the scraps, or bellies left empty here, tonight.

Once upon a time, he had been among the beggars waiting at a lord's gate with starving bellies and desperate hope, anxious to get even the smallest bit of bread or meat. The person doling out the remains—always a servant, never a lady—had usually dumped the food on the ground like so much refuse and looked at those eagerly awaiting as if they were worth even less.

Leaning back against the wall, his eyes closed, he tried to shove the memories of those days of hunger and need, loneliness and desperation into the back of his mind. Those days were long ago. He was a knight now, with an estate of his own. It wasn't a rich one yet, but in time, with effort—

"Sir Rheged?"

He opened his eyes to find Lady Thomasina standing in front of him, her empty basket over her arm, her brown eyes regarding him with grave concern. "Are you ill?"

He straightened. "I am never ill. I merely sought a breath of fresh air."

She frowned, her eyebrows drawing together, her full lips turning down at the corners. "You found the hall too smoky or stuffy?"

"No more than most."

"Nevertheless I shall see that more of the shutters in the hall are open." She turned as if she intended to do that at once, and by herself.

"I wouldn't bother. It's going to rain soon," he said as she started to hurry away.

She turned back. "Rain? The sky is clear."

"I can smell it on the breeze—not a heavy rain," he hastened to assure her. "Likely just a shower during the night, so not enough to delay the melee."

"I hope not."

"I'm fairly certain." He gave her a little smile. "I grew up where it rains much of the time, Lady Thomasina."

"Tamsin," she said quickly, then just as swiftly added, "That's easier to say than Thomasina."

"Tamsin," he quietly repeated.

She moved the basket in front of her. "I've heard you called the Wolf of Wales," she said, repeating the nickname given to him after his first tournament triumphs. "Are you so ferocious?"

"Not as much as I was in my youth."

"You're hardly an old man!"

"Older than some here."

"Surely that gives you the benefit of experience, as well as reputation."

"Experience, aye, and a reputation has its purpose, although it's not for fame I fight. Unlike your uncle, I'm not a wealthy man."

The moment he mentioned his poverty, he regretted it. She didn't need to know about that, nor did he want her to think the less of him because of it.

"You fight for money." To his relief, she didn't sound appalled or disgusted. She sounded…matter-of-fact. Practical. Accepting.

"I fight to earn more, to keep what I have."

She nodded slowly, thoughtfully. "Life gives us all battles to fight and we all try to win as best we can. I wish I could fight some of mine with sword or mace."

"I don't doubt you'd be a worthy foe. The clever ones are always hardest to beat."

"You flatter me, my lord," she replied, and not in the usual manner of coy young ladies.

She said it warily, with suspicion, as if she doubted his sincerity or perhaps wasn't used to receiving compliments.

Thinking it might indeed be the latter, he made a sweeping gesture encompassing the inner courtyard. "It takes intelligence to run a household the size of Lord DeLac's, and there's no doubt in my mind that falls to you. You do it well, my lady. I've never experienced such comfortable accommodations or fine food."

"My uncle is known for the excellence of his feasts."

"Because of you, I'm sure."

He saw the hint of a shy smile. Charmed and encouraged, he went on. "You have grace and beauty, too. That is a rare combination, my lady." He ventured closer. "I think you are a rare woman."

She stepped back and to his dismay, that suspicious wariness returned. "Are you trying to seduce me, sir, with empty words of praise?"

"I meant what I said."

"And now I suppose you will tell me that Mavis is lacking compared to me."

"She looks lovely, I grant you," he replied, "yet I do find her lacking. She seems almost a shadow compared to you. I doubt she concerns herself with anything more than what gown she'll wear or who she'll dance with at the feast."

The lady bristled. "Mavis is not such a ninny and you earn only my enmity if you criticize her."

Clearly Tamsin loved her cousin dear and he hurried to mend his mistake. "I admit I have little knowledge of her, and no doubt she's a fine young woman, but vitality and passion shine in your bright eyes, my lady, and you cannot deny that you take responsibility for the running of the household of DeLac."

His words didn't have the effect he desired, which was to make her linger.

"Thank you for your compliments, sir knight," she said, starting toward the kitchen once more. "If you'll excuse me, I do have many responsibilities, so I give you good night."

"Sleep well, my lady," he murmured in his low, deep voice as she hurried away.

It was all Tamsin could do not to break into a run as she left the unexpectedly grateful and flattering Wolf of Wales.

To think of such a man saying such things to her—plain, dutiful, responsible Tamsin! He was by far the most intriguing man she'd ever met, and not just because he was handsome, although he was the sort of man to make a woman look twice in spite of his stern visage. His eyebrows were like black lines above watchful dark eyes, and the planes of his cheeks and line of his jaw were as sharp as a sword blade. He dressed plainly in black, with no jewelry or other adornment.

He needed no adornment to draw attention to his powerful warrior's body, and as for those watchful and intense dark eyes, he obviously saw things others did not, like the way she worked—something no other guest had ever mentioned.

But she was no fool, just as she was no beauty, no matter what he said, and it would surely be wrong to let him know how much his words had affected her.

As she entered the kitchen to return her empty basket, Armond, the burly, aproned cook, red-faced after the efforts of overseeing the feast, looked about to have an attack of apoplexy. The shoulders of the exhausted scullery maids slumped from the effort of scrubbing the numerous pots and roasting pans and forks. Middle-aged Vila, who had been at Castle DeLac since her youth, wiped down the long table still snowed with flour that stood in the middle of the chamber. Baldur, the bottler, was excitedly urging Meg and Becky, two of the younger maidservants, to hurry as they headed to the door leading to the hall with more wine.

She followed the maidservants back to the even noisier hall. She swiftly surveyed the chamber and then the high table, where her uncle was comfortably settled with a goblet of wine in his hand. Mavis, attired as befit a wealthy lord's daughter in a gown of scarlet with embroidered trim of delicate blue and yellow flowers, sat with downcast eyes beside him, looking every inch the demure maiden. Later, though, when they were alone, she would have plenty to say about the guests. She could be surprisingly insightful and was very clever in her way, something Sir Rheged, like most men, failed to appreciate. The other nobles at the high table—lords of importance in the south and London—appeared to be well sated with food and drink. Old Lord Russford at the far end was already dozing in his chair.

Below the dais, several of the younger knights were moving about the hall, speaking to friends and being introduced to the other guests. Some of the mothers with daughters of a marriageable age looked like peddlers hawking their wares at any fair in the land.

Sir Jocelyn was Mavis's favorite of the moment, a handsome young man of good family, and the most expensively attired in emerald-green and bright blue velvet. He reminded Tamsin more of a peacock than a warrior, and he was also one of the most boring young men Tamsin had ever met. She was quite sure Mavis would tire of him soon, too.

Sir Robert of Tammerly was even younger, and not nearly so good-looking, but Tamsin didn't doubt that someday he would be a knight to be reckoned with. He seemed wary and watchful, and ate and drank sparingly, like Sir Rheged. He was very unlike the Welshman in one way, though. Like the others, Sir Robert wore his hair cut around his head as if a bowl had been placed upon it, which only seemed to emphasize the roundness of his face.

Although he was clean-shaven, Sir Rheged wore his dark hair—thick and wavy enough to make a woman weep with envy—to his shoulders.

She shouldn't be thinking about the one man who'd already left the feast, no matter how flattered she'd been by his compliments.

She spotted Denly, one of the stronger servants, and told him it was time to start taking down the tables to clear a space for dancing. Then she went to have a few words with Gordon, the minstrel, about the music for dancing. She herself never danced, but Mavis enjoyed it.

First, though, she would speak to Sally, a young and particularly voluptuous and overly friendly maidservant lingering at the table where the youthful squires sat.

Until tonight, Tamsin had never understood how any woman could give up the precious possession of her virginity to any man outside of marriage. There was too much to lose, even for a poor girl.

Now, though, when she remembered Sir Rheged's dark eyes and voice, she was beginning to understand how a woman could succumb to desire regardless of the consequences. His compliments had sounded so sincere, she could believe his words were not mere meaningless flattery, but spoken from the heart.

Even so, any pleasure to be gained from giving in to lust surely outweighed the risks, especially for a high-born lady. Bearing a child out of wedlock meant telling the world you were too weak to resist your base impulses. You were a woman of shame.

As for Sally, one of these days, she would probably come to Tamsin in tears to say she was with child and what should she do? Tamsin would see that some kind of dowry was provided and perhaps even a husband, if there was another servant willing to marry her.

But she would deal with that when and if it became necessary. In the meantime… "Sally!"

The maidservant with thick auburn hair and a pert

little nose knew better than to linger any longer and came forward at once. "Yes, my lady?"

"Open the shutters near the doors. The hall is getting too stuffy."

"Yes, my lady," Sally replied, doing as she was bid and wisely ignoring the obvious disappointment of the young squires.

Tamsin couldn't imagine Sir Rheged ever being like those boys, giddy with excitement over the tournament, trying their best to look manly and to persuade a woman into their bed.

Determined, even ruthless she could see, but never giddy. As for looking manly, she could well believe Sir Rheged had always exuded that sense of contained and controlled power. And when it came to persuading a woman into bed, she wouldn't be surprised to learn women had fought for the privilege.

"Careful, my lady!" Denly called out as she nearly stepped into the path of the servants moving the top of one of the trestle tables out of the way.

"I shall be," she murmured, and not just when it came to moving the tables. She would avoid Sir Rheged of Cwm Bron for the rest of his visit there. It would surely be better—and safer that way.

Late the next morning, after the light rain had let up just as Sir Rheged had said it would and the melee had commenced in the far field, Tamsin headed to the kitchen to check the progress of the preparations for the feast that would mark the end of the tournament. As she neared the entrance, she heard the unmistakable sound of a slap, followed by Armond's loud and angry voice. "Get up, you lazy, good-for-nothing scamp!"

Tamsin hurried into the kitchen to see Ben, the little spit boy, holding his cheek, while Armond towered over him, hands on beefy hips. "Armond!" she snapped. "You know I don't allow any servant to strike another!"

Armond glowered at her. "He was asleep when he has work to do."

"You know my rules," she replied. "If you don't wish to obey them, you may leave the castle."

"Your uncle—"

"Has no desire to be involved in any household disputes, as anyone will tell you. The servants are in my charge, and I keep the peace, not him. If you don't wish to obey my rules, there are plenty of other cooks who would be glad to have your place. Hit Ben or any other servant again, and—"

Mavis burst into the kitchen like a howling gale. "They're coming back! The melee's over already!" She came to a startled halt. "Oh, am I interrupting?"

Tamsin turned her back on the cook. "Are you sure?"

"Charlie says one of the guards saw their armor gleaming in the sunlight down the road, so they're coming back. Let's go to the wall walk and see if we can tell who won," Mavis eagerly suggested.

Despite Tamsin's avid curiosity, that news could wait. The returning knights would be wanting hot water and fresh linen to wash before the feast. Their ladies, too.

"I can't," Tamsin replied before she addressed some of the younger maidservants. "Sally, Meg and Becky, start taking hot water to the guest apartments."

The young women sighed in unison, for carrying the buckets of hot water was no easy task.

"Oh, please come with me, Tamsin!" Mavis pleaded. "There's time and you don't have to stand near the edge of the walk. They haven't reached the outer gate yet."

"Charlie could be wrong, then. Meg, Sally, Becky, don't bother with the water until we're sure, or it might be too cold when they return."

"That's right—we should be sure," Mavis agreed. "Let's go look ourselves."

"All right, but I can only spare a little time," she said, giving in. After all, she should know if the melee was really over or not, and she could stand against the tower, where she couldn't see over the edge to the ground below. She had always been afraid of being up high, even as a little child and before her parents died of the ague, and for no reason that she could name, other than a vivid notion of what a fall from a great height could do.

Together the two young women hurried through the corridor connecting the kitchen to the great hall.

Mavis wore a finely woven green gown with a lighter green overtunic, her blond hair gleaming like molten gold; Tamsin wore a plainer gown of doe-brown wool, the sleeves rolled back to expose slender arms and capable hands, her long braid of chestnut hair swinging down her back as always.

Skirting the excited and ever-present hounds, they walked quickly through the hall bustling with servants spreading clean linen on the tables and sprinkling fresh rosemary and fleabane on the rush-covered floors. Denly was putting new torches in the sconces. Despite their hurry, Tamsin made sure all was as it should be as she passed the servants, giving each a nod and a smile.

"I'm sure Sir Jocelyn won the day," Mavis said as they climbed the steps to the wall walk near the main gate in the inner curtain wall. "He was the squire of Sir William of Kent."

"He's very comely, too."

"That isn't why I think he'll win," Mavis replied with a toss of her head. "He's very well trained."

That might be, but he's no Sir Rheged, Tamsin thought, then silently chastised herself for even thinking of the Welsh knight.

As they came out onto the wall walk, Mavis went right to the edge, while Tamsin stood with her back against the solid tower. Her cousin pointed at the group of men in the area between the outer and inner curtain walls. Some were mounted, a few walked and behind them came the squires, carrying shields and swords. "There they are. I can't tell who won. Can you?"

Tamsin scanned the group. No man was obviously triumphant. No one rode out in front, or with a victor's proud poise.

She spotted Sir Jocelyn, his shoulders slumped. Clearly not the winner. Her gaze passed over a few others, until she saw Sir Rheged. He was among the last, walking and leading his huge black warhorse, while another man leaned on him for support.

She shouldn't feel so disappointed…but she did.

"There's the Wolf of Wales," Mavis said as if she'd been reading Tamsin's mind, "and that's young Sir Robert of Tammerly limping beside him."

"Sir Robert must not be badly hurt, or he would still

be in the tent or in a cart," Tamsin noted. She'd arranged for a physician and servants to be at the site of the melee to take care of anyone injured on the field.

"Sir Rheged doesn't look so fierce now, does he?"

"No," Tamsin agreed.

"Since he's lost, perhaps he'll cut his hair. He's clearly not another Samson."

"I wouldn't venture to suggest it."

"I wouldn't venture to talk to him at all if I could help it," Mavis said with a sniff and a second toss of her head. "I've never seen a grimmer fellow. I think he's barely said three words since he arrived."

He'd said more than three words to Tamsin, but she didn't bother to correct her cousin. She didn't want to tell Mavis about that meeting in the courtyard, or what he'd said, or how he'd looked at her, or how she'd felt when he looked at her, and she certainly wasn't going to tell Mavis about that dream.

"And he's so poor, he has absolutely no influence at court. Indeed, he's only got the small estate he has because Sir Algar gave it to him."

"Who is Sir Algar? I don't recall the name."

"A minor lord who used to be friendly with my father. He hasn't come here in years, though. The poor old man must be in his dotage, Father says. I gather the estate he gave Sir Rheged is barely enough to maintain a household and the fortress is a ruin. He can't have more than a few soldiers and servants. And he's called it Coom Bron, whatever that means in Welsh."

"Lady Thomasina!"

They both turned as Charlie came rushing up the steps. The lad was small for his age, lively and inquisitive, and often delivered messages about the castle. A lock of his brown hair was forever flopping over his forehead and a score of freckles spanned his wide nose. "Lord DeLac wants to see you, my lady," he panted, addressing Tamsin. "Right away, he says."

Chapter Two

Tamsin and Mavis exchanged glances. Such a summons on such a day could herald nothing good.

"Did you hear who won, Charlie?" Mavis asked as Tamsin started down the well-worn steps, wondering what she'd forgotten or failed to anticipate.

"Aye, my lady. The Welshman with the hair to his shoulders."

Tamsin came to an abrupt halt and glanced back at the grinning boy. "Sir Rheged?"

"Are you *quite* sure?" Mavis demanded.

"Aye, my lady. I had it from Wilf at the gate, who got it from the messenger himself come from the field. The Welshman bested seven knights and should be getting a pretty penny in exchange for their arms and horses, as well as the prize, o' course."

Tamsin started on her way again, smiling to herself as she headed to her uncle's solar. She stopped smiling when she reached the solar and knocked on the heavy oaken door, entering when she heard her uncle's gruff response.

A quick glance assured her nothing was amiss with the chamber itself. The brazier full of coals glowed brightly, the tapestries were clean and free of dust and the rushes on the floor newly laid. The candles, not lit during the day, had been well trimmed, and the cloth shutter over the arched window was open just enough to allow a bit of fresh air, but not enough to create a draft.

Her middle-aged, gray-haired, bearded uncle sat behind the large table polished with beeswax. As always he was richly dressed in a long tunic of finely woven brown wool, with an embossed belt around his ample middle and a long necklace of heavy silver links. Several rings adorned his thick fingers. The golden box studded with gemstones, which was to be awarded to the tournament champion at the feast that night, rested near his elbow.

Uncle Simon tapped the parchment open before him with his stubby index finger. She should have been relieved he didn't immediately launch into a litany of complaints, but there was something about the look in his beady gray eyes that did nothing to lessen her trepidation.

"You're finally going to pay me back for all I've spent on you," he announced.

Tamsin's heart leapt to her throat. She was a lady, a nobleman's daughter, and couldn't repay him in coin. There was but one way, and his next words confirmed her dread.

"I need an ally in the north, so you're going to marry Sir Blane of Dunborough. He's on his way for the wedding and should be here in a fortnight."

It was no more than she had expected, and yet—

a fortnight! Less than a month. And who was Sir Blane of Dunborough?

The answer crashed into her mind like a boulder. He was the bone-thin, lecherous old man who'd visited Castle Delac in the spring. She'd noticed at once how he'd stared at Mavis like an aged satyr, and she'd immediately declared that her cousin was feeling unwell. One look at Sir Blane, and Mavis had just as swiftly agreed, taking to her bed for the duration of his visit. Tamsin had kept the younger maidservants away from him, too, and even the oldest ones, who'd had years of experience fending off unwanted advances, had complained that he was the worst they'd ever encountered.

All the women of the household had breathed a sigh of relief when he had gone, and Tamsin had considered herself fortunate that she'd managed to avoid getting within ten feet of the man.

And now to hear she was supposed to *marry* him!

Her uncle's eyebrows lowered as he frowned. "Well? Where is your gratitude?"

She'd rather spend her days in the coldest, most barren, inhospitable convent in Scotland than marry Blane of Dunborough, but it surely wouldn't be wise to say so. "You surprised me, Uncle. I didn't think I would ever marry."

"What, you expected to live off my generosity forever?"

As if he hadn't begrudged every coin he'd ever spent on her and cast up her dependence on him nearly every day since she arrived after her parents had died when she was ten years old. "I had hoped I could remain in Castle DeLac."

"Living off my largess for life?"

There was no hope for it. "Or perhaps a convent…?"

"Good God, girl! It costs money to have the sisters take you. You expect me to pay for that?"

"Do you not have to provide a dowry to Sir Blane?"

Glaring, her uncle hoisted himself to his feet. "How dare you question me, you insolent wench? Where is your gratitude for everything I've done for you? Your thanks that I've found a man willing to take you?"

A man? Sir Rheged was a man. Sir Blane was more like a degenerate fiend in human form. "While I'm grateful for all you've done for me, Uncle—"

"You don't sound grateful! You sound just like your damned mother!"

The words stung like a slap. Nevertheless she had to object. If she didn't speak now, she might regret it for the rest of her life. "Sir Blane—"

"Is willing to take you off my hands and that's the end of it," her uncle said as he threw himself back into his chair. "Say nothing of this to anyone until I announce it tomorrow. I won't have you taking the attention from my feast, or the champion, even if he is an ignorant, uncouth Welshman. Now go."

She stayed where she was. "Uncle, I appreciate that I came to you with little, and you were forced to take me in. But to marry me off to a man like Sir Blane! Can you really be so callous and cruel, and to your own flesh and blood?"

Her uncle's face was like iron, hard and cold. "If you refuse him, another must take your place, so either you marry him or Mavis must, for the agreement has been signed and the alliance made. But if it must be Mavis, know that I'll marry you off to the first man I can find willing to take you for nothing except an alliance with me."

Her choice was no choice. Making the merry, gentle, loving Mavis wed Sir Blane would be like murdering her. "I shall abide by your agreement, Uncle, and marry Sir Blane."

"On your word of honor?"

She wanted to scream. She wanted to refuse. She wanted to tell him exactly what she thought of him. "On my word of honor," she replied, each word like a nail in her coffin.

"Aren't you going to thank me?"

She looked at the man who had never loved her, despite all her efforts, until his gaze faltered.

Then she turned and left him.

Feet planted, hands clasped behind his back, his stoic gaze sweeping over the hall and those gathered there, Rheged stood on the dais in the great hall of Castle DeLac waiting to receive his prize. The torches and expensive candles gracing the tables burned brightly, illuminating not just his prize and the fine clothes of the guests, but their less-than-pleased expressions, too.

His arms ached and he would have a few bruises come the morning, but what was that, or the angry and jealous looks from those who'd lost, if he received that valuable golden box?

Even so, it was not the box that commanded his attention most. It was Tamsin, far down the hall, half-hidden behind one of the stone pillars. Something had obviously upset or disturbed her. Gone was the lively gleam in her eye and the proud carriage of her head. The vitality that had seemed to shine forth from her slender frame and made him think she would be capable of managing everything and anything in a lord's castle, even to commanding the garrison if need be, had apparently ebbed away.

Lord DeLac came toward him holding out the prize.

Perhaps she was ill, but if so, surely she wouldn't be in the hall at all.

"A fine effort, Sir Rheged," Lord DeLac said, his smile more than half a smirk.

Maybe she was simply exhausted. It must be tiring running a large household, and there were many guests here, and feasts to arrange, with dishes of fish, fowl like swans and geese, roasted beef, pork and mutton, pottages of peas and leeks, greens and fresh bread.

"I congratulate you on your victory," Lord DeLac continued. "Not unexpected, given your reputation, but well earned nonetheless."

"Thank you, my lord," Rheged replied, not troubling to feign a smile in response when Lord DeLac placed the box in his hands. It was heavy, and the jewels decorating it glinted in the torchlight, reminding him of the reason he had come to Castle DeLac—to win this prize and collect ransoms. He needed money to begin the necessary repairs to his own fortress, to rise another step on the long ladder to power and prosperity.

He had not come here to concern himself with the troubles of Lord DeLac's niece.

An elderly priest appeared from the corner near the dais to bless the meal. When he finished, it was as if he'd given a signal for everyone to speak at once while they took their seats. Rheged had been given the place of honor to the right of Lord DeLac. Lady Mavis sat on Lord DeLac's left, with Lord Rossford beside her, while the elderly, stone-deaf Lady Rossford, who had been nursing a chill and seemingly recovered, sat on Rheged's right. He couldn't have conversed with her even if he'd wanted to, and her pursed lips made it clear she had no desire to speak with him, either.

The rest of the noble guests were seated below the dais, enjoying excellent wine as they talked and laughed, chatted and whispered and gossiped, while a bevy of servants tended to them under the ever-watchful eye of Tamsin, who barely touched her meal. Looking for all the world like a defeated general, she sat at a table that was far enough away to seem an insult.

Something truly serious must have happened to affect her so.

"Well, Sir Rheged, do you not agree?" Lord DeLac asked, his tone slightly impatient as the last course of baked fruit and pastries came to an end.

"I beg your pardon, my lord? The magnificence of your feast has taken all my attention," Rheged replied, thinking it probably wouldn't be wise to voice his concern about the man's niece now, or ever.

Wiping his greasy fingers on a pristine linen napkin, Lord DeLac smiled. "I said, between the prize I offered and the ransoms for horses and arms you captured in the melee, you have become somewhat richer today."

"The prize is a most magnificent and generous one, my lord, and your hospitality is without parallel."

Lord DeLac leaned back in his chair and reached for the silver goblet in front of him, the jewels in his

rings twinkling like the thick chain around his neck.
"I understand you have no wife. You must be thinking
of taking a bride soon."

"Thinking of it," Rheged agreed, certain the man
was not about to propose Rheged marry his daughter, or his niece. A man like DeLac would surely seek
rich, influential husbands for his female relatives, not
a Welshman who'd been born of peasant parents and
fought his way to a knighthood and an estate.

Nevertheless, to flatter the lady and his host, he be-
stowed a smile on Lady Mavis. Yes, most men would
call her beautiful, with her fair hair and milky white
skin, fine features and swanlike neck, but she was not
the one Rheged had thought about before falling asleep
last night, or when he was waiting for the melee to
begin. Nor, he was sure, would she be in his thoughts
tonight.

Nor would he be in hers, for although Lady Mavis
blushed, she did not return his smile.

On the other hand, that wasn't so surprising. Women
always responded to him in one of two ways: either with
fear and trepidation, avoiding his gaze like Lady Mavis;
or with avid interest and not a little indication that they
would enjoy sharing his bed. Sometimes he took one of
them up on their offer. Most times he did not.

Only Tamsin had ever seemed concerned about his
well-being and comfort.

He glanced down the hall again, in time to see Tamsin rise and leave her place. He continued to watch her
as she threaded her way through the hall to the corridor
that led to the kitchen, no doubt to give the remains of
this feast to the poor tonight, as well.

He was a knight sworn to protect women. She was definitely troubled or upset. Surely it was his duty to help her if he could.

"If you'll excuse me, my lord," he said, pushing back his chair, "I must retire. I have a long journey tomorrow and the opponents I faced today sorely tested my mettle. I am too weary to remain for the no doubt excellent entertainment."

"Oh, surely you can't be that tired!" Lord DeLac protested. "A fine young fellow like you! Why, in my youth, I could fight all day and drink all night and be none the worse for it come the dawn."

"Alas, my lord, I am not so fine a fellow then, for rest I must. I give you good night, and you, too, my lady," he added with a polite bow in Lady Mavis's direction.

The young woman nodded in acknowledgment but said nothing.

"If you must, then, Sir Rheged," Lord DeLac grudgingly and ungraciously replied.

Rheged rose and picked up his prize. Once more ignoring the hushed comments and disdainful whispers of the Norman nobles, he took the box to the chamber that he'd been assigned. It was on the second level of a long building near the hall and had a small window with wooden shutters opening about ten feet above the ground below. The chamber itself contained a bed, a washstand and a stool, as well as his armor on a stand and the two leather pouches he used to carry his belongings. There was nowhere to hide his precious prize, or so it seemed, but he had hoped to win and so had planned a way to conceal it. Moving swiftly, he put the box in the smaller pouch and removed the drawstring from the larger one, which he tied to the first. Then, getting up on the stool, he tied the free end of the string around the iron bracket for the shutter and lowered the bag out the window until it rested about a foot from the opening. He moved the stool away from the window and stepped back.

From where he stood, he couldn't see the knot or string, and even if someone outside noticed the pouch in the dark, it would be too high to grab.

Satisfied, he left the chamber and went back to the yard. He found a deep doorway in one of the many storehouses, a spot where he could watch the entrance to the kitchen without being seen from the wall walk or by any of the guards. It was also out of sight of the servants hurrying to and fro from the hall or kitchen or stables, and he ducked inside to wait.

The night was cool, with more than a hint of autumn in the air, and he wrapped his arms around himself for warmth. Not that he was as cold as most of those wealthy, coddled nobles would be in a similar situation. He'd spent more nights than he could remember sleeping beneath the open sky, or huddled in a doorway or an alley, often with no blanket or cloak to cover himself.

Nevertheless he was glad he didn't have to wait long before Tamsin emerged from the noisy kitchen carrying her basket. Once again he watched her cross the yard with that grace that could not be taught and deliver the remains of the food from the feast to the poor folk gathered there. He heard their thanks, recognized their heartfelt gratitude and admired her gentle voice as she assured them they were welcome to all they could take.

But he still saw defeat in her slumped shoulders,

and despair was evident in her slow steps back to the kitchen.

When she drew abreast of where he waited, he softly called her name.

She gasped and stepped back, clutching the basket before her as if it were a shield. "What are you doing here, Sir Rheged? What do you want?"

He spread his hands wide and kept his voice calm and gentle, as he would to a frightened horse. "I only seek to know if all is well with you."

"I am quite well, my lord."

"You're lying."

"How dare you, sir!" she demanded in a whisper. "How dare you make such an accusation?"

At least he'd brought the vibrant light back into her eyes. "Because something has happened to disturb you. You sat like a stone through the whole feast."

Her steadfast gaze wavered, but only for a moment. "I wasn't aware I was being studied with such scrutiny."

"What's happened to upset you so?"

"Nothing that need concern you. I give you congratulations on your victory today, Sir Rheged, and I wish you Godspeed on your journey home," she said before turning to go.

He put his hand on her arm to keep her there. "My lady, please. It's a knight's duty to help and protect women. If there's anything—"

"Let me go!" she ordered. "Or I'll call out the guard! Don't think I won't!"

Fearing she would indeed summon the guards who would likely take a dim view of anything a Welshman did even if he was the tournament champion, Rheged silenced her the first way that came to mind.

He kissed her.

Kissed her full on the lips. Kissed her first with hard, swift desperation and then, when she didn't pull away, with increasing need and desire. Kissed her as he had never kissed another woman, because until this day he had only ever wanted a woman for physical release.

Until tonight.

Until now, when he held Tamsin of DeLac in his arms and surrendered to the powerful, passionate yearning she aroused within him, as no other woman ever had.

Chapter Three

Tamsin knew she should protest. Make him stop. Push him away. Call out the guards if need be. Sir Rheged shouldn't be kissing her or embracing her in the dark. She was a lady. She was betrothed.

Yet she did not resist him. She could not. Not when his kiss gentled and his strong arms slid around her as if offering her sanctuary.

Not even when her empty basket fell unheeded to the ground and he opened the door behind him. Nor when he drew her into the deeper darkness of the woolshed, where the bundles of bound wool seemed to breathe, expanding and contracting with soft sighs as his lips found hers again.

But this thrilling embrace couldn't last, because duty must be done, or more than she would suffer.

Putting her hands on his broad chest, she pushed him back. "Stop," she commanded, her voice low and firm despite the quiver she couldn't suppress. "Please. Stop."

"As you wish, if that is what you truly wish," he replied, his deep voice like a caress in the darkness.

No, she didn't wish it, but it must and would be so. "It is."

"Very well. But something upset you before this, something that happened during the melee, or shortly afterward. Please, for my sake if not your own, tell me, and if I can help you, allow me that honor."

To have such a man make such an offer, at such a time, in such a voice, was nearly enough to make her weep. But she must not weaken. Nevertheless she simply couldn't resist the urge to tell him what her uncle had done. "I have been betrothed."

"Ah," he sighed, and she could read nothing in that long exhalation. "To whom?"

"Sir Blane of Dunborough."

He started as if she'd struck him. "That dog?"

His response, so like a curse, nearly undid her. But she had to be strong and do what she must, for Mavis's sake—and this man could not know her true feelings. After all, in spite of what he'd said about his knightly duty, there was nothing he could do. "I must remind you that you're speaking of a nobleman, and my betrothed."

"I know who he is," Rheged replied. "I know *what* he is. Does your uncle? Do you?"

"I've met him."

"And yet you'd marry him?"

"I've agreed to do so," she answered, although now more than ever she wished she'd refused.

"You said you've met Blane. Where?"

"Here, if it is any of your business—and it's not," she tartly replied.

"Not at his castle, then. You haven't witnessed him in his own household. You haven't seen how terrified his men and servants are of him—and with good cause. He's the most vicious, evil tyrant I've ever met. His sons, save one, are little better, and even Roland quarrels constantly with his brothers. Marry Blane, and you'll be walking into a nest of vipers at war with one another."

God help her if this was so, and yet she must marry Blane. For Mavis's sake she had agreed, and for Mavis's sake, she must honor that pledge.

And she had to get away from Rheged. It would do her no good to listen to him. To be with him. To let him take her in his arms and kiss her passionately.

Yet it seemed as if every muscle in her body had turned to water when she tried to leave. She stumbled and nearly fell, until Rheged took hold of her shoulders to steady her.

"I don't say these things to frighten you, my lady," he said quietly, his gaze searching her face. "I seek only to warn you, and protect you. If you don't believe what I've said about Blane, ask some of the other guests here about him. Even if they praise him, they will hesitate before they do, and the hesitation will tell you that I speak the truth." His grip on her shoulders tightened. "Whatever your uncle's promised, you have the right to refuse. You cannot, by law, be compelled to marry."

It was like a lifeline thrown to a drowning man who must choose whether to grab it himself or save the one member of his family who loved him, and whom he loved. "Let go of me, Sir Rheged."

He did, and then he moved to block the door. "I have talked with priests on my travels about many things.

I'm as certain as I'm standing here that you cannot be forced to marry against your will."

She believed him, yet if he spoke the truth about Blane, it was more important than ever that she marry him and not Mavis.

So Tamsin straightened her shoulders and faced Rheged squarely. "Did I say I was being forced? Did I complain the betrothal was without my consent? I am going to marry a rich man who will give me rank and a comfortable household, as well as create an alliance between my uncle and a man with power in the north."

"Who will make your life a living hell."

"What woman doesn't want a household of her own, and children?" she demanded, even though the thought of sharing Sir Blane's bed filled her with revulsion. "As for his alleged evil, surely you don't think my uncle would—"

"I think your uncle will do whatever he thinks will serve his own ends," Rheged interrupted, "and I think you, my lady, know that far better than I."

"So you say. But I may find it easier to please a husband than my uncle."

"How? In his bed? I doubt any woman has ever found happiness in Blane's bed."

"No doubt you would prefer I shared yours." She forced away the sudden, vivid image of being in Rheged's bed, in his arms, loving him and being loved, just like her dream last night. "You have a novel method of seduction, I grant you, but it will not succeed with me."

"I don't want to seduce you," he retorted. "I truly wish to help you, my lady."

His sincerely spoken words made it all the more difficult for her to pretend to be unmoved by his offer, and his compassion. "I thank you for your concern, sir knight," she said, keeping her voice cold, "but my fate is my own business, so unless you intend to keep me here against my will, you will let me go."

"Leave, then," he replied just as coldly, obviously angry now and with good cause—or so she thought until she put her hand on the latch.

"If you change your mind," he said with a quiet, yet firm, resolve, "send word to Cwm Bron and I will come for you and take you anywhere you choose to go, whether to a friend, or a relative's or a convent—any place of sanctuary where your uncle cannot compel you to marry against your will."

She had to get away from him before her resolve crumbled into dust, yet she couldn't go without some sign that she was grateful. That she appreciated and cherished his offer. That she respected and admired him for more than his looks and prowess in battle, although those were considerable.

That she wished they had met in different circumstances. That she was free, or even a maidservant, so that she could go to his bed and no one would bat an eye.

So she kissed him. Passionately. Letting loose, for just this once, all the need and longing and desire he aroused within her.

Just this once, so she would have something to remember in the long, lonely nights to come.

Just this once, since she would surely find nothing but selfish, demanding lust in Sir Blane's bed.

Just this once, to show Rheged how she truly felt

while he held her close and his lips moved over hers
with slow, sure deliberation and desire.

Nevertheless this kiss must end, lest she forget who
and what she was, and what she had to do to keep her
cousin safe. She simply could not succumb to the need
and yearning coursing through her, no matter how much
she wished he would lay her on the fleece and have his
pleasure of her, for loving him would surely give her
pleasure, too.

She forced herself to release him. "We will forget
we ever met here, Sir Rheged, and we will not speak
of my marriage again. Now I give you good night, sir,
and may you have a safe journey home."

"My lady—"

"Enough, Sir Rheged!" she cried, her words a plea as
much as an order. "I will marry Sir Blane and you will
go back to Cwm Bron." Her voice softened. "It must be
so, my lord, so please respect my wishes."

"Very well, my lady, and may you have more joy in
your marriage than I foresee," he replied as she opened
the door and left him.

Rheged slumped back against one of the large bundles of wool. Perhaps the lady truly did want to marry
a man of wealth and position, regardless of who he was,
or the toll it might take upon her. If so, that was her decision, and he must abide by it.

He went to open the door, then hesitated. He was sure
no one had been watching when he called out her name
and that they'd been shielded from prying eyes in the
doorway. Nevertheless it might be wise to wait awhile
yet before leaving. It could mean trouble for them both

if people knew they'd been together in the woolshed, even for a short time.

With a sigh, he climbed onto the bundles of fleece and stretched out, sinking down with a sigh. He would to stay here a little longer. After all, he'd wanted to save her from her troubles, not add to them.

Still holding the empty basket, Tamsin hurried to the small chamber she shared with Mavis. She didn't go back to the kitchen where a host of servants would be, nor to the hall, where all the lords and ladies were still gathered. She ran like a frightened deer or a mouse that sees a cat to the servants' stairs leading to the family chambers. Mercifully she met no one as she dashed up the steps, or in the corridor. Panting, she opened the door—to find her cousin already there, her hands clasped anxiously before her and a worried expression on her lovely face.

Mavis's expression grew even more concerned as she looked from Tamsin's startled visage to the empty basket in her hands.

"I was so busy thinking about all the guests leaving tomorrow, I forgot to return this," Tamsin said, her excuse sounding weak even to herself.

"I was right—you *are* ill!" Mavis cried, taking the basket from Tamsin and setting it down on the nearby dressing table. "You're flushed and out of breath and you were so quiet during the feast."

"I'm not usually a font of merriment," Tamsin noted with a smile only slightly forced as she picked up a taper and stuck it in the brazier warming the small chamber.

"I was thinking about the cook. Armond may have to go. He struck the spit boy, and if he does it again—"

"I've seen you worried about household matters many times before, and this is different," Mavis interrupted, blocking Tamsin's way as she went to light the rushlight beside Mavis's curtained bed. Tamsin's smaller cot was on the other side of the room, along with the small chest that held her few gowns. Mavis's clothes were in a much larger chest at the foot of her bed.

Mavis put her hand on Tamsin's forehead before she could move away. "No fever, thank God, but you must go to bed and rest before you fall seriously ill. I'll do what must be done tomorrow while you rest—and I won't allow you to refuse!" she added, looking as stern as it was possible for cheerful, pretty Mavis to look.

Which was not nearly so stern as Sir Rheged. But Tamsin would not, must not, think of him. And it would be better if she kept busy tomorrow, away from the guests.

"I'm quite all right," she replied, moving farther into the room.

"No, you're not," her cousin insisted. "Something is wrong." She went to Tamsin and put her hands on her shoulders, turning her to face her, her anxious gaze searching Tamsin's face. "Please, Tamsin, won't you tell me? I come to you with all my troubles, as if you were my sister. Won't you treat me like a sister and tell me yours?"

If she had demanded the truth, Tamsin would have resisted. But this tender, heartfelt plea, from the cousin who had been the only one to welcome her with kindness when she first came to Castle DeLac, and from whom she would soon be parted, proved irresistible. "Your father was going to wait until tomorrow to make the announcement."

Mavis's blond eyebrows drew together in a query as Tamsin forced another smile onto her face. Mavis must never know what her father had threatened if Tamsin refused the betrothal. Mavis was a loving, loyal soul and Tamsin didn't doubt that she would insist on taking Tamsin's place if she knew the truth. "I am to be married."

"Married?" Mavis repeated, as shocked as Tamsin had been. Or Sir Rheged. And no doubt as everyone else in Castle DeLac would be, too, when the news got out. "When? To whom? Is it one of the visiting knights? Sir Jocelyn?"

"No, it's—"

"Not young Sir Robert. He's barely twenty."

"It isn't one of our guests. It's Sir Blane of Dunborough."

"Sir Blane of…" Mavis repeated. Then her eyes widened and a look of horror came to her face. "Not that terrible old lecher! It made my skin crawl just to look at him! Surely Father wouldn't be so cruel!"

Tamsin drew herself and spoke as she had to Sir Rheged, with pride and resolve, so that Mavis would believe her. "He's rich and powerful. It's a much better match than I could have hoped for."

"But you yourself saw the way he went after the maidservants. If you hadn't kept them—and me—away from him—"

"Surely once he has a new, young wife he won't want to dally with servants."

"I don't think marriage would ever stop a man like him from trying to take advantage of any woman. And he wouldn't have *a* wife," Mavis said. "He would have *you*. *You* would be in that disgusting old man's bed, Tamsin."

Better her than Mavis, Tamsin thought, her cousin's compassionate concern making it all the more necessary that she wed Sir Blane. "I'm aware of a wife's duties— all of them," she said, meeting her cousin's gaze with all the cool composure she could muster.

"It may not be pleasant, but if I'm to have children, I will do what I must, and I do want children," she continued, trying not to imagine little boys with flashing brown eyes and dark hair, or little girls with thick lashes and long, waving black hair.

She took Mavis's hands in hers. "This may be the only way I'll ever have a household and children of my own. I'll no longer be a beggar at my uncle's table, a glorified servant who must be grateful for every mouthful."

Mavis regarded her questioningly for a long moment, until at last she lowered her head and pulled her hands free. "If that's how you feel, Tamsin, then I must be happy for you, and wish you well on your betrothal."

"Thank you, my cousin, who is more than a sister to me," Tamsin said, embracing her.

Mavis threw her arms about her and hugged her close.

Rheged awoke to pitch-darkness and the scent of wool. God's blood, he'd fallen asleep in the woolshed.

He rolled off the bundle and onto his feet at once. Moving his stiff arms, he bent his knees and straightened, then brushed any bits of fleece from his tunic before raking his fingers through his hair.

He opened the door and peered into the yard. It was barely dawn, the yard empty and quiet, with only the footfalls of the guards on the walk to break the silence. Like a shadow, Rheged crept out of the shed and along the wall, stealthily making his way back to his quarters, more glad than ever that he had a chamber to himself.

On the other hand, he thought as he slipped through the outer door into the guest quarters, he might not be the only man sneaking into his chamber in the wee hours of the morning. If anyone saw him, they would likely think he'd been sporting with one of the servants, like that pretty wench with the pert nose who'd spent most of the feast near the squires. Nevertheless he was relieved to get to his chamber without encountering anyone else.

Once there, he checked to make sure his prize was safe, washed, changed his clothes and packed his belongings, including his mail, helmet, plain surcoat devoid of any devices or crest, and gambeson, the padded garment worn beneath his mail. That done, he went to the hall to break the fast.

The only people in the large chamber were some servants cleaning after last night's feast, a few soldiers finishing their early meal of bread and ale and the hounds. Tamsin was not there, nor were any of the guests, Lady Mavis or Lord DeLac. No doubt the lords and ladies were still abed.

As one of the maidservants—not that pretty pert one, but an older one—brought him bread and ale, stifling a yawn as she did so, he told himself to be glad Tamsin wasn't there. She had made her feelings quite clear, so there was nothing more to say to her.

Trying to put Tamsin from his thoughts, he ate slowly, savoring the excellent bread and fine ale, better than anything he would have at his own castle. He watched with hidden amusement as some of the other knights and squires stumbled into the hall, clearly the worse for feasting too much and too long last night. None of the ladies appeared.

That was to be expected, he supposed. But he did hope to see Tamsin bustling about, giving orders and seeing that all was well later, when he was preparing to depart. Yet he never so much as caught a glimpse of her in the hall, the guest quarters or the courtyard.

It was as if Tamsin had disappeared off the face of the earth. Or been locked away.

Chapter Four

Rheged immediately went back to the hall. If Tamsin was being punished because they'd been together last night, he must and would make certain Lord DeLac knew the lady was innocent of any indiscretion.

Well, perhaps she wasn't entirely innocent, but she'd certainly done nothing worthy of punishment.

When he entered the hall, he saw at once that Tamsin wasn't there, although more of the guests were, including a few of the ladies.

Deciding he would wait until Tamsin appeared or Lord DeLac arrived, Rheged sat on one of the benches halfway down the hall, away from anyone else. Not surprisingly, no one moved to sit near him. Only the servants addressed him, hurrying to offer him bread, honey, wine or ale. He waved them away and paid no heed to their curious regard any more than he did to the sideways glances the Normans gave him.

"Not like her at all," he heard a woman say behind him. "Normally she's calm as can be, even after a feast, but I swear to you, Denly, she fair tore a strip off Baldur this morning for not telling her they was running short of wine."

Rheged moved farther back in the shadow of the pillar and looked over his shoulder. Two servants, a man and a woman, were replacing the torches in the sconces.

"No wonder she's snappish," the man remarked as he lifted down a burned-out torch. "Poor thing's bone-tired. Not that she's resting. She's been in the store-rooms all morning, checking the stores as if the king himself were coming."

So it seemed Tamsin wasn't being punished. She was going about her daily business, as if nothing at all had happened.

And so should he.

So Rheged was still telling himself early the next morning as he rode the last mile toward his fortress. He had spent the night encamped in a wood halfway between Castle DeLac and his estate, in a ruin of a coal burner's hut he'd spotted when he ventured from the road seeking water for his horse. As was his habit after years of being on his own, he always carried flint and steel, and had a loaf of bread he'd slipped into his tunic before he left the hall at Castle DeLac that morning. That meant he was able to save the cost of a night at an inn, as well as the worry that some outlaw or thief might guess that he carried something of value and try to rob him. Not that any thief or highwayman would have succeeded. None ever had before, not even when he was a boy. He fought fiercely to keep what was his, and had first learned to fight not from some honorable knight, but on the streets and in the alleys of more places than he could remember. He could use anything that came to hand to defend himself, or simply his bare fists, if need be.

Thank God those days of living hand to mouth, of never knowing if he would eat that day or starve, of fighting over scraps or holding off any who would take what little he had, were over.

His heart swelled with pride and satisfaction when he rode over the ridge and saw his fortress rising from the autumn mist in the valley—the White Valley, Cwm Bron. To be sure, compared to Castle DeLac, his castle seemed small and more than a half a ruin, but this was only a beginning. One day, he would build a new and better fortress with a moat, at least two curtain walls, an inner and outer ward and a gatehouse with a portcullis. Inside, there would be a larger keep, stables, a hall and a chapel, too. The family apartments would be spacious and comfortable, finely furnished with beds and perhaps even a carpet in his own chamber. Farmers, tradesmen, craftsmen and merchants would feel safe and secure under his protection, and the village beyond the castle walls would grow and prosper, too.

Now, though, only a very small village of wattle-and-daub cottages and wooden buildings had grown around the single outer stone walls of his fortress. Inside the wall only the ancient round keep and one other building were made of stone. The others were wattle-and-daub, or timber, and several were in a sad state of disrepair. So far, he'd managed to have the work on the keep completed and the mill, farther down the river, repaired. Recently his men had started on the outer wall.

Later, when it was finished, the work on the rest of the interior buildings would begin.

He could achieve his goals faster if he wed a wealthy woman. Not a titled lady, who would likely look down on a man of his origins, but a rich merchant's daughter or sister.

With snapping brown eyes and hair to her waist.

He must stop thinking of Tamsin of DeLac. She must be nothing to him.

He surveyed the wall walk nearest the gate and thought he could make out the stocky Gareth, his friend and garrison commander. Gareth had no doubt been watching for his return, ready to ply him with questions about the tournament, the fighting and, being Gareth, the women.

Gareth had lost three of his bottom teeth in a skirmish, most of one eyebrow was nothing but a scar and his visage had been none too pretty to begin with. Despite his lack of physical attractiveness, however, he rarely had trouble finding female company, for he was as merry as Rheged was serious. Nevertheless they had been friends and comrades-in-arms for over fifteen years, from the time a half-drunk Gareth had tried to knock Rheged down and instead had fallen, laughing, into a horse trough.

As Rheged raised his hand in greeting, Sir Algar, white-haired and agile despite his years, came hurrying out of the open gate of Cwm Bron. Rheged hadn't expected to find his overlord waiting for him, and he was pleased and flattered. And relieved, too, a little, for now Gareth's questions would have to wait.

"Greetings, my lord!" Rheged called out, riding

closer. Unlike Lord DeLac, Sir Algar was slender and although his long tunic, embossed leather belt and polished boots had surely been expensive, he wore few jewels.

"I couldn't wait to find out who the champion of the tournament was," Sir Algar cheerfully explained when Rheged swung down from his horse to walk beside him.

"I was."

"I knew it!" Algar cried, slapping his thigh with delight. "I knew nobody'd beat you!"

"Nobody at that tournament anyway," Rheged replied.

They'd no sooner entered the yard than Dan the groom hurried out of the stable as fast as his short legs could take him. Between his lack of height, potbelly and red face, the groom was rather like an apple with limbs. He was also honest and good at his job, and that was what counted with Rheged.

"Rub Jevan down well, and have my mail and surcoat taken to the armory for cleaning," Rheged said, stroking his destrier's nose.

Dan nodded and took hold of the reins while Rheged retrieved the smaller leather pouch that had also been tied to his saddle.

"Well, then, no limbs missing, I see," Gareth noted wryly after he joined them, running his gaze up and down Rheged's frame, which was as long and lean as his was short and brawny.

"No," Rheged replied, apparently equally serious. "Only a few bruises."

"And he won!" Sir Algar exclaimed.

"Can't have been much of a competition, then," Gareth observed.

"Not much," Rheged answered with a shrug. "I see the fortress is still standing, so no trouble while I was gone, I take it?"

"Not a thing."

Rheged noticed Sir Algar fidgeting. "Good. Tell the guards the watchword for the night is…woolshed."

Gareth looked a little surprised, but he nodded and strolled off toward the men standing near the gate while Rheged, with Sir Algar beside him, started toward the keep.

"What did you make of Lord DeLac?" Sir Algar asked as they went up the steps to the second level in the building that served as Rheged's hall. The chamber where he slept was on the third level, just below the new slate roof.

"Rich and prosperous and pleased with himself," Rheged replied as they entered. This room was half the size of Lord DeLac's great hall, and had no tapestries or other decoration. The tables were scarred and none too clean, the benches likewise. There was one chair, also old and not in the best of condition. Compared to Lord DeLac's hall… There was no comparison, but then, he had no wife to rule it.

Sir Algar chuckled. "That's one way to put it, I suppose. He always was a vain fellow, and arrogant. Who else was there? Anyone to give you trouble?"

"It wasn't my easiest victory," Rheged conceded while they walked toward the smoking central hearth. "A few of the younger knights decided to try me, and one or two will be formidable when they've had more experience."

Hopefully by the time those young bucks were skilled enough to be serious competition, his estate would be so prosperous that he wouldn't have to travel to tournaments to augment his income like some kind of entertainer.

Sir Algar slid him a grin. "And the ladies? Any beauties among them? Did any quarrels break out over you?"

"I was thinking about the battle before the melee and was too tired to pay much attention afterward," Rheged replied, deciding there was no need to tell Sir Algar about Lord DeLac's niece and his encounters with her.

"What, you saw no one to make you think of marriage? What of DeLac's daughter? I hear she's very beautiful."

Rheged wondered if that was why Sir Algar had been so keen that he go to this particular tournament. If so, he was going to be disappointed. "I don't think Lord DeLac would consider me a fitting son-in-law, and Lady Mavis didn't seem at all interested in me."

The older man chuckled and settled into the chair. "I find that hard to fathom."

Rheged sat on a nearby bench and called out for Hildie, a middle-aged maidservant with a mole on her cheek who was lingering near the door to the kitchen, to bring wine.

"I'm far from wealthy," he said to Lord Algar, "and I'm Welsh to boot—hardly attributes to attract a Norman bride."

"Plenty of women wouldn't care about wealth or nationality when they look at you. Good God, man, you're any maiden's dream!"

"I didn't appear to be Lady Mavis's dream."

Sir Algar sighed. Then his eyes lit up again. "What of the man's niece? Is she not of marriageable age?"

"Yes."

"What sort of woman is she?"

"Betrothed."

"Betrothed? To whom?"

"Sir Blane of Dunborough."

"That old reprobate?" Sir Algar cried with a disgust that matched Rheged's own.

"I gather DeLac needs an ally in the north."

"DeLac must truly be desperate if he'll give his niece to that black-hearted villain!"

"Or she wants a rich and powerful husband," Rheged answered, for was that not what she herself had said?

"Ah." Sir Algar leaned back in the chair and stroked his beard. "That could be—and it would be understandable, too. She came to DeLac with nearly nothing as a child after her parents died of a sickness and has been dependent on his charity ever since. That cannot be a comfortable existence. But Blane! Surely there must be someone else she could marry in the north."

"The lady has already agreed."

"Well, then, there's an end to it," Sir Algar said with another sigh. "At least Blane is old, so she may soon be a widow. Perhaps she's already considered that."

"Perhaps," Rheged agreed, although he found no comfort in that thought. He didn't want to believe the passionate woman he had kissed could be so cold-hearted that she would eagerly anticipate widowhood, any more than he wanted to see her in Blane's household. As for spending even a single night in the man's bed...

"But what of the prize, man?" Sir Algar demanded, his query breaking the silence. "And how much did you take in ransoms for arms and horses?"

From his belt Rheged drew out a purse of coins that would have delighted him at any other time and set it on the bench. "Fifty marks in coin, and this." He opened the leather pouch, pulled the golden box from the leather bag and held it up. "This was the prize I won."

"God be praised!" Sir Algar gasped, his light blue eyes widening as his white eyebrows shot up. "I can't believe it! Either the man's richer than I ever suspected or he's grown generous over the years."

Sir Algar reached out for the box and took it almost reverently. Then he squinted and rotated it slowly in his hands, examining it closely.

"What is it?"

"Did you think this was solid gold?" Sir Algar asked slowly.

"Isn't it?"

Sir Algar shook his head. "The gems aren't real, either. Could you not—"

"Tell? How could I?" Rheged retorted, taking the box from him and studying it just as intently. "I've never had any jewels, or anything solid gold, either. Are you certain?"

Sir Algar took the knife from his belt and scraped the bottom of the box. The gold peeled off, revealing the dull gray of some other metal underneath. "I suppose

I shouldn't be surprised. DeLac's always been a miser, unless he wants to impress his guests."

Rheged grabbed the box, shoved it into the leather pouch and started for the door.

Sir Algar jumped to his feet. "What are you—"

"That damned miserly bastard won't make a fool out of me! I'm going to get my proper prize!"

"Perhaps it might be wise to accept—" Sir Algar began as he followed Rheged.

"Being cheated? Never!" Rheged paused and turned to face the older man. "What would you do if a merchant sold you bogus goods?"

"I would either get my money back, or demand the goods I paid for."

"I am going to seek the goods I paid for," Rheged replied.

"Lord DeLac is a powerful man, Rheged," Sir Algar said warily.

"And I am not. I realize that, my lord." He managed a grim smile. "I am well aware that I lack sufficient power to risk the man's enmity, my lord, but I must try to get a more proper prize, or I will have deserved to be cheated."

Sir Algar nodded. "Farewell, then, and good luck—but be careful."

"I will, my lord."

His mouth a grim, hard line, his knuckles white as he gripped the pouch, Rheged left the hall and marched across the yard to the stable. Gareth, standing near the well talking to one of the maidservants—the quiet one whose name was Evie or some such thing—saw him and immediately hurried to meet him at the entrance.

"What's wrong?" he asked gravely, clearly realizing this was no time for jesting.

"I'm going back to Castle DeLac," Rheged replied. He went into the stable and called for Dan, whose head appeared over the wall of Jevan's stall, surprise on every feature.

"Saddle Myr," Rheged ordered. Jevan was for fighting; Myr, his gelding, was for speed.

"Forgot something, did you?" Gareth asked.

"Not me," Rheged grimly replied. "Lord DeLac." He glanced at his puzzled friend. "He forgot his honor, and what is due a knight."

"Want some company?"

Rheged shook his head. "I need you here." He put his hand on Gareth's shoulder. "The man will either do what's right or he won't, and if he won't, I'll come back and fetch you."

Gareth grinned and nodded. "As you will, my lord."

Tamsin shivered, pulled her cloak more tightly about her and checked the figure for the total number of baskets of neeps in the kitchen storeroom against the list in her hand. On other shelves were apples drying on racks, baskets of peas and leeks and clay jars of honey. Sawdust covered the floor and scented the air along with the vegetables and fruit. A few dust motes danced, and one or two must have gotten into her eyes, to make them water.

Thankfully the total of all the stores here was correct, so she could be sure she was leaving a good count for Mavis. She wanted to be certain all was in good order before Sir Blane arrived and she was taken away to the north, where it would be even colder.

Unfortunately what should have been a simple task was taking far too long. Her thoughts kept drifting to what she might encounter in her future, and what she would be leaving behind. She wouldn't be sorry to see the last of her uncle, but she would sorely miss Mavis, and the servants. Even Armond. And she knew how to manage this household. What would Sir Blane's be like? she asked herself as she wiped at her eyes. Because of the dust, of course.

A commotion outside jerked her back to the present. It seemed to be coming from the yard, near the gates. They weren't expecting any visitors today, at least none that she...

Surely it couldn't be Sir Blane! Her uncle had said he would arrive within the fortnight, not today—unless her betrothed had traveled more swiftly than expected, anxious for the alliance. Or the marriage.

Although that thought was enough to make her queasy, Tamsin put down the list, gathered up her skirts and hurried to the yard.

To see Sir Rheged of Cwm Bron standing near the gates, feet planted, his hands on his hips and obviously angry.

That explained why the guards were watching him so closely, even though he wasn't dressed for battle. He wore a white shirt open at the neck beneath a boiled leather tunic, the attire of common men-at-arms. Despite the autumn chill in the air, the long sleeves of his shirt were rolled back to reveal skin bronzed brown by the sun. His breeches were of wool, his boots splattered with mud and he stood beside a foam-flecked gray gelding, not the powerful destrier he'd ridden in the melee. He did, however, carry a sword, the scabbard resting against his muscular thigh.

Despite her determination to keep certain memories locked away forever, she vividly recalled the thrill of being in his arms and the sensation of his lips on hers, especially when his gaze swept the yard and settled upon her.

Then he started toward her, as if his business was with her alone.

That must not be. That could not be. She must marry Blane, regardless of what this man said. Or did.

Straightening her shoulders, she walked forward resolutely, determined to send him on his way. "Greetings, Sir Rheged," she said, managing to sound calm.

"I wish to see your uncle."

So he hadn't returned to offer her aid again, or sanctuary. Or so she thought, until she saw something deep in his eyes that revived her hope of rescue.

Her useless, wistful hope that must be nipped in the bud. "He rode out this morning, sir knight," she said with cool detachment.

The Welshman skeptically raised a dark eyebrow. "*He* went riding?"

She, too, had been surprised to hear her uncle's plan, until it had occurred to her that he might wish to avoid his niece as much as she wanted to be far away from him. "You're welcome to wait in his solar, or you may tell me your business and I will see—"

Sir Rheged turned on his heel, went to his horse and took a leather pouch from the saddle. He opened it and, like a conjurer at a fair, held up his prize. "This is not gold, but painted metal and the jewels are false, too. Your uncle lied to every knight who fought here, and I demand a proper prize."

Oh, she *was* a fool to harbor such romantic notions of rescue by a knight she barely knew!

Whatever her uncle had done, this was no place to discuss it, where so many could see and hear. Not only were the guards within hearing distance, but a quick glance around the yard confirmed that several servants and not a few curious guests were watching from doors and windows, including Mavis. "Please come to the solar, Sir Rheged. I will send a man to find my uncle. I'm sure he can—"

"Explain?" Rheged scornfully interrupted. "What explanation can there be? He played me, and every other knight who came to his tournament, for a fool." He leaned toward her, close enough to kiss, except that wasn't desire burning in his eyes. "And I assure you, my lady, I do not take kindly to being made to look a fool."

"Nor do I," she snapped, her own ire rising. If he could speak so to her, and in public, too, she'd been right to suspect that his motive for complimenting and kissing her had been seduction all along. "I had nothing to do with the prize, yet you stand here and upbraid me as if I were a naughty child. Now either follow me to the solar or get back on your horse and go!"

For an instant, she thought he was going to leave, until her uncle came strolling out from behind the chapel. He was clad in his thick cloak with the ermine collar and lined with fox fur, his silver broach glittering in the September sunlight, his hair sleek and smooth as his voice.

"Greetings, Sir Rheged," he said genially, although his eyes were far from friendly. "I didn't expect to see you again so soon. Have you forgotten something?"

"Not I, but apparently you forgot you are supposed to be an honorable man. You played me false, DeLac, and all who fought in your tournament. This box is no more made of gold than I am, and the jewels are just as false. If you have a drop of honor in you, you'll give me a more worthy prize."

With a shrug of his beefy shoulders, her uncle answered as if he were innocence itself. "You received the prize that was offered. *I* never said it was real gold, or that the jewels were gemstones. It was on display in the hall the night before the melee, and you were quite welcome to examine it then. If you did not..." Her uncle spread his hands wide, as if to say, "What fault is it of mine?"

"And why such anger?" he continued. "Have you not won another victory? Will that not add to your fame and fierce reputation? Surely that was worth the effort."

Rheged regarded the man with undisguised disdain and answered in Welsh. Whatever he said, it was obviously no compliment.

"Leave my castle, Sir Rheged," her uncle ordered, all vestige of amiability replaced by indignant anger, "or I'll order my guards to—"

"What?" Rheged demanded, his voice low and hard. "Try to make me go? If that's your notion, think again, my lord. I have my sword."

"And I have twenty archers with arrows nocked and aimed right at your head," her uncle returned.

A quick glance at the wall walk confirmed the truth of what he said.

Rheged threw the box onto the ground with such force the lid flew off and it skittered to a halt inches from her uncle's toe. "Twenty men to one. Why am I not surprised?"

He gestured at the windows surrounding the yard, proving that he, too, was aware that they were being watched by more than the men and servants in the yard. "Soon all will know what kind of *honorable* nobleman you are. Then we shall see how many friends you have at court."

"More than you, at least," her uncle retorted. "More than some peasant of a Welshman will ever have, no matter how well he fights or how many walls he climbs. Indeed, a monkey could have done what you did to earn your knighthood, so don't think to threaten me. Now get out, Sir Rheged, before I have you shot."

He would do it, too, Tamsin knew. *Leave, Rheged,* she silently urged, instinctively stepping forward.

The Welshman glanced at her, his expression unreadable, before he turned his attention back to her uncle. "Perhaps I shouldn't have expected better from a man who'll give his niece to a greedy, lecherous lout like Blane."

"My niece's marriage is no business of yours!" DeLac cried as Tamsin stood frozen where she was, rooted to the ground, afraid to move a muscle lest she make things worse. "And you've got the only prize you deserve. Now go, before I order my men to kill you where you stand!"

"Very well, my lord, who has given a prize worthy of the giver—false and cheap, good for show, but lacking any true value," Rheged replied as he threw himself into the saddle. "Keep your prize and be damned!"

"Get out and never return, you stupid, stinking Welshman!" her uncle shouted.

Rheged lifted his horse's reins, but instead of heading for the gate, he rode right at Tamsin, turning his horse at the last moment.

In that same moment, he reached down and grabbed the back of her gown. Gasping with shock and dismay, she kicked and struggled as he hauled her over his lap.

"Put me down! Let me go!" she cried with desperate panic. Ignoring her, he punched his horse's sides with his heels and, with her slung over his horse as if she were a sack of grain, rode out through the gates.

Chapter Five

"Stop! Let me down!" Tamsin cried, noise and confusion surrounding her as she fought to get off the swiftly moving horse, despite the fear of falling to her death.

But Rheged held her tight, and as they passed beneath the portcullis, she could understand nothing of the shouts, except for Mavis calling her name.

And then her uncle ordering his men to shoot.

Something hit her calf. Like a bee sting, only worse. Her leg was wet. With blood?

"Stop!" she gasped again, trying to be heard over the pounding of the horses' hooves and shouts from the castle. "Please…stop…."

Regardless of her desperate cries, Rheged didn't stop.

He wouldn't until they were well away from Castle DeLac, when it would be safer, Rheged thought as he held on to Tamsin with all his might so she wouldn't fall. Thank God they had some time before DeLac's men could mount and give chase.

At least she'd stopped struggling. Because she'd fainted, apparently. No surprise, that, considering how shocked and frightened she must have been at his impulsive act. He had never been impulsive in his life. Until today. Until he'd…

The magnitude of what he'd done hit him like a rock thrown from a great height. He'd abducted a woman, a noblewoman, stolen her away from an uncle with wealth and power and influence with the king. He'd acted without thinking.

Foolishly.

Although he hated the thought of Tamsin—or any woman—married to a man like Blane, he had no right to interfere. Regardless of the consequences, he must take her back at once, he told himself as he began to turn his horse. Perhaps there would be no serious repercussions if he left her near—

Myr suddenly shied, as if there was a snake at his feet. Or he was hurt.

Rheged slipped from the saddle, his motion making Tamsin moan. She must be waking up from her swoon. Then he saw the blood dripping from her foot onto the road beneath.

God help him! She'd been struck by an arrow! He could see the shaft protruding from her cloak where it had pierced her calf. He knew from experience that such a wound must be tended to at once. They had to return to Castle DeLac immediately, even if the jostling of the ride would make her bleed more and although every sense told him it was about to rain.

He grabbed Myr's bridle and started back just before the rain began to fall. It wasn't droplets or a drizzle, but a downpour. They would both be soaked through unless…

The coal burner's hut! It was little more than a ruin, but it was a shelter.

Leading his horse from the road into the wood, he hurried toward the hovel. He looped Myr's reins around a bush and lifted Tamsin down. She groaned softly as he carried her to the hut and kicked open the ramshackle door. The hard-packed floor was bare, and a circle of stones with a few charred and half-burned sticks were all that remained of the fire he'd built before. The pile of branches he'd slept on was still there, too, and he laid her on it. He unbuckled his sword belt and set it on the ground nearby before tugging off his leather tunic. He put that down beside her, then gently shifted her onto it.

Cold air blew in through chinks in the rough walls and rain began dripping through the hole in the roof made to let the smoke from the fire escape. They needed a fire tonight, both for warmth and should he have to cauterize the wound.

Thank God he had his flint and steel. He hadn't taken the time at Cwn Bron to remove the pouch he always wore at his waist when he traveled. He grabbed some leaves from the branches and got them alight. He used a few of the sticks to build a fire, then ran out into the rain, seeking larger pieces of wood under the trees. He could get water from the stream nearby.

Gathering up a few more sticks, he made his way through the bracken, ferns and underbrush toward the stream. This time he spotted a broken pot on the bank. Fortunately there was enough of it left to hold water, so with his free hand he filled it and then hurried back to the hut. Crouching, he fed the wood into the fire, then put the broken pot near the flames to warm the contents.

Only then did he glance at Tamsin, to discover she was watching him, her brown eyes huge in her pale face, one hand clutching the arrow in her leg.

He rose and approached her cautiously. "I'm sorry, but I'm going to have to tend to that," he said, nodding at the arrow.

"I'm sorry you ever came to Castle DeLac," she retorted, her teeth clenched. "Take me home!"

"I can't. It's raining and it's going to be dark soon."

"I don't care if it's pouring. Take me back!"

"As soon as the water's heated, I'm going to have to wash your wound."

"You're no physician."

"No, but I've dealt with such injuries before, my own and other's. The sooner it's tended to—"

"Take me home!" she commanded, but now there was a tremor in her voice. "You must take me back. I have to marry Blane." She moved as if she was trying to stand, then gasped, her face growing even more pale.

"Sit," he commanded, "or you'll bleed more."

She didn't answer. She didn't say anything, her lips a thin line of anger and pain, but at least she didn't try to move again.

He reached for the warm water. "It's good you're wearing a heavy gown," he said as he knelt down and got a good look at the spot where the arrow had pierced her garments. "I'm going to break the shaft so I can pull the fabric of your clothes away from the wound. Stay still. It won't be easy. Fletchers use the hardest wood for strength."

"I know that," she snapped.

"I suspect there isn't much you don't know," he replied. He held the shaft against her leg with one hand and gripped the other end of the shaft near the feathers with the other. "How many days until Christmas?"

"What?"

"How many days until Christmas. That's got to be a busy time for you."

"I don't—"

In spite of his efforts to distract her, she stiffened and cried out in pain when he broke the shaft. Panting, she lay back.

"I'm sorry, my lady."

"You should be!"

"I didn't shoot the arrow," he said, carefully maneuvering the fabric of her gown and shift up and over the broken shaft.

"It wouldn't have happened at all if you hadn't taken me." She jerked as her skirt caught on the shaft. "For the love of God, be careful!"

"I'm doing the best I can."

Her stocking was the most difficult of all, but at last he managed to uncover her calf. The wide end of the arrowhead, he saw with great relief, was visible, so it hadn't gone too far into the muscle, probably because of her clothes and the distance it had traveled. It would be easy enough to remove the tip and clean the wound. Although that would be painful enough, he need not do more.

"This isn't too bad," he said, sitting back on his haunches. He had three scars himself from similar wounds and treatment, and knew enough to believe the damage wouldn't be severe, or lethal. Thank God.

Tamsin didn't hear him. Pain, nausea and dizziness had overwhelmed her, and she had swooned once more.

She was cold and shivering and her leg hurt.

Tamsin's eyes snapped open as she remembered that she was in a decrepit hut off the road from Castle DeLac, brought here by Rheged of Cwm Bron, and she'd been hit by an arrow. He'd been angry with her uncle because the tournament prize had been almost worthless and he'd taken her by force, probably intending to hold her for ransom or perhaps for vengeance.

"You're awake."

She turned her head to see Rheged rising from beside the fire where he'd been crouched like some kind of demon. He was clad only in woolen breeches and worn leather boots, with his plain sword belt around his narrow waist.

"Don't touch me!" she cried, gasping in pain as she scrambled back against the rough wall of the hut. "Don't come near me!"

Rheged crossed his arms over his bare chest. "I have no intention of touching you except to check your wound. If you fear for your virtue because of my state of undress, my shirt is bandaging your leg where your uncle's man shot you, and my tunic is beneath you, covering the branches that wouldn't be very comfortable otherwise."

She glanced down and saw the edge of his tunic beneath her. Carefully raising her skirt, she saw white fabric wrapped around her lower leg, fabric that was now stained with blood.

She swallowed hard and raised her eyes. "You touched my leg?"

"It was that or leave the arrowhead there to fester."

"Take me home."

"To the man who almost got you killed?"

"*You* almost got me killed when you took me by force. If you have any shred of chivalry as a man and as a knight—"

"Because I have a shred of chivalry, I'm taking you to Cwm Bron come the morning."

She stared at him with horror and dismay. "In the *morning?* That's too late!" Trying to ignore the pain, she started to stand. "I have to go back *now!*"

He shook his head. "We can't risk riding in the dark, especially when it's raining."

She blinked back tears not just of pain but of frustration as she limped past him toward what was supposed to be a door.

"Stop," he growled, taking hold of her arm.

She couldn't stifle a little moan of agony as she tried to pull free.

"It's dark and it's wet," he said, his tone more gentle. "You'll swoon or get lost before you find the road."

She wrenched herself free and nearly fell, but managed to stay upright. "If I'm not back before the morning, it will be too late! Everyone will know you had me alone all night."

"So what of that? I'm a knight sworn to protect women and children. I would never take a woman against her will."

"So *you* say! But what will people believe? And you half-naked, too!"

"I had to make a bandage out of something, lest you bleed to death—and you might do so anyway if you don't sit down and keep still. Would you rather I'd torn off a piece of your shift?"

She could barely stand, but that didn't matter. "Rumors will fly when people hear you've abducted me and that we were together for a night. That's all they will need to hear to believe I'm no longer a virgin. Your selfish act of vengeance has quite likely rendered me unmarriageable and for what? A prize at a tournament."

"I've hardly touched you, except to attend to your wound."

"And grab me and throw me onto your horse with no more care than you would a sack of flour."

"Sit down before you swoon."

She did, but not because he told her to. She was feeling sick and dizzy again, so she hobbled toward the fire and sat as best she could. She must return to Castle DeLac before it was too late, but she couldn't try while he was awake. But Rheged would have to sleep sometime.

He came around the fire and squatted at her feet. "Try not to move while I look at your leg," he said, starting to raise the hem of her gown.

She slapped his hand away. "Leave me alone!"

He regarded her with a frown of frustration. "I may not be a physician, but I've tended plenty of wounds, including my own, my lady, so whether you want me to or not, I'm going to examine your leg."

His tone would brook no refusal, so she bit her lip

and looked away, staring at the gaps in the door and listening to the rain hitting what remained of the roof.

"The bandage isn't soaked through, and that's a good sign," he said as he moved her skirt and shift back into place. "I'm going to fetch more wood, if I can find any that's dry. Stay where you are and don't move about."

She glared at him with all the majesty of an outraged monarch before he shoved open the door and went outside. So what if he was half-naked and the rain was pouring down and the air was cold? If he caught a chill, it would be small recompense for the pain and trouble he'd caused her.

Later, when he fell asleep, she would get away. It might be dark and raining, but she could take the horse and surely she could find some sign of the way to the road.

If he didn't fall asleep, or woke up before she could get to his horse, she must be prepared to fight.

Looking around, she spotted a loose bit of wood at the base of the wall within reach. She had to lean to get it, but with a little effort, it came away. She shoved her makeshift weapon under the straw just before Rheged returned. He'd found a few more sticks, and he shoved them into the dwindling flames before sitting back on his haunches. In that position, with the water dripping down his broad shoulders and naked chest, and his long damp hair brushing his shoulders, he looked not so much like a demon as a warrior king from the days of the Celts and Picts.

A handsome, savage warrior king, with corded muscles and scars of battle, the wet cloth clinging to his powerful thighs. But a savage nonetheless.

She reached for his tunic, ignoring the twinge of pain. "Put this on," she said, tossing it at him.

It nearly landed in the fire and he had to lunge to save it. "You need it more than I," he said, throwing it back at her.

"You are in a state of undress that I find offensive," she retorted. "Isn't it enough that you stole me away without forcing me to look at your nakedness?"

"If my *state of undress* offends you, my lady, don't look."

"Very well, stay that way, and catch your death of cold."

"I've been plenty colder in my life, and I never get sick."

"Not even if you're soaked through?"

"Not even then."

"How miraculous," she replied, her voice dripping with sarcasm as the water dripped from him.

"I suppose," he said with a shrug before he shook his hair back from his forehead. "But I don't get sick. I've never had a fever in my life." He stirred the fire so the flames shot higher. "I don't think you're the sickly sort, either. Although you swooned, you seem very robust otherwise."

Robust? Hardly a compliment for a lady, but this was hardly the time for compliments.

"I'm sorry I can't offer you anything to eat. I left Cwm Bron in a hurry."

"I'm not hungry."

"Rest, then."

She lay down and feigned sleep as best she could, occasionally opening one eye to see what he was doing.

For a long time, he simply sat and stared at the flames. Eventually he drew up his knees, wrapped his arms about his legs and laid his head down.

If he wasn't asleep, he would be soon, for he was clearly exhausted. So was she. If she didn't move, she might fall sleep herself, so Tamsin very slowly, carefully and quietly pulled the stout stick from under her makeshift bed. Very slowly, carefully and quietly she sat up and inched her way forward, ignoring the pain in her leg. When she was near Rheged, she raised the stick, ready to clout him.

He sat up with a jerk and grabbed her upraised arm, forcing it—and her—down, until his body pinned her to the ground.

"Are you mad?" he demanded, his face barely an inch from hers, his dark eyes full of anger and his lips a thin and angry line.

Chapter Six

"No, I'm not, but you may be," Tamsin retorted as she tried to shove him away. Unfortunately she could no more move a boulder than Rheged of Cwm Bron. "Taking me from Castle DeLac was the act of a madman. Or perhaps you took a severe blow to the head during the melee."

"A person would have to be mad to think she could get back to Castle DeLac alone in the rain and the dark and with a wounded leg," he charged. "Are you truly so determined to marry Blane that you'll risk your life for it? Or perhaps you're seeking death rather than marriage."

"I have no wish to die," she answered just as forcefully, "but you have no right to keep me here—or do you intend to prove that you don't, after all, possess a shred of chivalry?"

"I would never take a woman against her will," he repeated as he finally moved away from her.

She began to breathe easier and levered herself up on her elbows. Meanwhile, he grabbed her makeshift weapon and shoved it in the fire. The flames leapt higher, lighting his stern visage and bronzing his naked chest.

"I may be humbly born, but I possess more honor than the man you're so keen to marry," he growled, glaring at her with his grim brown eyes. "Let me enlighten you a little more, my lady. No serving woman or village wench is safe from his lust. They hide when they see him coming—and from his oldest son, too. A woman Blane and Broderick can't take by seduction, they take by force. If he weren't a lord and Broderick his heir, they'd have been hanged—or worse—long ago, by outraged fathers, husbands and brothers."

"Many noblemen are the same," Tamsin said. She hated that it was so, but it was the truth.

"Aye, it is, and some say King John is of that ilk, but if that isn't bad enough, that isn't all Blane does. He punishes any infraction, however slight, to the utmost, and isn't above bending the law for his own end. John's as greedy as Blane, so as long as Blane pays him off, he's free to do what he will."

"He's not alone in that, either."

"So you would make excuses for him?"

She simply couldn't let Rheged think she condoned such behavior or immorality. "No. But perhaps when I'm Blane's wife, I can persuade him to be more just and merciful."

If she could do that, it would make her sacrifice even more worthwhile, and might bring her some peace.

"That would be as difficult as convincing John to give up the throne."

"I can try," she replied, even though she suspected

Rheged was right about her chances of persuading her future husband to be more merciful. Nevertheless she clung to the desperate hope that she could help the people of Dunborough, as well as save Mavis. "I've spent years trying to please and appease an uncle forced to take me in. Surely I can have some influence on my husband, especially if I give him children."

Although thinking about what she had to endure to make that happen made her feel sick again.

"Bearing Blane children will more likely only bring you more pain, to say nothing of what they might suffer with such a father. Blane delights in setting one child against the other, lest they conspire against him. He's so determined to keep them at each other's throats that he won't even tell his twin sons who is the elder."

That had to be a lie, or idle gossip. "Surely someone else would know."

"The twins' mother died giving them birth. Shortly after, the midwife slipped and fell on some stairs. Her neck was broken and she died before she could tell anyone what she knew of the birth. So now only Blane knows for certain who is the eldest, and his sons are constantly at war. Nor should you think a daughter will be any safer. Blane will use her as your uncle's using you, selling her to the highest bidder or the man with the most influence at court, regardless of his reputation."

The more terrible a picture Rheged drew of Blane and his sons, the more Tamsin knew she had to prevent Mavis from taking her place as the bride. "I have given my word that I'll marry Blane and so I will, if he'll still have me. You *must* take me home in the morning. If you

don't, I'll see that you're arrested and charged with abduction as soon as I'm able."

Rheged's eyebrows lowered and his frown deepened.
"Have you heard *nothing* of what I've said?"

"Nothing you've said—or will ever say—will make
me break my word."

"Then I hope your stubborn pride and sense of honor
will give you comfort in the long years to come, for your
husband certainly won't."

"Nor shall I expect it of him. So will you take me
back to Castle DeLac, or will you prove yourself an
outlaw?"

"I'll return you to Castle DeLac when it's light."

As dawn broke in the eastern sky, Mavis stared at
her father slumped in his large chair on the dais, a goblet in his hand and a wineskin on the table at his elbow.
The fire in the hearth was nearly out. The candles and
torches, too. All of the remaining guests and most of
the servants were still abed, and even the hounds slumbered.

Mavis hadn't slept at all, and neither, apparently, had
her father. Yet while she had spent the night restlessly
pacing, fearing the worst for Tamsin, all he had done,
it seemed, was drink.

"Father, you must send your men to rescue her!"
Mavis insisted, her voice rough with exhaustion. Although she hadn't been able to hear the argument, the
distraught servants had quickly told her the reason for
Rheged's return and how enraged he'd been. "It may already be too late to save her. She might even be dead!"

"That Welshman may be a peasant and uncivilized,

but he wouldn't be stupid enough to kill the niece of Lord Simon DeLac," her father replied, lifting the goblet for another gulp of wine.

His declaration brought Mavis a little relief, but only a little. It was too easy to imagine what other terrible things might be happening to her beloved cousin.

"It'll be a ransom he wants," her father muttered more to himself than to her. "Not the wench. Some sum he thinks he deserves. Fool!"

Mavis knelt before her father, trying to get him to look at her. "But you'll pay whatever he asks, won't you, Father?" she pleaded.

Lord DeLac sniffed. "I won't pay a ha'penny for her. She's ruined. Worthless. No good to me now."

"Father, you *must* pay or try to rescue her!" Mavis cried. "You're her uncle, her guardian. Even if she's been…" Mavis blinked back tears as she thought of what Tamsin might have been forced to endure. "*Especially* if she's no longer a virgin, it's your duty to—"

"Duty!" her father snarled as he pushed her away. "I've done my duty! I took the brat in! I got her a husband. And for what? Nothing! She was worthless then and she's more than worthless now!" His eyes bloodshot, he glared at his daughter as she got to her feet. "What are you so worried about? Can't you guess what's really happened? She didn't want to marry Blane, so she got that Welshman to take her away. Probably seduced him first, or paid him. For all I know, the little whore's been sleeping with half the servants and most of the garrison, too."

"Father!" Mavis gasped. "Tamsin is the most honorable, virtuous—"

DeLac sat up abruptly and glared at his daughter. "More virtuous than you? Are you a whore, too?"

"No, of course not, Father, and neither is Tamsin!"

Lord DeLac threw himself back in his chair and reached for the wineskin at his elbow. He lifted it to his lips and drank, ignoring the wine spilling down his already stained tunic. "Well, whatever she is, she's gone and now you have to marry Blane." His mouth slid into a terrible smile when he saw the look on Mavis's face. "Yes, my daughter, an agreement has been made, a contract signed. One of you has to marry the man, and since Tamsin has found a way to avoid it, you must take her place. Not so loving toward her now, are you?"

"You have no proof she wanted to go with Rheged, and I'm sure she didn't."

"Doesn't matter. She's gone and her reputation is ruined, and I must have the alliance with Blane, so you'll have to marry the man—and don't even think of trying to run. I'll lock you in your room. Maybe I should anyway, just to be sure. Who knows what that little slut's put into your head?"

He was right to think Tamsin had influenced Mavis, but not in the way he imagined.

She straightened her shoulders and regarded him with calm dignity and resolve, just as Tamsin would. "If I agree to marry Sir Blane, will you pay a ransom for her?"

"I don't need your agreement. And I told you, she's worthless to me."

"But I'm not, and although the betrothal contract has already been signed, surely you can seek better terms if I am the bride, especially if I make myself pleasing to the groom. I give you my word that I shall do my utmost to do that if you bring Tamsin home before Sir Blane arrives. If you don't agree, I may have to marry the man, but I don't have to pretend to like him. What do you think he'll do if I refuse to speak to him? Or bar the nuptial chamber door?"

"You wouldn't dare!"

"There is more I could do, too," she continued, desperate and determined to save her cousin. "It's not difficult for a pretty girl to make herself ugly—and I will. I can feign a squint, or lisp. Or forget to wash."

Simon DeLac stared at this daughter he didn't really know and who had always meant far less to him than a son would have. It was like discovering a puppy had the fangs of a wolf, and every intention of biting. And if she chose to make trouble with Blane... "I'll pay whatever the Welshman demands for Tamsin's safe return. Within reason."

"*Whatever* he asks," Mavis insisted.

Her father scowled, until he realized that with Mavis for the bride, he should be able to lower the dowry, or perhaps even forgo it entirely. "Very well, but if you refuse to marry Blane, or make any difficulties about the marriage, I'll leave Tamsin with the Welshman, or any other man who wants her."

Mavis nodded. "Then, Father, we are agreed."

"Good. Now get back to your sewing or whatever it is you do all day."

"Yes, Father," Mavis replied humbly.

As whatever love she bore him began to slip away.

* * *

In the faint light of early dawn, Tamsin gingerly unwound what was left of Rheged's shirt from her throbbing calf. She had spent a restless, nearly sleepless night watching the half-naked Rheged as he sat on the far side of the hut. He was equally awake but still as a statue, and mercifully silent. She didn't want to hear more words of warning or descriptions of her future husband and his family. She didn't want to think about the future at all, or Rheged, either.

Wincing, she pulled the bandage away from the wound, and what she saw made her feel worse. Her calf was swollen, the wound red and angry-looking, and there was pus around the edges. Wiping her sweat-slicked brow, she swallowed hard as she began to re-bandage it. She would be home soon. Her uncle would send for the apothecary and he would make her well.

A shadow loomed over her. "Stop," Rheged commanded as he squatted down in front of her. "I need to see."

"It's all right. I'm sure—"

"I'm not." He took hold of her ankle, and she bit back a cry of pain.

He quickly undid the bandage and drew his breath in sharply when he saw the wound. He felt her forehead, his touch surprisingly gentle, even though he muttered what must be a Welsh curse. "You're feverish."

"My uncle will send for an apothecary when we return."

Rheged took a knife from his belt.

She skittered backward. "What are you doing?"

"This needs a fresh bandage, at the very least,"

Rheged replied. "I require some of your shift after all, my lady."

"No! I can't return with a torn shift or people will be sure—"

"I don't give a damn what people will think, and neither should you. If this isn't tended to immediately, you may lose a limb, or even your life. Now sit still and let me make a new bandage."

Gritting her teeth, she said no more as he lifted her skirt and, with the tip of his sword, cut her shift just below her knee. He sheathed his sword, then ripped her shift all the way around. He tore it all the way around again, and tossed away the muddy hem.

He glanced up at her while he rewrapped her leg. "You need a physician, my lady, not an apothecary. Sir Algar's doctor is one of the best in England, and we can get to Cwm Bron faster than Castle DeLac, so we're going to Cwm Bron."

"You said you'd take me home!"

"I will brook no argument in this, my lady," Rheged said as he finished tying off the bandage. "I won't risk your leg or your life on a point of honor. When is Blane expected to arrive?"

"Soon!"

"Tomorrow?"

"Yes, tomorrow," she lied. "Maybe even today."

His wry expression revealed his skepticism. "I'm sure Blane will stop at every brothel and tavern along the way, so I think we should have time enough to get your wound seen to and you back to Castle DeLac before he arrives."

She wanted to insist that they return to Castle DeLac,

but she remembered the servant whose wound had festered and turned to gangrene. In the dark hours of the night, she'd heard his howls of pain as they cut off his leg. The poor man had died anyway, in agony, a few days later.

Blane would surely balk at marrying a woman missing a limb and she would be no use to Mavis, or anyone, if she were dead. "Very well," she said. She pulled his tunic from beneath her and held it out to him. "But once my leg is healing, you will take me home."

He nodded and rose, put on his tunic and buckled his sword belt around his waist. He kicked the fire out, then bent down and scooped her up into his arms as if she weighed no more than a child.

She opened her mouth to protest, but she wasn't sure she could make it to the horse on her own, so she wrapped her arms around his neck and let him carry her out of the hut to his horse. After he lifted her into the saddle, she grasped the saddle board with both hands, dizzy once again.

"Are you going to be sick?" he asked warily.

"No," she replied, determined not to tell him that she hated being off the ground, or up high, and this horse seemed very tall.

"Good," he muttered, and mounted behind her. She shrank away from him as he reached around her for the reins and turned the horse toward the path leading north. "I'll go as fast as I can when we're in the open. Tell me if it hurts too much."

"I can endure a gallop if it gets me to a physician all the sooner," she said, gritting her teeth and holding on for dear life.

* * *

Rheged rode as quickly and easily as he dared, yet by the time they had reached the river that flowed past Cwm Bron, Tamsin had slipped into another swoon and he muttered the earthiest Welsh curse he knew.

At the same time he spotted Gareth waiting on the wall walk of his fortress. Unlike the last time he'd returned, though, the gates were closed. No wonder, given his anger and the way he'd ridden off. Gareth must have been afraid he was going to make an enemy and start a battle.

So he had done, in a way, God help him. Over a golden box and a woman betrothed to another.

He never should have returned to Castle DeLac, regardless of the bogus prize. He never should have tried to reason with that sly cheat DeLac, and he should have ignored the impulse to take Tamsin. She had nothing to do with the prize, and although he wanted to save her from a terrible marriage, surely he could have found some other way. If she lost her leg—or worse—she would never forgive him and he would never forgive himself.

He heard Gareth order the gates to be opened and ignored the few staring villagers who watched him ride past. By the time they rode under the portcullis, Gareth was in the yard, with Dan by his side, and several soldiers nearby.

Rheged's friend trotted toward him, his eyes wide. "God save my beating heart," he murmured when Rheged pulled Myr to a halt. "What the devil—"

"She's hurt," Rheged interrupted. Answers to Gareth's questions could wait. "Take her, will you?"

Rheged lowered Tamsin's limp body into Gareth's arms while Dan held Myr's reins to keep him steady.

"Who is she, Rheged?" Gareth asked.

"I'll explain later," Rheged said, dismounting. Once on the ground, he took Tamsin in his arms. "Close the gates."

Gareth's eyes widened. "You're being chased?"

"Maybe." He'd heard nothing in the night like the sound of a mounted party riding past, but it was well after dawn now, and DeLac's men could be on their way.

"God, Rheged, what—"

"Later," he repeated as he turned and strode quickly toward the hall. He had to get Tamsin inside and to bed, then send for Sir Algar's physician.

He was nearly at the keep when Sir Algar himself appeared at the door. "Blessed Savior, Rheged!" he cried, staring. "Who is that and what have you done to her?"

"This is Lady Thomasina, Simon DeLac's niece," Rheged replied as he started up the stairs of the keep. "She's been wounded."

Sir Algar swiftly moved out of his way. "My God!"

"I fear the injury's infected and beyond my skill," he continued. "We need your physician at once."

"Yes, yes, of course! I'll send a man for Gilbert immediately!"

Sir Algar rushed down the steps as Rheged kicked open the door to his hall in the middle level of the keep. "Hildie!" he bellowed. She was the oldest and presumably wisest of the maidservants, or so he hoped.

The brown-haired serving woman with a mole on her left cheek appeared at the entrance to the kitchen, her green eyes widening when she saw Rheged's burden.

"Fetch plenty of hot water and clean linen for bandages," he ordered as he hurried toward the stairs that curved around the inside of the keep and led to the chamber on the upper level. The upper room that served as both his solar and his bedchamber was the only place that offered any privacy.

He gently laid Tamsin on his bed and wished that it was new and as comfortable as the one he'd had at Castle DeLac.

Her eyes fluttered open. She raised her hand as if to push him away, then almost immediately fell back into a restless slumber, crying out when she moved her leg.

"Oh, God," he muttered, wondering what more he could do to help her until the physician arrived.

"My lord?"

He turned to see Hildie waiting at the threshold, a ewer of steaming water in one hand and a pile of linens over the other. "Fill the basin and bring it here. And the cloths," he said. He raised Tamsin's skirt and began to undo the blood-soaked bandage, and nearly groaned himself when he saw the wound. It was definitely worse.

Hildie approached warily. "That looks bad, my lord."

"Help me hold her still while I wash the wound again."

"Going to take more than washing to fix that, I think, my lord," Hildie said as she obeyed.

"Which is why Sir Algar's sent for his physician. Now try to keep her from moving," Rheged commanded.

He set about cleaning as much of the blood and pus as he could. Although Tamsin struggled a little, he was sorry she didn't struggle more. Her lack of reaction had to be a bad sign.

He rebandaged her leg and then, sitting on the side of the bed, wiped his brow with his sleeve while Hildie heaved a sigh and stepped back. "I'll fetch Elvina to help me undress her. We should do that, my lord, shouldn't we?"

"Aye," he muttered.

After the servant left the chamber, he took a clean cloth and wiped Tamsin's perspiring face, then her neck.

And he prayed. Fervently, as he never had for himself either before a battle or when he was wounded, or even when he'd been scaling that castle wall in France. The last time he'd prayed this hard, he was a boy trying to wake his parents, thinking they were only asleep. Praying that they were, although they were so cold.

Sir Algar entered the room and Rheged swiftly rose. "I've sent a man for Gilbert asking him to come at once. He should be here before nightfall. Now, what happened at Castle DeLac and why is this young woman lying on your bed with a wound in her leg?"

Chapter Seven

Rheged quickly and briefly told Sir Algar what had happened when he returned to Castle DeLac. "And I was so angry and disgusted with the man," he finished, flushing with shame, "I took her."

Sir Algar's thick white eyebrows drew together in a frown. "What do you mean, you took her?"

"I pulled her onto my horse and rode out of the gates with her."

"Good God, man!" Sir Algar cried. "You *abducted* her and right out of DeLac's courtyard? What in God's name were you thinking?"

"I wasn't," Rheged admitted. For once, he'd only been feeling. "DeLac is a cheating rogue and she deserves better than Blane. You know the lord of Dunborough. Would you want to see any woman married to him?"

"I *know* that it was not your place to interfere, unless she asked you for aid. Did she ask you?"

"She believes she must honor the agreement. In fact, she insisted that I return her to her uncle as soon as possible and she threatened me with imprisonment if I don't."

"Justly so," Sir Algar replied. "Would *you* not seek to honor any agreement you made and threaten anyone who tried to stop you?"

"This is different."

"To you, perhaps." Sir Algar's eyes narrowed. "And last night? Where were you both last night?"

"We had to take shelter in the wood. I found the remains of a coal burner's hut and we stayed there."

"Despite her wound?"

"It was pouring rain, my lord, and dark. I tended the wound as best I could and bandaged it with my shirt."

Sir Algar paced with agitated steps. "My God, man, whatever your reasons, you've put both the lady and yourself in a terrible situation! Her reputation may suffer and DeLac is a powerful man, with influence at court."

A low cough interrupted him, and they turned to see the slender, middle-aged physician standing at the door. Gilbert was plainly attired in a long black woolen robe of fine quality belted about his waist, and he carried a wooden box with leather handles, his medicinal chest.

"Ah, Gilbert! Thank you for coming so swiftly," Sir Algar said, moving to meet him. "Sir Rheged will explain what's happened. I'll be below."

"Explanations can wait," Gilbert said after Sir Algar had left the room. The physician's voice was deep and soothing in spite of the shrewd interest in his deep brown eyes. "First I want to examine the lady."

Rheged nodded and told Gilbert where she'd been wounded.

"The blood has dried," the physician noted as he began to untie the makeshift, bloody bandage. "She might awaken from the pain when I remove the bandage, so please stand by her shoulders and, should it be necessary, hold her still."

When Rheged put his hands on Tamsin's slender shoulders, she opened her eyes and stared at him with confusion. "Where am I?" she asked like a lost child.

"Cwm Bron," he replied softly, her vulnerability making another dent in the wall around his heart. "You will be safe here, my lady. A physician has come to help you."

"My leg hurts so…."

"He will help you," Rheged repeated.

Despite Gilbert's efforts to be gentle, Tamsin screamed and tried to twist away as Gilbert pulled the bandage from the wound. Biting his lip, hating himself for being responsible in any way for her pain, Rheged laid his body across hers to prevent her from moving, until he realized she was no longer trying to, and her eyes were closed.

"I hank God she's swooned again," Gilbert said as he examined the wound carefully and probed it with his fingertip. "This could be worse, my lord, much worse. Fortunately, thanks to your immediate attention, the infection has been confined to the area around the wound. It will need to be cauterized, but that should be all that's necessary for her to heal, except for rest."

Relief filled Rheged, but only for a moment. "Will her leg be permanently damaged?"

"I think not, although she'll have a scar."

Gilbert took a clay vessel from the wooden medicine chest he'd set down by the washstand and measured a powder into a small metal cup to which he added water.

"This will dull the pain and reduce her fever," he explained as he gently raised Tamsin enough to drink. When he poured some of the potion he'd prepared into her mouth, she coughed and spluttered a bit but didn't wake up.

"Why doesn't she awaken?" Rheged asked, some of his anxiety seeping into his voice.

"I would say because she's exhausted as well as wounded," the physician replied.

"How soon will she be able to travel?" he asked, although he'd like to forget he'd ever promised to return her to Castle DeLac.

"A sennight at the earliest. A fortnight would be better."

So she had to stay in Cwm Bron for a few days, whether she wanted to or not.

"You may go now, Sir Rheged," Gilbert said. "A serving woman can help me with the rest."

There was undeniable dismissal in the man's tone, so Rheged nodded and took his leave.

He found Sir Algar pacing anxiously by the central hearth in the hall below.

"What happened? I heard her scream," the older man said at once, concern on every feature.

"She cried out when Gilbert removed the bandage. He has to clean the wound again and burn it, but he thinks she'll recover and there should be no permanent damage."

"Thank God for that!" his overlord exclaimed as he sat heavily.

"She has to stay here for at least a sennight."

"So we shall have to deal with DeLac, and perhaps Blane, too."

Rheged took some measure of comfort from the fact that Sir Algar had said "we," but he wasn't about to have his friend and overlord, or anyone else, suffer because of his impulsive act.

"If you'll excuse me, my lord, I should go back to Castle DeLac to tell Lord DeLac that his niece will be returned to him as soon as the doctor says she may travel," Rheged said, rising.

"I'll go with you."

Rheged shook his head. "Although I'm grateful for your offer, my lord, this was my doing and mine alone, so I alone should meet DeLac and face the consequences, whatever they may be."

"You'll at least take Gareth and some of your men."

Again Rheged shook his head. "As always, I'll leave Gareth in command of Cwm Bron."

Regarding him intently, Sir Algar put his hand on his arm. "That's madness, Rheged! DeLac will either arrest you or kill you outright."

"I'll take my chances," Rheged grimly replied. "It's bad enough the lady's been hurt because of what I did. I won't ask anyone else to risk the same or even, perhaps, their lives."

Sir Algar sighed but made no further protest as Rheged strode from the hall, determined to do just what he said and meet DeLac alone.

He hadn't reckoned on Gareth.

His friend had clearly been waiting for him and swiftly fell into step beside him.

"Where are you off to now?"

"Back to Castle DeLac, to tell Lord DeLac that his niece has been wounded and will return when she is well enough to travel."

Gareth came to a startled halt. Rheged didn't pause, so his friend had to trot to catch him up at the stable door. "His niece, is it? How the devil did she get hurt?"

By now, Dan had joined them, too. "I'll saddle Mythrin myself," Rheged said, naming the second-fastest horse in his stable, and starting forward again with Gareth by his side.

Dan moved back a pace, then followed in their wake.

"Come, man, you can't be leaving it at that! What's she doing here?"

"I took her to get back at her miser of an uncle. The tournament prize was almost worthless and when he wouldn't provide a better reward, I lost my temper and took her instead. It was his men who shot her."

"Mary's sacred heart! *You* lost your temper?"

"I was justly angry."

Gareth looked over his shoulder at the groom. "Dan, fetch Rob and Alec and the Big Scot—"

"I'm going alone," Rheged interrupted. "This was my doing, so it's my battle, Gareth, if it comes to a fight."

"I haven't saved your skin a score of times to see you throw it away now!" Gareth protested. "DeLac's garrison must be a hundred at least and—"

"You have to stay here in command. If DeLac does arrest me, he'll probably try to take Cwm Bron. It'll be up to you to see he doesn't."

"And if you're killed?"

"Then I'll be dead and you'll have to take the lady home."

Rheged rode swiftly back to Castle DeLac, stopping only once to let Mythrin eat and drink, so that he reached the castle while it was still light. As he drew his tired gelding to a halt in the outer ward, several soldiers hurried through the inner gate to intercept him and he could hear more gathering on the wall walk above.

"I have business with Lord DeLac regarding his niece," he announced.

A flurry of movement from just within the gates told him the summons was being relayed to the lord inside. Now all he could do was wait to see if DeLac would meet him there, or if he would be surrounded, captured and thrown into the man's dungeon.

Not that he intended to allow that without a fight.

At last the inner gates opened. More mounted soldiers rode out, followed by Simon DeLac himself seated on a fine gray horse with costly accoutrements. The nobleman wore a bright blue velvet cloak with a collar of jet-black fur over a tunic of darker brown wool, a thick leather belt buckled around his waist and calfskin gauntlet gloves. A golden cloak pin glinted on his shoulder, and a thick necklace of silver hung about his neck.

Despite the fine attire, all was clearly not well with the man. His face was red and mottled, and he could hardly sit straight in the saddle. If he wasn't already drunk, one more drink would do it.

"Where's my niece, you cur?" Lord DeLac demanded, his words slightly slurred as he tried to look fierce.

Tried and failed, for Rheged had spent years among men who made DeLac seem like a petulant child. "Safe at Cwm Bron," he replied, "under the protection of Sir Algar and being attended by Sir Algar's own physician, who assures me she'll recover."

"Recover? From what? What have you done to her, you rogue?"

"I have done nothing. One of *your* men shot the arrow that wounded her. I have come to tell you she's safe and I shall bring her back to you when she is well enough to travel."

DeLac's bleary eyes narrowed. "Just like that, eh?"

"Just like that."

"No ransom?"

"I want nothing from you, my lord, now or ever."

"You expect me to believe that?" DeLac scoffed.

"Believe it or not as you will, it is the truth. As soon as the physician gives her leave, I shall bring her back."

"You give her up so easily, this woman you stole? Why? Have you had your way with her and so are willing to give her back like used goods?"

It was all Rheged could do not to draw his sword and strike the man down. "Your niece's virtue is intact."

"I am to take your word for that, am I," DeLac scornfully replied, "when you've had her a day and a night— all night?"

"I give you my word as a knight of the realm, she is as she left here, except for the wound in her leg."

DeLac's lip curled. "*Your* word!"

"My word—and that is worth more than the word of some I could name."

"Don't try to play the honorable knight with me, Welshman," DeLac retorted, "not after what you've done. I would be within my rights to imprison you here and now."

"As she would be within her rights to refuse this betrothal you've arranged for her."

"What gives you leave to talk of her marriage? Or say anything at all about my niece?" Again DeLac's eyes narrowed. "Did she plan this little escapade with you? Has she run away just like her whore of a mother?"

Rheged swung down from his horse, his sword slapping his thigh as he walked toward DeLac. "Are you so lacking in chivalry you'll insult your own flesh and blood, and one who has done nothing wrong? Who, in spite of her pain caused by your orders, insists on coming back here, and even though she knows as well as you or I that Blane is a lecherous, evil old man. Yet because she's given her word—her word that truly means something—she will come back and fulfill the bargain you made."

DeLac straightened his shoulders and adjusted his cloak. "Of course she will. I am her uncle and she must obey me."

Rheged had met all kinds and conditions of men in his travels, but never had one so disgusted him as the lord of Castle DeLac. "Perhaps I *will* keep her."

"You can't!" DeLac cried angrily. "If you do, the king will hear of this outrage and more than you will suffer. You are Algar's liegeman and he will pay, too, I assure you!"

"If I return the lady," Rheged began, loathing the man with every fiber of his being, "you must give me your word, such as it is, that there will be no charges or other repercussions against me or my overlord for my rash act."

"Rash act? Is that what you call it?"

Before Rheged could answer, there was a commotion on the wall walk nearby that signaled the arrival of Lady Mavis. She glared down at him as if he were the devil incarnate.

A flush stole over his features and guilt replaced his anger, for she did have some cause to hate him.

It seemed her presence gave her father new determination, for his voice was somewhat stronger when he spoke, in spite of his inebriated state. "Seven days, Sir Rheged. Have Tamsin back in seven days, untouched save for that wound, and all will be forgiven."

Gilbert had said she might be well enough to travel by then, but also that she might not. "She will return when the physician says she may, and not a day sooner," Rheged replied. "If you're worried about Blane arriving first and finding his bride missing, I doubt he's traveling with any speed, even for his wedding."

"A sennight," DeLac insisted, "and no more, or I *will* have you arrested and Algar, too."

"You can try," Rheged replied, his voice like cold metal as he returned to his horse and mounted. "But I will not risk the lady's health, so she will return when the doctor says she may, and only then."

He said no more before he spurred Mythrin into a gallop and rode out of Lord DeLac's castle.

* * *

After Rheged had gone, Mavis rushed to the hall and found her father seated by a blazing fire, his cloak carelessly tossed over a bench and a silver goblet of wine already in his hand, a large carafe containing more on the table beside him.

"Where is Tamsin?" she demanded.

"Oh, for God's sake, girl, be quiet!" her father commanded. "Your cousin is in that Welshman's castle. Where else?"

Mavis tried to speak softly, lest her father refuse to answer or order her to go. "How much does he want for her safe return?"

Her father gave her a scornful smile. "Nothing. He wants to keep her for a time, and then he'll bring her back. For nothing. I told you she was worthless."

"Why does he want to do that?"

Her father raised an eyebrow.

"No! Oh, Father, you mustn't let him have her! You *must* send your men to rescue her."

"I will not. She's useless to me anyway, and you said as long as I paid the ransom, you would marry Blane. I was willing to pay, but if Rheged asks no ransom, well, so much the better, and Blane will still have a bride."

Mavis stared at the man who'd sired her, wondering how they could be of the same flesh and blood that he could be so cruel and callous, while her heart was breaking to think of the indignities Tamsin must be suffering. "I will keep my word, Father, and I shall marry Blane, but I will never speak to you again."

Her father straightened. "What nonsense is this? Of course you'll speak to me! You'll have to."

Mavis turned on her heel and walked away, her embroidered overtunic and gown of soft, smooth green wool swirling around her slender ankles.

"Come back here! Who do you think you are?" Lord DeLac demanded.

He threw the goblet at her and even though it hit the floor beside her, Mavis still did not look back.

"Damn all women to hell!" her father muttered as he watched her disappear into the kitchen corridor, her back straight, her fair blond head held high, just like that damned whelp of his ungrateful, selfish sister.

Then he drank more wine.

Her eyes still closed, Tamsin reached down and delicately felt her calf. It was sore and swollen but mercifully not as painful as before.

She slowly opened her eyes and found herself in a dimly lit room with round walls. A tower or keep, then. Two narrow windows with wooden shutters closed off any light from outside, while a brazier held a small amount of glowing coals to warm the room. A scarred table, a wooden chest of the sort used to store garments, its blue paint peeling, and a stool and washstand completed the simple furnishings. There were no tapestries on the walls, no candleholders, no chair. The ewer and basin were plain, undecorated metal vessels. The blanket covering her was old, and the featherbed beneath her so thin, she could feel the ropes beneath.

She turned her head the other way and gasped when she saw the stranger sitting in the shadows by the bed. "Who are you?" she demanded, pulling the worn sheet up to her chin.

The man with black hair graying at the temples, dressed in a long, plain tunic and with a kindly mien, rose and smiled down at her. "Good morning, my lady. I'm Gilbert, a physician, and I'm very glad to see you awake." He lightly placed his soft hand upon her brow, and his smile grew. "No more fever."

She licked her dry lips. "My leg…?"

"Should heal well," he replied as he raised her up and put a metal cup of water to her lips.

Never had water been so welcome. "Thank you."

Gilbert moved back and spoke to someone else—a serving woman, rather slovenly dressed, with brown hair and a mole on her cheek. She must have been waiting just outside the door. "Tell Sir Algar the lady is awake."

Sir Algar? Wasn't that Rheged's old and feeble overlord?

The serving woman went out, closing the door behind her. Meanwhile, the physician put a small clay vessel back into what had to be his medicinal chest.

"Where am I?" she asked warily, starting to sit up. "Is this Cwm Bron?"

"You mustn't move so much, my lady," the physician said. "Yes, this castle is called Coom Bron."

Sir Rheged's fortress, then. "Is this the dungeon?"

Gilbert gave her another smile. "No, my lady. I understand this is Sir Rheged's private chamber."

Then he must indeed be poor. The servants at Castle DeLac had better quarters than this.

Gilbert's expression changed to one of grave concern. "Did you not know where you were going?"

"Sir Rheged told me his intentions, but I've never been here before. Did he send for you?"

"Gilbert came at my request," an older man announced as he walked into the chamber.

The stranger wore a soft leather tunic with a pristine white shirt beneath, brown breeches and red boots polished to a high gloss. His white hair was brushed back from a high brow. His equally white eyebrows were bushy and his beard likewise, but his shrewd blue eyes were as bright as a bird's, and his smile warm and pleasant. "Good morning, my lady. I am Sir Algar. I can't tell you how happy I am to know that you'll soon be well."

This was the man her uncle claimed was in his dotage? Simon DeLac was clearly not just a miser and a cheat, but a defamer, too, for Sir Algar was obviously very far from feeble.

"I'm delighted to meet you, my lady," Sir Algar continued, "although I wish the circumstances were better. I knew and admired your mother years ago, before she married."

Tamsin wished she'd met him under other circumstances, too.

"The lady needs rest, my lord," Gilbert cautioned.

"Of course. I'll only stay a little while," Sir Algar replied as he pulled out a purse and took out a few coins. "Thank you, Gilbert."

With a nod, the doctor left the room.

"I appreciate your kindness, my lord," Tamsin said, "but is it not Sir Rheged's responsibility to pay for my care?"

"I'm sure he would agree, if he were here. He's gone

to tell your uncle that although you've been hurt, you'll soon be well."

Rheged had gone back to Castle DeLac without her? Then he was likely either imprisoned or dead. Despite what he'd done, she didn't want that. "When did he leave?"

"Yesterday, after Gilbert told him you would be all right."

"And he's not yet returned?"

"He would be lucky to get there before nightfall, so I suppose he had to take shelter for the night."

Then he might still be safe. Perhaps he'd stayed in that hut. Perhaps he'd slept on that same makeshift bed, shirtless and—

She wouldn't think about such things.

"Hopefully he'll return soon," Sir Algar continued.

"How many men did he take?"

"He went alone."

"Alone?" she cried, aghast. "He must be mad! He'll be killed or thrown in the dungeon."

"Rheged said he wouldn't risk any of his men getting hurt or killed because of what he'd done. He said it was bad enough that you were hurt."

Sir Algar drew up the stool and sat near the head of the bed. "I fear you, my dear, are suffering not just because of a hotheaded young man, but because of an older one who should have shown more wisdom. It was I, you see, who told Rheged that his prize wasn't real gold and sent him angry back to Castle DeLac. I shouldn't have blurted it out the way I did."

Tamsin picked at the edge of the sheet and took a deep breath. "What's happened is my uncle's fault, too," she replied, determined to be just. "Sir Rheged was right to say my uncle had played all those at the tournament for fools with that bogus prize—although that still didn't give him leave to take me."

"No, no, of course not. I don't approve of what he did, my lady, but I wouldn't want to see him arrested for it, either, although I can easily believe Simon would do exactly that.

"You see, my dear, I used to know your uncle well, years ago, when the two of us were younger men. He was a good companion then, or at least an entertaining one, although he rarely paid for food or wine. I can well believe your uncle thought he was being clever with a counterfeit prize, but he's never been poor, so he cannot understand what a valuable prize means to a man like Rheged who's had to fight for everything from childhood. Still, that doesn't excuse Rheged, although I must say I am surprised that he acted so impulsively. Usually he's the most levelheaded of men, even in battle, or so I've heard."

Usually but not always.

As she was usually levelheaded, except when she was near Rheged.

"Whatever came over him, though, I'm not going to excuse him. I give you my word that whatever has happened with Rheged at Castle DeLac, you shall be returned as soon as my physician says you can travel. Until then, you are under my protection."

Shouts and the sudden clatter of hooves came from the yard below.

"Let's hope that's Rheged now," Sir Algar said as

he went to the window while Tamsin moved to put her feet on the floor, until the pain forced her to stay still.

"It *is* Rheged, thank God!" Sir Algar said, turning toward her.

She sighed with relief, although she couldn't venture to guess what had transpired at Castle DeLac.

Then Rheged himself was there, his powerful body filling the doorway, his hair disheveled, his boots caked with mud and his expression grim. By rights, she should despise him. She should not be thinking that even exhausted and stained with travel, he was still the most handsome man she'd ever seen and she would have mourned if he'd been killed.

"Thank God you're back!" Sir Algar cried, hurrying toward him. "What happened with DeLac?"

"As long as I return the lady in a sennight, all will be well."

She should be glad that her uncle was willing to be merciful, for his sake and Mavis's, too.

Yet in spite of her need to save Mavis, Tamsin's heart sank. She didn't want to go back to Castle DeLac, or to marry Blane. Nevertheless, she wouldn't reveal her true feelings, not here, and especially not to him, lest he once again interfere and make more trouble for them all. "The marriage will proceed?"

Only then did Rheged turn his dark-eyed gaze to her. "I assume so. But I told him you would not return until the physician said it was safe for you to do so."

As if that was his responsibility. "*I* shall decide—"

"Gilbert—"

"Now, now, there's no need for an argument," Sir Algar interjected. "After all, Gilbert may well say she's able to travel in that time." He put his hand on Rheged's shoulder. "What Gilbert *has* said is that the lady requires rest, so we should go and let her do so."

Rheged gestured to someone outside and that maid-servant with the mole peered around the door. He made another impatient gesture, and she sidled into the room.

"While you are my guest, Hildie will be your servant, and you'll have all the comforts I can provide. I regret they will not be as fine as those you're used to, but I am not a wealthy man. Until later, my lady," Rheged finished before starting for the door.

"Sleep well, my lady," Sir Algar said. He followed his liegeman out of the chamber and to the hall below.

"Now, then, Rheged," Sir Algar said sternly as he joined the younger man near the hearth. "What *really* happened with DeLac?"

Chapter Eight

"It is as I told you, my lord," Rheged replied. "If I return the lady in a sennight, all will be well."

"You seem to forget that I know DeLac as well as you know Blane and his brood," Sir Algar said grimly. "There has to be more to this. He made threats, didn't he? He said he would go to the king if she's not returned, or he would have you imprisoned. And me, too, no doubt."

Rheged had to admit that he was right. "But it will not come to that, my lord," he finished, "or if it does, I will insist that I alone did the deed, so I alone should be brought before the king."

"I would like to hope your assertion would be treated with the respect it deserves, but unfortunately DeLac and John are not honorable or reasonable. They are greedy, ambitious men, and should this matter come to trial, DeLac will surely bribe whoever is necessary, including the king, to get the judgment he wants." Sir Algar sat in the chair by the hearth. "So I fear we must hope that for once, DeLac will be as good as his word and Tamsin will be well enough to travel in a sennight. We shall also have to pray that Blane is willing to overlook what's happened for the sake of the alliance."

"He's greedy and ambitious, too, my lord, so I think he will," Rheged said, sitting and running a hand through his long, dark hair. "But to think of Tamsin married to that man! The law would be on her side if she refused. Perhaps I can persuade her—"

"No, Rheged!" Sir Algar said firmly. "As distasteful as it is, what must be must be, for your sake as well as mine. You do not have to like or approve of her choice, but since the lady has apparently accepted her fate, you must, too."

The man who had never accepted the fate decreed for him by birth and status said, "If you will excuse me, my lord, I should give Gareth the watchword for the day."

"Of course. Then get some rest yourself, Rheged. You look exhausted. Where *did* you sleep last night?"

"Where I did the night before," Rheged replied before he bowed and went to find his friend.

Gareth had not been on the wall walk when Rheged had returned, and he could guess why. So much watchful waiting would make the soldiers and servants anxious, and anxious soldiers meant quarrels and perhaps a fistfight or two.

That didn't mean Rheged hadn't seen him when he returned to Cwm Bron. He'd spotted Gareth, along with a company of soldiers, in the large meadow closer to the mill engaged in sword practice.

They must still be there, he reasoned, heading to the gate where the guards on duty were warily watching him. He nodded in passing, just as he would under any circumstances, and continued toward the meadow with his usual steady and determined pace.

Drawing closer, he could hear Gareth, in the time-honored tradition of commanders of foot soldiers, loudly instructing and insulting the men under his tutelage. Like Gareth, they were dressed in boiled leather tunics and breeches and leather helms as they practiced with wooden swords.

"Damn me, lad, you'd have lost an arm if that sword was real!" Gareth chided one of the younger soldiers who'd failed to block a blow.

Since his friend's back was to Rheged, the blushing, blond-haired soldier saw Rheged before Gareth did and stiffened to attention. Gareth immediately swiveled on his heel.

"Come to see the poor sods you're stuck with, my lord?" he asked, his tone jovial but with a serious look in his eyes that told Rheged he was concerned about recent events. "Pathetic, mostly, but there might be a wee bit of hope for some of them."

"A word with you, Gareth, if you please," Rheged said.

This time, Gareth made no amusing reply. He nodded and gestured for one of the older men to come forward. "Rob, I'll let you have a go at trying to get it through their thick heads we're not playing patty fingers here."

The man whose face bore evidence of more than one skirmish nodded as Rheged led Gareth a short distance away, where they couldn't be heard over the clash of wooden weapons and Rob's forceful corrections.

"So DeLac didn't drag you into his dungeon," Gareth noted with genuine relief, telling Rheged just how worried he'd been.

"No, and as long as I return the lady in a sennight, he won't cause any trouble."

Gareth grinned. "Well, that's good." His grin faded. "Isn't it?"

"She'll go home when she's fit to travel and not before."

"Am I to take it you don't think that'll be in a sennight?"

"I don't know. But I won't risk her health if moving her is dangerous."

"Not even if DeLac takes exception? The man can afford to hire an army to take her back."

"I know." Rheged gave his friend the ghost of a smile. "But I have you."

"I appreciate the compliment, but we'll be no match for an army. Is she worth a battle? Is she worth losing Cwm Bron?"

"I have hope she'll either recover enough to go home in the time he demands or DeLac will agree to a delay."

"I guess we'll find out in seven days," Gareth said grimly.

"What are the men saying?" Rheged asked. Gareth might be their commander, but like Rheged, he'd come from nothing, and the men considered him one of their own, albeit one with authority and worthy of respect.

"They were baffled, of course, when you came back with a wounded woman and wondering what was afoot. Nervous, the lot of them, so I told them it was a Welsh tradition to abduct a bride."

Rheged stared at him. "You...what?"

"Well, I had to tell them something, didn't I? You coming back, then riding out again at once like a madman, coming back the second time with a woman, and her with an arrow in her leg to boot. And then you go riding off again with barely a word to anyone. Bound to cause them to wonder and worry and not just the soldiers. I heard Hildie talking to that quiet girl, the pretty one, Elvina. Hildie thinks you must have fallen in love with the lady at the tournament and she with you. She wanted to come away with you, but her uncle protested so you had to fight your way out. Very romantic, Hildie thinks. That gave me the idea to tell the men about the custom."

"It was a bad idea."

"Would you rather I told them the truth? That you lost your head and abducted the woman against her will and made an enemy of a man like DeLac? They'd be seeing soldiers around every tree and calling an alarm every time a branch moved in the breeze."

Rheged raked his long fingers through his hair. "If they know she was shot trying to get away from her uncle, how does that lessen their worry?"

"I told them you took back the prize for a bride price and to make peace with the man. Since you came back safe and sound, they'll believe it."

"Except that we aren't going to be married and she has to go back. And DeLac may attack us anyway."

"So we say she changed her mind. I wouldn't advise telling them anything more until we have to."

His men and the servants would think him a jilted suitor. Given what he'd done, that would be a small cross to bear. "All right. Let the soldiers and servants gossip as they will, but say no more about weddings and Welsh customs. And *don't* say anything like that to Sir Algar."

"Perish the thought—not that the man talks to me. He's a fine fellow, for a Norman, but he's a Norman nonetheless, and since I'm not a knight…well, his loss, I'm sure you'll agree."

"I do," Rheged replied, regretting that although Sir Algar was friendly to him, he was like most other Normans when it came to those beneath him in rank or heritage.

Gareth glanced back over his shoulder at the men still practicing. "Anything more? I should get back to those louts."

"I should give you the password for the night."

Gareth's eyes brightened with mischief. Nothing, not even the prospect of a battle, could dim his spirits for long. "Blast the bastard?" he suggested with a grin. "Death to DeLac?"

"No." Rheged smiled grimly in return. "Fate be damned."

The stocky young man sneered with disgust as he looked around the messy room in the inn on the road to Castle DeLac. Clothes and stockings and boots lay scattered on the floor. A carafe of wine, two goblets and the remains of a meal littered the table. The bed was little better, a tangled heap of sheets and blankets wound around and about the two occupants.

"Get out, slut," Broderick of Dunborough said to the woman lying beside the gray-haired man.

Eying him with dread, the slatternly woman quickly

gathered up her ragged, dirty clothes, clutched them to her sagging breasts and fled.

After she was gone, the stocky knight with the hard eyes and thick lips in a fleshy face shook the carafe, finding it nearly empty, before he went to the bed to rouse the old man sleeping there. "Father! Wake up!"

"What is it?" Sir Blane demanded querulously. He raised his head, his Adam's apple bobbing, his small, rheumy eyes dots of rage, his body as thin as his son's was prone to fat.

"I have news about your bride," Broderick replied. He strode to the door and grabbed the man waiting outside. Holding the fellow by his shoulder, Broderick dragged the young man with light brown, curling hair and weak chin into the room and shoved him toward the bed. "Tell him what you told me down below."

The minstrel clasped his hands and swallowed hard while the old man sat up in the bed and regarded him with annoyed expectancy, not even bothering to hide his nakedness.

"I...I..." the minstrel stammered "...that is, I was there...and I saw..."

"You woke me up to listen to the gibbering of an idiot?" Sir Blane demanded as he got out of bed. Still naked, he struck his son hard across the face. "Fool! Call the wench back—and you'll pay her this time, not me. Then find me another one, too. Younger. For later."

Hatred smoldered in Broderick's eyes, but he stayed where he was, despite the red welt growing on his cheek. "Tell him what's happened," he ordered the minstrel, who was sidling toward the door. "Or was all that a lie? If so, you'll rue the day you—"

"No, no, it's true, it's true!" Gordon cried, looking from the angry young man to the irate, thin old one whose lips were tinged a cold blue.

He quickly told them all that he had seen and heard when Sir Rheged had returned to Castle Delac with the prize. "Lady Thomasina was taken right out from under Lord DeLac's nose," he finished. "The Welshman just grabbed her and rode away!"

"He's talking about your bride, my lord," Broderick said to his father, whose expression betrayed neither shock nor outrage. "She's been abducted."

"Aye, aye, that's right," the minstrel confirmed. "He—the one who took her—he was angry about the tournament prize and so he came back and took Lady Thomasina."

Blane finally picked up his bedrobe lying over a chair and drew it on over his scrawny body. Even then, he didn't look angry or upset. If anything, he looked... pleased. "Her uncle did nothing to stop it?"

"He tried," Gordon answered. "He ordered his men to stop them, but Sir Rheged was gone before his soldiers could get to their horses and by the time they gave chase, they'd disappeared."

Blane darted a look at his son before he addressed the minstrel. "Sir Rheged, you say?"

"Aye, my lord, Sir Rheged of Cwm Bron, him they call the Wolf of Wales."

Blane wrapped the bedrobe about himself and slid into the chair. "Well, well, Broderick. Sir Rheged of Cwm Bron. Your very dear friend."

Gordon thought that if Sir Rheged was Sir Broderick's friend, he'd hate to see how Broderick would regard an enemy.

"So he's taken my bride," Blane continued. "For vengeance, or his own lascivious ends, perhaps." The old man froze the minstrel with his gaze. "When was this dastardly deed done?"

"Four days ago, my lord."

"You hear that, my son? Rheged has had her for four days." Blane turned his attention back to the quaking minstrel. "Has he demanded a ransom?"

"I...I don't know, my lord. I left Castle DeLac just after she was taken."

"Understandable. I'm sure no one was in a mood for entertainment after that." Blane again addressed his eldest son. "Does this fool have any other news we should know?"

Broderick shook his head.

"Then he can go," his father said, and with that, Broderick grabbed the minstrel by his collar and pushed him out the door, slamming it behind him.

"That Welshman is as good as dead!" Broderick declared as the minstrel's clattering footsteps died away.

As if he had all the time in the world and nothing else to do, Sir Blane picked up the heel of a loaf and began to tear it apart with his long, gnarled fingers. "Is that any way to repay a man who's done us such a favor?"

"Favor?" his son repeated with disdain.

"Favor," Blane replied, dropping what remained of the loaf and dusting off his hands. "If DeLac wants an alliance with me, simpleton, he'll have no choice now but to give me his pretty virgin daughter, and a larger dowry, too."

Which would be a waste of a pretty virgin, Broderick thought, unless his father wanted to share. He did that sometimes, when the mood was on him.

As for the Welshman... "I'm still going to kill Rheged," Broderick declared.

"I suppose this time you might succeed."

"I know his tricks now."

Sir Blane laughed the wheezing, mocking laugh that all his sons hated. "Go ahead and try, my son. If you're successful, all well and good, and if you're not, I don't suppose Roland or Gerrard will mind it if you fail."

The old man's wheezing laugh turned into a hacking cough. "Don't just stand there, you oaf!" he said as he gasped for breath. "Fetch me some wine!"

Broderick obeyed, even as he wondered how much longer it would be before the old man was in his grave.

"You're healing quite well, my lady," Gilbert said as he finished tying the new bandage around her calf a day later. An anxious Hildie hovered nearby, having come with the physician and a bundle in her arms. Tamsin had yet to discover what was in the bundle, but that question was far less important than Gilbert's verdict.

"Then I can get out of bed?" Tamsin asked. For years she'd been awake and dressed and about her duties as soon as the first cock crowed. This forced rest was almost beyond bearing.

"Yes, and you may walk about a bit, as long as your leg isn't too painful. If it begins to ache, though, you must sit down and rest at once."

"I shall," she promised, glad she could at least get out of bed.

"I shall return in two days' time, my lady," Gilbert said as he picked up his medicinal chest, "to check again."

"Thank you, Gilbert," she replied. "I appreciate all your care."

The physician nodded and left the room. The moment he was gone, Tamsin threw back the sheet and blanket and put her feet on the floor, paying no heed to Hildie setting the bundle on the foot of the bed and opening it.

Tamsin eased herself upright and took a tentative step. Not too painful at all, she thought with relief, then glanced at the end of the bed to see Hildie standing with a broad smile. Three woolen gowns—one a very pretty shade of green, one of dark blue and one a light brown with darker bands of brown around the cuffs and bodice—two linen shifts, some stockings, a dark woolen cloak and an ivory comb were spread out on the bed before her. A pair of light leather slippers stood on the floor.

Tamsin's eyes widened as she sat back down. "Where did all this come from?"

"They're a gift from Sir Algar."

Tamsin reached out to touch the prettiest gown of soft green wool. "It's too much. I will accept the shifts and stockings and slippers, but I have the gown I came in. Has it not been washed?"

Hildie's face fell. "Yes. I suppose it's dry by now."

Tamsin thought a moment. She might be considered ungracious if she refused the gifts, and since they weren't from Rheged... "I've never had such pretty dresses," she admitted. Unlike Mavis, she was never on display, like an article in a stall at a market. "I wouldn't want to disappoint Sir Algar after he's been so kind."

"Or Sir Rheged. He'll think you're a vision in these gowns."

"What Sir Rheged thinks is no concern of mine," she decisively replied. She was well aware that servants gossiped, and she must nip any sort of romantic notions in the bud. "However, I wouldn't want Sir Algar to think me ungrateful."

"I think he'd be a tad miffed if you refused, my lady," Hildie confirmed gravely.

"I shall need some help to dress."

Hildie hurried to help her change into one of the clean, soft linen shifts and the lovely green gown.

"This fabric is marvelous," Tamsin said, smoothing down the skirt as Hildie tied the laces at the back of the fitted bodice.

"That's my sister Frida's work," Hildie replied proudly. "She's a wonderful weaver, my lady. She's married to the miller and expecting her first, so she hasn't been weaving for a while. She'll be happy to hear you like her work, though, I promise you."

"Has she thought of selling it in Salisbury? Or London? It would surely fetch a good price."

"Do you think so?" Hildie replied, her eyes wide as she came around Tamsin to face her.

"Indeed, I do."

"I'll be sure to tell her so. Now sit ye down on the stool, my lady, and let me run this comb through your hair."

Tamsin walked slowly to the stool, sitting carefully and easing her calf forward.

"You've lovely hair, my lady. I bet the young noble-men have been pestering you for locks of it for years."

Tamsin had to smile at that. "Not once has anyone ever asked for a lock of my hair."

"No? God save me, are they all blind at Castle DeLac or what?"

"Blinded by my cousin's beauty, perhaps," Tamsin answered without rancor. "Mavis is very beautiful, with hair like gold."

"The only woman Sir Algar and Sir Rheged's been talking about since he got back from Castle DeLac is you."

Tamsin flushed, and yet there had to be only one explanation—she was the only woman from Castle DeLac Rheged had abducted.

"Help me to the window, please," she said after Hildie had tied her braid. "I'd like a breath of fresh air."

Hildie put her arm under Tamsin's shoulder and helped her limp to the window. Thankfully her leg didn't hurt too much. When she opened the shutters and took a deep breath, she felt almost normal as she surveyed the rest of the castle.

It was small and old, with a single curtain wall and four towers, one at each corner. Parts of the west wall had crumbled away, and although there was some scaf-folding erected, indicating repairs were under way, it was likely to be some time before such a job could be completed. The round keep she was in was at least as old as the wall, and she could see the wooden steps that led into the second level, below this one. The lowest level in a keep was usually the dungeon, or perhaps a store-room. She could also see what had to be the kitchen,

judging by the smoke coming out of the louvered opening in the roof, as well as the wooden walkway to the
keep. The kitchen was wattle and daub, and so were a
few of the other buildings, such as the stables. One other
building was made of stone—a long, tall building close
by the kitchen. Another storeroom, perhaps, although it
seemed large for that. Otherwise, all the other buildings
were made of wood, and all the roofs were thatched.
The yard itself was fairly muddy, so likely missing a
few cobblestones in places.

It would be expensive to repair this fortress completely and make it siege-worthy. No wonder Rheged
had been upset that the prize her uncle had offered
wasn't worth as much as it seemed.

But it wasn't the sympathy she felt for Rheged, or the
state of his fortress, that kept her riveted to the window.

Rheged stood in the middle of a line of soldiers at
the far end of the inner ward, in a relatively large open
area where livestock would be penned if the villagers
had to seek safety. Dressed exactly like the others, he
held a bow in his hand and had a quiver of arrows on
his back. Also like the other men in the line, he faced
butts of straw with targets of cloth, a bull's-eye drawn
on them with charcoal. More soldiers waited nearby,
talking and laughing and calling out encouragement.

This was clearly a practice, but it also seemed to
be some kind of competition. It was also obvious that
Rheged was far more comfortable among the common
soldiers than he'd been in the great hall of Castle DeLac.

"Maybe you ought to sit down, my lady," Hildie said
with a hint of anxiety.

"In a moment," Tamsin said as Rheged nocked his arrow.

Apparently nobody else intended to shoot, for they all watched the lord of Cwm Bron who, with one fluid motion, drew back the arrow and bowstring and, seemingly without aiming, let fly. She held her breath as his arrow arched high in the sky before coming down and she gasped with delight when it struck a bull's-eye.

The men began cheering, although a few looked a little disgruntled as they reached into their belts, no doubt having lost a wager. She'd lived in a fortress long enough to know that soldiers bet all the time, on almost anything.

Rheged smiled and accepted their praise with a shrug of his broad shoulders.

He looked years younger and even more handsome when he smiled.

"Please, won't you sit down and rest a bit, my lady?" Hildie pleaded. "Sir Algar and Sir Rheged might be angry with me if you don't."

"I shall take any blame," Tamsin assured her just as Rheged looked up at the window, as if he somehow knew that she was there.

Blushing, Tamsin turned away. "Yes, I believe I should sit down," she said, trying to sound calm and composed as she limped back to the stool. "Hildie, I'm not used to being so idle. There must be *something* I can do."

What was Tamsin doing out of bed? Rheged wondered, momentarily oblivious to the excited men around him. Surely she should still be resting, unless Gilbert had pronounced her fit enough to stand.

"Look you, stunned by his own success, he is!" Gareth declared, forcefully reminding Rheged that he was not alone.

"That's enough archery for now, Gareth," he said as a slight drizzle began to fall.

"I'm pleased with your efforts," he called out to the rest of the men, noting that a few of them were rubbing their shoulders. "But I'm not so pleased I don't see plenty that needs to be better. Still, you've earned your meal tonight, so those not on watch, enjoy. Those on watch, I'll see you've a hot meal waiting when your watch is done."

The men gave a cheer, although there was a somewhat subdued response from the more exhausted among them.

"Give the youngest the task of dealing with the butts," he said to Gareth. "They need to build up their strength."

"Aye, Rheged, aye," Gareth said. "Anything else?"

"Not now," Rheged replied.

"I'll see you in the hall, then."

"Aye," Rheged replied, turning to head back to the keep.

As he walked toward it, he couldn't help wondering what Tamsin thought when she saw him with a bow. No doubt even less than she did already, given that she was nobly born. Most Normans considered bows the weapons of peasants. He, however, had no prejudices against any weapon. If it was effective, he would wield it, and as best he could.

Nor should he trouble himself with what Tamsin thought about him, or anything else. She would be gone soon, back to her greedy uncle and the marriage that she wanted.

Chapter Nine

When Rheged entered the hall, he found Sir Algar nodding in the chair by the hearth. He tried to pass him quietly, but the man awoke with a start. "How was the practice, then?"

"The men are much improved," Rheged said as Sir Algar gestured for him to sit and join him by the fire.

"So is Lady Thomasina," Sir Algar said. "Gilbert was very pleased with her progress."

"I saw her standing at the window."

A frown came to Sir Algar's face. "He didn't tell me she could get out of bed."

Rheged spotted Hildie coming down the stairs from the upper chamber and summoned her. "Did the physician give Lady Thomasina leave to get out of bed?"

"Aye, my lord, he said she could walk about a bit, as long as her leg didn't trouble her too much. She's to rest if it does. She was that pleased, I must say. I think she was weary of being abed. She was only on her feet a little while, though, just long enough to get a breath of fresh air at the window. She's sitting now and wants to do a bit of sewing and sent me to find needles and thread. I don't think the lady's used to being idle, my lord."

Given the way Tamsin had bustled about Castle DeLac, Rheged could well believe she would find enforced idleness as bad as imprisonment, just as he had the few times he'd been wounded. "Do as she asks," he said, "so long as she's careful not to overtax her strength. If you see her tiring or in pain and she refuses to return to bed, come to me at once. Now you may go and fetch what she requires."

"Aye, my lord," Hildie said with a bob of a bow.

As the maidservant hurried away, Sir Algar sighed and smiled wistfully. "Granted we wouldn't want Tamsin to do more damage to her leg, but if she's at all like her mother—and I do believe she is—I don't think we'll have much chance trying to force her to rest. Her mother was the most stubborn woman I've ever met."

"You knew her mother well?"

"I knew the whole family well," Algar replied, "until old Edward DeLac tried to force his daughter to marry. Cordelia refused and ran off with another man. After that, I kept my distance."

"Until my hasty act put you in jeopardy. I am truly sorry for that, my lord."

"I'm not. I would never have met Cordelia's daughter otherwise. Still, it's an unfortunate situation. Her mother's passions ran strong and deep, and I suspect her daughter's similar in that, as well. Her love would be a great prize and her hate…well, it will last a lifetime."

"I don't doubt that, my lord," Rheged replied.

* * *

"You're having us on," Dan the groom declared from his place by the big hearth in the kitchen of Cwm Bron. "She ain't."

"She is," Hildie retorted. "Sitting there in his bedchamber mending that old tunic of his like she was already his wife."

Shy Elvina sighed as she chopped some turnips before putting them in a pot of boiling water hanging from the pothook over the fire.

Foster, the lean and youthful cook, stopped kneading the dough for the crust of a beef pie. "I th-thought l-ladies only d-did em…em…fancy work," he stuttered.

"Well, not her," Hildie replied. "She wanted to be doing something, and finally suggested mending. I could hardly say no to that, could I? So she had me fetch needles and thread, and then open Sir Rheged's clothes chest."

Elvina gasped and Foster's ladle hovered in midair. "What did you do?" Dan demanded, leaning forward.

"He said she was to be treated with respect as an honored guest, didn't he?" Hildie replied defensively, "and she was looking at me like…well, like *he* does when he wants something done, so I opened the chest and grabbed the first thing I could—that old tunic. I swear I was that relieved it had a torn seam, or she might have had me rooting through all his things. I hate to think what would happen if he found out I'd done that!"

Dan shook his head as if the very thought was too terrible to contemplate.

"And then he asks me what she's doing!" Hildie continued. "I swear I nearly swooned!"

"Wh-what did you s-say to h-him?" Foster asked breathlessly.

"I said she wanted to do some sewing. Thank the good Lord he didn't ask me what kind of sewing!"

The others all nodded in sympathy.

"I'll say this for her, she's not lazy, not like some of them ladies I've heard of," Hildie went on. "Sir Rheged could do a sight worse."

"Then you…then you think he really wants to marry her?" Elvina asked, her voice as quiet as if they were in the chapel.

"Why else would he bring her here?" Hildie replied. "Besides, he's mad in love with her. And she with him."

Elvina's eyes grew wide as a waterwheel. "How can you tell?"

"I got eyes," Hildie replied as if their lord's feeling should be obvious to all save the sightless.

"Aye, it must be true," Dan said. "Gareth told the men it's a Welsh custom to abduct the bride and that's what Rheged's done."

"But there's been no talk of a wedding," Elvina protested.

"Yet. They have to decide about the dowry and the bride price, no doubt," Dan explained. "That's why Rheged's been back and forth."

Hildie dropped her voice to a whisper and regarded them knowingly. "I'm sure they're already lovers."

Elvina's delicately featured face reddened. Dan looked like a man trying to appear so worldly that Hildie's observation was no shock to him, while Foster regarded Hildie as if she'd just announced he'd been summoned to cook for the pope.

"Aye, Foster, me lad," Hildie declared with a brisk nod, "you'd best start planning a wedding feast, and I'd best get back to my lady."

The rain fell steadily harder as the afternoon progressed. Tamsin thought the sound of it pounding on the slate roof would drive her mad, so when Hildie said it was time for her to go to the hall to help serve the evening meal, Tamsin also left the upper chamber to join the others below, even if that meant enduring Rheged's stony silence and even grimmer visage.

Making her way down the curved stairs, she noticed at once that, like the rest of Cwm Bron, the large, round chamber was in need of some work. The hearth apparently hadn't been swept in weeks, cobwebs hung from the torch sconces and the rushes on the flagstone floor looked and smelled days old. The simple, bare furnishings were rough and unpolished, and it seemed there was but one chair, which Sir Algar was currently occupying. Rheged sat beside him on a bench. Other men were likewise seated on benches at the tables, while hounds and serving women moved among them.

His expression impassive, Rheged rose when he saw her. Sir Algar beamed a smile as he, too, got to his feet. Although his tunic was dark and plain like Rheged's, it was made of obviously finer fabric, and tonight he sported a wide gold chain around his neck.

"This is an unexpected pleasure, my lady!" he cried as he pulled out the chair for her to sit.

Rheged said nothing. However, he glanced at a man sitting at another table nearby. At that look, the equally long-haired, bearded fellow with a scar where an eyebrow should be jumped to his feet. All the other men rose, too, with expressions that varied from frankly curious to suspicious.

While she, who had never before been the center of so much attention, blushed to the soles of her feet.

"Gilbert said you were doing well," Sir Algar remarked as they all returned to their seats and Rheged made a place for his lord on the bench beside him. "But perhaps it's a little early for much exertion."

"My leg is only a little sore, Sir Algar," she assured him, "and I confess I'm desperate for company. I'm not used to spending so much time alone."

"No doubt, no doubt," Sir Algar agreed. "We're delighted to have you dine with us, aren't we, Rheged?"

"Delighted."

"I'm sure Foster's outdone himself, as usual," Sir Algar noted as Hildie brought another trencher and a goblet and spoon and set them in front of Tamsin. "I tell you, my lady, Rheged need never be ashamed of his cook. Foster was trained in the king's own kitchen. Rheged did Foster a service once, so when the fellow heard Rheged had been given this estate, he appeared one day and asked to cook for him. Isn't that right, Rheged?"

"Yes, my lord."

"What did you do for him again?" Sir Algar prompted.

"He was being set upon by some ruffians and I suggested they leave him alone."

"Suggested?" Sir Algar repeated with a laugh. "I can imagine—at the point of your sword!"

"There was no need to offer violence. They were cowards and ran away when I challenged them."

Tamsin could well believe one look from Rheged of the sort he'd given her when he was angry would be enough to send all but the most hardened rogues and vagabonds fleeing.

"So now he has one of the best cooks in England."

"Men fight well when they're well fed," Rheged coolly observed, "and servants serve better when they're not starving."

"I quite agree," Tamsin said, not at all surprised that a man born poor would want good meals and be willing to pay for them.

"Why don't you tell her about the tournament in Kent, the one where we met?" Sir Algar suggested.

Hildie brought a basket of fresh, fragrant bread to the table, and another, more bashful maidservant ladled a thick, rich beef stew into the trenchers before them.

"You should have seen him, my lady!" Sir Algar continued as they started to eat the best beef stew Tamsin had ever tasted. "His armor was the most motley collection of metal I'd ever seen."

"It was all I could afford."

"So naturally all the other participants in the tournament assumed that he'd be as poorly trained as his armor was made. If they'd taken a good look at his horse, they might have known better, eh, Rheged?"

"I spent my last coin on Jevan, and he was worth every penny."

"Now perhaps, but then? The poor beast had been half-starved. He was nearly as skinny as you were, Rheged."

"I wasn't skinny."

"You looked like you hadn't had a decent meal in

months. Anyway, there he was, in his collection of bits and bobs of armor, seated on a most unimpressive mount, facing some of the finest young nobles—"

"Richest," Rheged interjected. "Not necessarily finest."

"Very well, *richest* young nobles in the land," Sir Algar amended, "and everyone expected him to fall in the first tilt. Instead, he hits his opponent's shield one blow and off the fellow tumbles. Who was that?"

"I don't recall."

"Whoever it was," Sir Algar continued, sopping up some of the thick gravy with his bread, "down he went with a crash. Broke his shield in the fall and was knocked right out. After that, it was a different story, although nobody thought Rheged would win the day."

"Nobody else had so much to gain."

"Or lose, eh?" Sir Algar replied, reaching for more bread while Tamsin took a sip of wine that wasn't nearly as fine as the bread or stew. "I tell you, my lady, you never saw such tenacity. He sat on that saddle like his life depended on it and never did get unseated. But that's not the best part. The best part is at the feast that followed. Rheged appears without even a scratch—"

"I had plenty of bruises."

"Not on your face," Sir Algar noted. "The young ladies were like bees to flowers, and a few of the older ones, too. Naturally the young noblemen were not well pleased, especially when they'd not only been defeated, but had to pay to get their horses and arms and accoutrements back from Rheged. So one of them finally insulted Rheged to his face—who was that again?"

"Sir Francis Bellegardie."

"What exactly did he say to you?"

"He questioned my parentage and suggested I didn't belong there."

"Not like that," Sir Algar chided.

"His exact words aren't fit for a lady's ears."

"I've met Sir Francis," Tamsin said, remembering the young guest of her uncle's who'd tried to back her into a corner. She'd managed to evade his clumsy groping, but only just. "He's a most vain and stupid fellow, so I can imagine the sort of thing he'd say."

"Rheged laid him flat with one blow, right there in the hall. Didn't say a word, just hit him, then apologized to the host for disturbing the peace of his hall, sat down and drank his wine like nothing at all had happened."

She wished she could have seen that.

"I was tired, or I would have ignored him."

"That wasn't all," Sir Algar continued gleefully. "When it came time to dance, who was the most anxious to dance with you? Who hovered around you all night until you practically had to shoo her away?"

"I don't remember."

"If you don't, I do—Lady Angelica, Sir Francis's own sister! And you should have seen the way she looked at the other women he danced with! I was afraid there'd be a murder done before the night was out. How many times did you dance with her? Two times? Three?"

"I'd rather fight than dance."

"What a thing to say with a lady present!"

"Nevertheless it's true." Rheged slid from the bench and rose with the same athletic grace with which he'd drawn the bow. "Now if you'll both excuse me, I need to speak to the commander of my garrison. One of my shepherds found three of his flock dead, their throats and bellies torn open, on the far pasture on the ridge. We'll be fox-hunting tomorrow as soon as the rain lets up."

"You're sure it was a fox?" Sir Algar asked. "Not wolves or outlaws?"

"It's the work of a fox to kill and leave the bodies lying. Wolves or wild dogs would have eaten more of what they'd killed. Men would have taken the carcasses and the shepherd would have found only blood and maybe footprints, if he found anything at all."

"And you're equally certain the rain is going to stop?"

"Before dawn, my lord, so we'll be riding out at first light. Would you care to join us?"

"God save me, no! I hate riding in the wet."

"Then good night, my lord. My lady." Rheged bowed, then went to join the man without an eyebrow.

"That's Gareth," Sir Algar explained to Tamsin. "He and Rheged served together for years. After Rheged was knighted and I gave him this estate, he sent for Gareth and offered him the command of his garrison."

"He's a Welshman, too?"

"Yes, and like Rheged, born a peasant."

There was no need for her to know more about Rheged, and yet she wasn't able to completely subdue her curiosity. "How did the son of peasants become a knight?"

Sir Algar twisted the stem of the goblet in his long, slender fingers. "It's rather remarkable, really. He was a foot soldier in the king's army in France and they were besieging a castle. The siege had dragged on for days until Rheged scaled the wall in the dark, alone. He got a rope around a merlon so others could follow before he was discovered. The castle fell to John's troops and the king was suitably grateful."

She shivered as she envisioned Rheged climbing up a wall with a coil of rope around him, his face intense with concentration while he sought hand- and footholds. "It's a miracle he didn't fall to his death."

"He was wounded in the side during the fight and took several weeks to recover. After that, he left the king's army and returned to England. He was poor, but he had a knighthood and enough money to pay for a license to participate in tournaments. That's how I met him, at that tournament in Kent. He was clearly better than any other man I'd seen that day and I had an estate that needed an overlord, so I offered it to him if he swore allegiance to me. He agreed before he even saw the fortress, provided he could name it what he wished. I have no objections to the name he chose, although we aren't in Wales."

Sir Algar raised a hand as if he thought she was about to speak. "I warned him the place was in sad disrepair, but he didn't hesitate. Nor have I regretted making the offer. I would do the same again even after his abduction of you, I must admit." He smiled. "Otherwise, I'd never have met you."

"You said you knew my mother. Did you know my father, too?" Tamsin asked, seizing a rare opportunity to talk about her parents.

"Not well. Did your mother ever tell you why she and her husband never visited your uncle?"

"I knew they were not on friendly terms, but that was all I knew."

"Your uncle didn't approve of their marriage, and neither did your grandfather. He had made a betrothal agreement for your mother, you see, and your uncle was all for the match. It would have created a valuable alliance and given the family more influence at court."

As her own marriage would.

"Then your mother told them she loved another. They were angry but thought they could compel her to marry whoever they wanted, until she told them she was with child."

Tamsin stared at him in dismay. "Me?"

Sir Algar regarded her with equal distress. "Forgive me, my dear. I should have spoken with more care."

She reached out to touch his arm. "It's all right. It explains something my uncle said to me the last time we spoke. And other things, too."

Like the way he'd scowled at her the first day she arrived at Castle DeLac and many times since, and seemingly without reason, or at least not one that she could fathom.

Sir Algar put his hand over hers. "Unfortunately, instead of making her father and brother release her from the betrothal, that only made them angry. They tried to force your mother to tell them who her lover was, but she wouldn't. She was so beautiful and charming and sweet, she'd had no end of suitors, and it could have been any one of them. Not that her virtue had ever been in question, not until then. She treated all her admirers the same, or so it seemed. So her father beat her and locked her in her chamber, intending to keep her imprisoned until she told them everything. One night she escaped and one of her admirers, a visiting knight named Sir Renard de Salacourt—"

"My father!"

"He risked his life for her—and when I say he risked his life, my dear, he did. Your grandfather and your uncle would surely have killed him if he'd been caught. He was a very brave fellow, Sir Renard de Salacourt."

"I wish I could remember my parents better," Tamsin said softly, trying to picture her parents and failing. "My uncle would get angry if anyone even mentioned them."

"To see your mother's face you need only look at your own reflection, my dear," Sir Algar replied with a gentle smile. He toyed with his goblet a moment before speaking again. "I hope you can overlook Rheged's abrupt manner. He's a little unpolished, but he has a loyal heart, and a good one. That's how I know he hasn't touched you, other than to tend to your wound and bring you here."

Except that he had touched her, and kissed her, too— but Sir Algar didn't need to know about that. "No, he hasn't hurt me."

"And you are adamant about returning? Blane is not a good man, or a worthy one."

She didn't want to discuss her future husband. "I don't relish the prospect of marriage to Sir Blane, but I won't go back on my word."

"No, no, of course not. I understand completely. And so does Rheged."

Chapter Ten

"So it's only one fox, you're thinking?" Gareth asked as he rode beside Rheged the next morning. The newly risen sun made the wet grass and bracken glisten, and puddles dotted the well-worn path up the wooded ridge.

"Probably," Rheged replied.

They rode on in silence, and so did the men behind them. Only the hounds were noisy, barking and yipping with excitement as they strained on their leashes.

"Sir Algar didn't want to come?" Gareth asked, his tone carefully noncommittal.

"He doesn't like to ride in the wet."

"Aye, there's that, I suppose."

"What else?"

"The lady."

Rheged darted a glance at his friend. "What do you mean?"

Gareth regarded him with wide, apparently innocent eyes. "Nothing, except she's a damn sight more pleasant to look at than me or these louts, and it's likely a lot more enjoyable to sit by the fire with her than riding about chasing a fox."

Rheged knew Gareth well enough to realize exactly what he was implying and be appalled by it. "Sir Algar's old enough to be her father!"

"She's lovely and keeps a good household, or so I hear, so who could blame the man for wanting to wed? He'd have a nursemaid in his old age, if nothing else, but not being dead, he's likely thinking of something else, too. And Sir Algar's rich, so it'd be a good match for her. Better than Blane anyway, from all I've heard about the man."

"You're mad."

"Just practical, and there's no need to glare at me like you're a poked bear in a cage, Rheged. I see what I see, that's all, and you're not planning to marry her, are you?"

"I'd never wed a relative of DeLac's and I need a woman with a large dowry to make Cwm Bron strong. DeLac's a miser."

"So you'll be looking for a wealthy merchant's daughter or widow perhaps, is it? Well, that'd surely be easier than courting some Norman nobleman's daughter. Or niece."

"Nothing I've gotten has ever come easy, Gareth. You know that."

"Aye, Rheged, aye, I do. And all the better for it when you get it, eh?"

The hounds suddenly leapt on their leashes and started to bay.

"Let them go!" Rheged called to the huntsmen, at the

same time spotting a flash of red fur among the rocks higher on the ridge.

The fast-moving, lithe fox led them an exhausting chase over the rough terrain. It easily slipped under and around rocks and fallen trees and more than once they seemed to have lost it completely. Fortunately the dogs caught the scent again, until they finally had it cornered in a narrow crevice between some rocks on the riverbank a few miles from the mill. The dogs, tired but still excited, surrounded the crevice that was too narrow for them to enter. Some of the dogs were in the front, while others crowded at the sides and the far end above the opening.

There was no doubt the fox was there, though. The eyes of the cornered animal gleamed in the shadowy darkness and they could hear it snarl.

There was no doubt about what had to be done next, either.

Rheged dismounted, took his hunting spear and made his way through the pack of panting, barking dogs. He straddled the crevice and plunged his spear into the darkness. There was a brief yelp from the fox, and the deed was done.

He twisted the shaft of the spear, then waited a moment to be sure the beast was dead before he drew out the body. The large fox's slack mouth gaped and blood dripped from the wound in the back of its neck. Despite that, the fur could still be used, perhaps for the collar of a lady's cloak—a gift to Tamsin as a way to make amends for bringing her to Cwm Bron.

"Well, that's one less nuisance," Gareth remarked,

holding the fox while Rheged cleaned his spear. "Not the most thrilling hunt I've ever been on, though."

"The fox is dead and that's all that matters," Rheged replied as he took the fox and went to his horse. Meanwhile, the huntsman began gathering the dogs and leading them back to Cwm Bron, joined by the other men who'd accompanied them.

When Rheged tossed the dead fox over his saddle, Myr whinnied in protest and tried to back away. He kept a firm hand on the reins and murmured a few words to quiet the gelding before mounting and heading for home. Gareth rode with him, keeping up a stream of meaningless chatter about more exciting hunts he'd been on, narrow escapes he'd had and the wild boars and stags he'd killed almost single-handedly. Since Gareth needed no encouragement to keep talking, Rheged was free to think about other things.

Including things he would rather not think about.

Like Tamsin. At least when he was chasing the fox, she hadn't been in his thoughts. He hadn't been remembering how regal and beautiful she looked in the green gown that clung to her shapely figure like water flowing over a rock, or haunted by the memory of her slender body in his arms.

As for Sir Algar's reasons for staying behind, Gareth had to be wrong. The older man just didn't want to ride in the wet and the mud.

It wasn't that Rheged was jealous of his overlord and what Sir Algar could offer a woman like Tamsin. He'd meant what he said to Gareth. He needed a woman with a sizable dowry to prosper, to be safe and secure in this dangerous world, and Simon DeLac would surely never give Tamsin a penny if she were betrothed to him or any Welshman.

If she would even consider the idea, which she surely wouldn't.

"That was the last time I tried that, I can tell you. I suppose you'll be saying I was a fool to even think of... Rheged, have you heard even one word I've said?" Gareth demanded as they rode through the gates of Cwm Bron.

"I heard..." Rheged began, then fell silent as he surveyed the courtyard.

Across the yard, that pretty, quiet serving woman named Elvina stood at the well, turning the handle as fast as she could while another serving woman waited with empty buckets at her feet. Smoke churned out of the kitchen chimney as if it were aflame, or Foster had decided to feed the entire county. Despite the woman's hasty drawing of water at the well, the kitchen couldn't be on fire, or more people would be in the yard with buckets, although there were certainly more people there than usual. Three men with mortar and stones knelt by one of the large holes in the cobblestoned yard, filling and repairing it. An old man—one of his soldier's fathers, he thought   was seated on a stool near a storeroom making what appeared to be a broom. Other servants rushed about carrying baskets and bundles and tools as if they were about to be besieged.

Gareth, too, reined in his horse. "God save us, what's going on?" he muttered.

As Rheged and Gareth looked around in confusion, Dan came hurtling out of the stable, and Hildie appeared at the door of a storeroom. Her head down, her arms full of linen, she began to hurry across the yard as if she were pursued by all the hounds of hell.

"What's going on here?" Rheged demanded of the groom as he dismounted and lifted the fox's carcass from the saddle.

His voice low as if he feared being overheard, Dan nodded in the direction of the keep, which was a good thirty yards away. "Nothing's amiss, my lord. No attack or anything. It's…it's *her*."

There was only one possible person to whom he could be referring. Nevertheless Rheged said, "I assume you mean Lady Thomasina?"

"Aye, my lord." Dan looked about furtively, then leaned forward and whispered, "The moment you were out of the gates she comes down to the hall and starts giving orders right and left. You didn't say whether we was to obey or not, but she weren't taking no for an answer, if you follow me, so we all thought we'd better do as she says."

Rheged called out to Hildie, who hurried over to him. "Yes, my lord?"

"What are you doing?"

"I'm to wash this linen, my lord. *All of it,*" she added incredulously. One would think she'd been asked to wash every piece of linen in England.

Gareth started to laugh, until Rheged silenced him with a look.

This was *his* home, by God. His castle, his hall, his servants, earned with his blood and sweat and risk. She was a guest here, not his wife or chatelaine.

As Rheged marched toward the keep, the fox's tail still gripped in his hand, Gareth let out a low whistle.

"Our Rheged's in a foul humor, Dan, and I fear he's likely to stay that way until the lady leaves."

With a mournful frown, Dan nodded his agreement.

Rheged strode into the keep, then came to an abrupt halt. It was as if he'd marched into the wrong hall, one that smelled of beeswax and fresh herbs instead of sweaty men, beef stew and leather.

The tables and benches had been washed and polished, the rushes covering the flagstones swept out, replaced and sprinkled with rosemary, and every single cobweb had disappeared.

Sir Algar slumbered in the chair by the hearth, which had also been swept clean, and a fire of dry, snapping wood warmed the chamber.

Most disconcerting of all, standing by the hearth and dressed in that pretty gown of green wool was Tamsin, her hands clasped before her, regarding him expectantly and looking for all the world like she'd been waiting for his return.

He stood motionless until she started to limp toward him. He immediately walked toward her. "You should be sitting down."

In the chamber above, not waiting here as if you were my wife.

"I'm feeling even better than yesterday," she replied. She nodded at the carcass still in his hand. "You were successful, I see."

"Aye. I thought you could use this." He held out the dead fox. "The fur, I mean. For a collar for your cloak, perhaps," he added, feeling like a bumpkin, but not wanting her to think he meant it to be eaten.

"Thank you, my lord," she replied, taking the fox gingerly by the tail, her arm stretched out away from her.

"It's quite dead," he assured her.

"Yes, I can see that. And I'm sure the fur will be very warm. Elvina," she called to the maidservant who had entered the hall and was sidling past them, "take this for me, please."

The slender young woman grabbed the beast by the tail. "Yes, my lady," she whispered, blushing and nodding a bow before she hurried off with the carcass.

Fortunately their exchange had given him a chance to compose himself. "I see you found a way to occupy your time."

"I noticed a few tasks that needed doing. I also had a bath prepared for you in the upper chamber."

"I don't need a bath."

"God save me, that's not a very gracious response when the lady's gone to so much trouble," Sir Algar declared, rising from the chair, and obviously wide-awake.

"The bath is to keep you from taking a chill, not for any other reason," Tamsin explained.

He hadn't thought she was implying that he smelled, although maybe he did.

"There's mulled wine waiting there, too," she added.

"Thank you, my lady," he replied, bowing. "I am indeed grateful for all your efforts, and now, if you'll both excuse me, I'll enjoy the comforts you've provided."

"I'll send one of the servants to tell you when the evening meal is ready." Her tone was just the same, but he saw the tinge of a blush on her cheeks and a sparkle in her eyes that told him she was pleased.

Such a little thing it was to say thank you, and yet it meant so much to her, he thought as he hurried up the steps and pushed open the door to the upper chamber.

A brazier full of glowing coals heated the room. A linen-lined tub of water stood steaming in the middle of the room, with the stool beside it bearing more linen and a chunk of soap. Another curl of steam drifted up from a carafe on the table, and there was a goblet nearby. He glanced at the bed and noticed a clean tunic, breeches and stockings laid out in readiness. An old pair of boots that had been cleaned and polished was on the floor beneath it.

No one had taken care of him, in any way, since his parents had died all those years ago. Ever since that terrible time, he'd been alone in the world.

Self-sufficient, and beholden to no one. Needing no one.

He went to the carafe and poured some of the warmed spiced wine into the goblet and took a sip. God, it was good, and warmed him all the way down. He drank some more, then walked to the tub and ran his hand through the hot water. How long had it been since he'd had a hot bath? Weeks, at least.

Suddenly eager for the caress of hot water on his body, he put down the goblet, drew off his tunic and shirt, then tugged off his boots and stockings. He stripped off his breeches and gingerly stepped into the tub. With a sigh, he sat down and leaned his head back against the linen-padded edge.

It felt good.

Very good…

* * *

Surely he must have bathed and dressed by now, Tamsin thought as she knocked softly on the door of the upper chamber. Her leg was beginning to ache, so although she would have preferred to dine in the hall below, she thought it best to retire to the upper chamber before it got much worse.

Rheged didn't answer, so she knocked a little louder.

It was possible he had dressed and left the chamber and she hadn't seen him come down the stairs. She'd tried to keep watch for him, but Sir Algar had distracted her more than once with his enthusiastic demands to hear all about the fox hunt from Gareth and the others.

Perhaps Rheged had suffered some kind of wound during the hunt and hadn't told her about it. Maybe he'd even lost consciousness. She'd seen no sign of injury, but he was a proud man and would probably make light of a wound he didn't consider serious.

She immediately pushed open the door, to be greeted by the sounds of gentle snoring and the sight of Rheged still in the tub, his head leaning back against the rim, his eyes closed, his mouth slightly open and his broad chest rising and falling as he slept.

She should leave, Tamsin told herself, except that she might not be able to climb the stairs so easily later. Besides, he had surely been in that water long enough. It must be cold by now. He could get sick if he remained in the tub. She ought to wake him.

She took a few steps into the room. He looked so different when he was asleep—so much younger, as if he lost years when he was sleeping, or the cares of the world were forgotten.

Perhaps if he could feel completely at ease when he was awake, he would look like that.

Her gaze flicked lower, beneath the water.

He suddenly sat up, sending water splashing over the sides of the tub and onto the stone floor.

"I'm sorry!" she cried, reaching down to grip her aching calf as she backed away. "I knocked but you didn't answer." She pointed at the wooden tub. "You should get out. The water must be freezing by now."

"Aye, it's a little chilly," he agreed as he reached for one of the large squares of linen she had set out on the stool and began to rise.

She averted her eyes before she saw…too much… and heard him step out of the tub.

"Thank you again for all this," he said, his tone unexpectedly calm. "It's been many years since I've had anyone concern themselves with my comfort, although if I'd known the price was seeing me naked, I might have reconsidered."

She risked a glance. He'd wrapped the linen around his narrow waist. His chest was still bare, though, the water glistening on his naked skin as if he were Neptune newly risen from the sea, and reminding her of the night they'd spent together. "I thought you would be dressed."

"Surely you didn't expect me to bathe fully clothed?"

"I was certain you'd be out of the tub by now. It's nearly time for the evening meal."

"Then I'm glad you woke me, or I might have slept right through it."

A more disturbing reason for his heavy slumber came to her. "Are you not feeling well, that you're so tired?"

"I never get sick," he replied as he reached for his shirt. "It's just that I'm not as young as I used to be."

"You're far younger than Sir Algar."

Some expression she couldn't decipher flashed in his eyes. It might have been triumph, but why would he be pleased when she'd simply stated the obvious?

"I'm nearly thirty. How old are you? Eighteen?" he asked before he pulled the clean shirt over his head.

"I'm almost twenty," she replied, "and that *is* old for an unwed woman."

"Not so old you need throw yourself away on the first man who asks for you."

"I have no wish to discuss my marriage."

"I don't doubt that," he replied, reaching for his breeches.

She started toward the door, but forgot her wound, and when she put her weight on her injured leg, she had to bite back a cry of pain.

"Sit on the bed," he ordered.

"I'll return after you've dressed."

"I'm dressed enough," he declared, and the next thing she knew, he'd picked her up and carried her toward the bed.

At least he had his breeches on, but still—! "Put me down!" she commanded, pushing at his rock-hard chest.

"As you wish," he said, letting her slide out of his arms, so she was standing close to him beside the bed.

Very close to him. Beside the bed.

His gaze locked on to hers. "I've heard some women prefer older men. Are you such a one?"

"Preference has no place in my decision. My pledge has been given, and I will not go back on my word."

"What if a new arrangement could be made, for a different alliance, with a man equally powerful and with even more friends at court?"

He couldn't be speaking of himself. "What do you mean?"

"Sir Algar is rich and has more influence than Blane at court."

Sir Algar? The thought had never crossed her mind, and yet it was possible her uncle could be persuaded to break the betrothal agreement with Blane to make a new one with Sir Algar.

But there was still Mavis to consider—and that had to be the reason his proposal was so distressing. "Have you made this suggestion to Sir Algar?"

"I believe he's already thought of it."

Tamsin fought to keep the dismay from her features. She hadn't, not for one moment, had any inkling that Sir Algar harbored that sort of feeling for her. He treated her like a daughter, not a potential wife.

But no matter what he thought, she had to marry Blane. "If Sir Algar ever mentions such a notion to you, please advise him I won't break the original betrothal contract with Sir Blane."

Rheged took hold of her shoulders and regarded her sternly. "There is doing a thing because honor demands it and there is being honorable to the point of madness. I tell you, it's madness to marry Blane."

"I must because of honor and necessity both!" she retorted, twisting away. "You cannot possibly understand."

"Explain it to me."

"Why? What am I to you but something you took in place of a bogus golden box? And a few stolen kisses."

"I took you because I won't see you wed to that monster from Dunborough!" He ran his hand through his long, dark hair and growled, "I'd rather see you wed to Sir Algar."

There was something in his voice, in his eyes, in his stance, that rooted her to the flagstones. "Is that the truth, Rheged? Do you want me to marry your overlord?"

"It would be easier than seeing you married to Blane."

She looked into his dark eyes. She saw pain there, and a longing that matched her own. "Do you truly want me to marry Sir Algar, Rheged? Would that make you happy?"

"God, no!" he said through clenched teeth. "I would rather—"

He fell silent.

"What?" she pressed, his manner and the look in his eyes making her heart race and her breathing quicken. "What would you rather?"

"What I want does not matter, except that I would see you safe. You won't be safe with Blane."

"I would be safe with Sir Algar, though," she replied, "and cherished, no doubt, as well as given whatever material goods my heart desires."

"Yes," he snapped.

"That would be enough, do you think? And I should

be content to be the substitute for the woman he loved and lost?"

"No!" he said, his voice husky with need as he tugged her into his embrace and captured her lips with his own.

Chapter Eleven

Desire, lust and longing seized Tamsin.

This was the man she dreamed of in the night, taking her to his bed and claiming her for his own. This was the man whose kisses stirred her, whose arms she yearned for, whose body she craved. This warrior, this man in his prime, not some ancient villain or heartbroken older man.

Yet there was more than lust in her heart as she returned his kiss passion for passion. For so long she had yearned to be loved, and when she had dreamed of marrying, she had hoped it would be to a man she could admire and respect as well as love.

Rheged had begun with even less than she. He'd worked and struggled and survived, overcoming deprivation, hardship and the disadvantage of his lowly birth. Yet she could see beyond the face he showed the world, to a heart as full of loneliness and longing as her own. Yes, he was hard and tough and proud, but so was she. In that, they were equals, as she was with no other.

And so she would surrender to this man, this warrior, and give herself up to the pleasure and desire and need coursing through her, at least for a few all-too-brief moments.

Sliding her hands under his shirt and tunic, her palms brushed lightly over his broad chest and around his back, his scars like ridges beneath her fingertips. His hand grazed her bodice, sending a new wave of excitement coursing through her—dangerous excitement. She wanted more; she wanted him. They were alone, with his bed behind her.

Yet she must not ask for more. If she gave Rheged her body, she would have nothing left save her title. That loss would be too much to exchange for a few moments of bliss, even with him.

"No!" she cried as she pushed him away, the command as much for her as for him. "This must stop. You mustn't kiss me. Or touch me, ever again!"

His eyes narrowed. "What game is this, my lady?"

Game? She wasn't toying with him like those silly noblewomen who flirted and preened and pranced about when there were men to see them. "This is no game to me, sir, nor should it be to you. I'm not free and neither are you, I have my name and reputation to think of, as you have yours. Have you not done enough to harm both of ours—and Sir Algar, too?"

Ire replaced desire in his eyes as he sat on the bed and tugged on his boots. "I have never sought to harm you, my lady, as you should know by now," he said, then rose to finish dressing, "nor have I any inclination for flirtation and other such sport."

He started for the door, only to turn back on the threshold and regard her with that cold reserve she had seen before. "Nor have I acted without encouragement, either here or on the road or in your uncle's castle. Nevertheless, we shall call an end to…" Although he hesitated for an instant, his expression did not change. "To whatever it is that exists between us. Good day, my lady."

"Good day, my lord," Tamsin said as he shut the door behind him.

Then she sank down on the bed and covered her face with her hands. If she didn't leave soon, she would beg Rheged to let her stay. To love her, even if he didn't offer marriage.

Late the next afternoon, Gareth stood at the end of the makeshift tilting ground in the barren patch beyond the meadow and Rheged brought his destrier to a snorting halt close by. A quintain at the other end of the long, bare area was still spinning from the blow from Rheged's lance. The small shield on one arm of the wooden dummy had been shattered and a mace that had been at the end of the other arm lay on the ground a few feet away, past the remains of the end of Rheged's practice lance.

"That's the last, I see," Gareth noted, nodding at the pile of broken and splintered lances near Jevan's prancing hooves. "Destroyed them all, have you?"

Rheged didn't answer before he swung down from his horse and started down the field to gather up the broken bits of what was indeed the last of the practice lances he possessed.

Gareth fell into step beside him. "You've been out here since the noon."

"So what of that?"

"So I'm wondering why. Your shoulders have got to be aching, and you've tired Jevan out, too."

Rheged glanced back at his warhorse. Jevan *was* tired. He shouldn't have worked him so hard in what had proved to be a wasted attempt to get over his anger at Tamsin. That woman was like all the rest of her kind. Arrogant. Selfish. Using him. To her, he was just a wild Welshman, a bit of rough for sport.

But he wasn't about to explain, not even to Gareth. "Jevan can rest tomorrow."

"I know you can push yourself nearly to death, but it's not like you to work Jevan so hard."

Rheged didn't reply to that, either, before he bent down to retrieve the last of his broken practice lances.

"What's wrong?" Gareth asked, concern written all over his face.

"Beyond having DeLac's niece take command of my household without so much as a by-your-leave?" he replied and gathering up as much of the broken wood as he could carry.

"Aye, there's more afoot than that," Gareth said, picking up the mace and chain. "You've been like a bear with a thorn in its paw ever since you went to that tournament. Did more happen there than you've let on? Is it worse than you've said with DeLac? If there's a battle to come, Rheged, I ought to know."

"There'll be no battle if I can help it," Rheged said. He started back toward Jevan, doing his best to keep the pieces of wood from falling out of his arms. "You know all there is to know about my troubles with DeLac."

"Then it's her, Lady Thomasina. You don't want to

take her back. You're falling in love with her, aren't you?"

Rheged threw down the wood near Jevan, who whinnied and refooted. "Steady, Jevan," he murmured, sorry he'd disturbed his horse. And overworked the poor animal. And been too wrapped up in his own troubles to see it.

But he didn't need Gareth's council. Not in this.

Clearly, he ought to avoid Tamsin as much as possible in future, or others might mistakenly suspect him of such feelings, too. "I am *not* falling in love with that woman, and I'll take her back as soon as I can. Do you think I want a shrew like her in my household?"

"Shrew?" Gareth repeated with obvious surprise.

"Scold. Harpy, call her what you will," Rheged said, grabbing hold of Jevan's bridle.

"I'd never call her those things, Rheged. To be sure, she's a bit high-handed, but—"

"But that's enough," Rheged declared, then started back toward Cwm Bron. "I don't want to talk about the woman. She'll be going home soon and that'll be the end of it, thank God. I'm sorry I ever laid eyes on her!"

"God help us," Gareth murmured as he watched his friend march back to the fortress. "He's mad in love with her, all right."

That night Sir Algar stood beside Tamsin as they waited for the evening meal. Several soldiers were also waiting in the hall, standing near the tables in small groups, or leaning against the walls and pillars. Those servants not at work were also there, eager to eat.

"I must say, my lady, this seems a different hall!" Sir Algar exclaimed, looking about.

"It only wanted a little cleaning," she replied, wondering if Rheged would sup with them, and what all those gathered here would think if he didn't.

She had no idea where he was. She hadn't seen Rheged since he'd angrily left her in the upper chamber yesterday. He'd been gone when she ventured below to break the fast in the morning after another restless night and she'd spent the rest of the morning alone in the upper chamber doing a little more mending. She'd met Sir Algar in the hall for the noon meal, where Rheged did not join them, and spent the rest of the afternoon talking about castles and fortifications, meals and minstrels, her parents and the past. Perhaps Rheged was avoiding her on purpose. If so, she should be pleased. She had no wish to have another quarrel with him, although she had to wonder what Sir Algar and the rest of the household would make of that avoidance.

She also kept wondering if it could indeed be possible that Sir Algar was thinking of her as a possible wife. Surely he would give some indication if his thoughts were tending that way, yet despite what Rheged had said, she hadn't been able to detect a single sign that Sir Algar considered her anything but the daughter of a woman he'd admired long ago.

They were about to take their places at the table when the door to the keep opened and Rheged strode in, his expression grave and grim.

As he made his way forward, a sigh seemed to waft about the chamber, as if more than she were relieved to see him. Unfortunately, and in spite of what had so recently passed between them, she felt more than mere relief. Simply seeing him caused her desire to kindle.

"My lord, my lady," he said, nodding as he joined them, his tone even and measured.

Obviously he didn't intend to act as if there was anything amiss between them.

Therefore, neither would she. Sweeping back her skirts, she sat on the bench. Sir Algar sat also and so did Rheged, followed by the rest of the soldiers and servants in the hall.

"Tamsin and I have been discussing a most excellent idea she's had about Cwm Bron," Sir Algar said while Hildie ladled roasted chicken floating in a thick sauce of leeks onto their trenchers. "Tell him, my dear."

Rheged slowly turned to look at her, one eyebrow raised in question, his dark eyes unreadable.

She *never* should have stayed in the chamber with him yesterday. She should have fled the moment she'd seen him asleep in the tub, or when his lips touched hers—and every time they did.

"Have you given—" God help her, she was squeaking like a mouse! She cleared her throat and began again. "Have you given any thought to using your armory as your hall and storing your weapons in the keep instead?"

Sir Algar had told her that the large, tall building near the kitchen was used to store and repair weapons, and that seemed a waste of a building to her.

"The armory is closer to the kitchen," she went on, "so the food would be warmer when it's served. The building might require a good cleaning and liming and whitewash, but the keep would surely be better for storing weapons. If the castle did come under attack and you and your men had to seek refuge in the keep, you would be well armed and your attackers couldn't get to your weapons unless you were defeated."

"I didn't realize the lady was an expert in castle defenses as well as the running of a household," Rheged replied before breaking off a piece of bread and using it to wipe up some of the sauce.

She couldn't tell if he was angry or not. "I've lived in a large fortress for the past ten years, among men who talked often of such things."

"She makes a good point, Rheged," Sir Algar noted, apparently seeing nothing unusual in Rheged's response. "The armory would certainly make a more spacious hall."

"There could be a fireplace with a chimney built into the wall, as well," Tamsin said.

"A most excellent and modern idea," Sir Algar agreed.

"A very expensive idea, my lord," Rheged replied, his tone even and measured. If he was still annoyed with her, he hid it well. "The necessary repairs to the walls and keep must come first. After that, I have my other plans that we've already discussed."

Sir Algar raised his bushy white eyebrows. "Ah, yes, the new castle."

"It would be money better spent than doing extensive alterations to the buildings here."

"You should talk to Tamsin about those plans, Rheged. I'm sure a woman's perspective will be helpful, especially about where the kitchen and family apartments should be."

"Those decisions can wait until I have a wife," he replied brusquely, effectively ending that discussion.

The rest of the meal passed in mostly uneasy silence. Sir Algar tried to speak about the latest news of King John and his troubles with his barons, but Tamsin had no heart for a political conversation, especially when she could feel the curiosity of the soldiers and servants watching them. It was like being on display at the market, and she had even more sympathy for Mavis, who must often feel that way at feasts and other gatherings.

Not able to stand the strain any longer, Tamsin got to her feet when Elvina and Hildie brought baked apples to finish the meal. "If you'll both excuse me, I'm feeling rather tired and believe I should retire."

"Your leg isn't troubling you too much, is it?" Sir Algar asked, rising and offering her his arm. "I'll send for Gilbert."

"There's no need to fetch him, my lord," she said hastily. "I'm just a little tired."

"Nevertheless you must allow me to escort you to your chamber, my lady," Sir Algar said as if he were addressing a queen.

As if she were a queen, Tamsin inclined her head and took his arm.

While they made their way to the stairs, Rheged concentrated on drinking and not watching Sir Algar help Tamsin. He should have lingered longer brushing down Jevan, who asked no questions, offered no opinions and obeyed without complaint.

As for her idea about the armory… If he intended to keep this fortress as his main defense, her idea might have merit. But that was not his plan. He wanted a new castle, stronger, and in a better defensive position. Something that would last for years and after he was dead and buried, to show that he'd existed.

"Have you lost what manners you possessed, Rheged?"

He started and looked up to find Sir Algar glaring down at him. "You're as sullen as a whipped dog. I don't ask you to be the merry minstrel, but by God, you were as close to rude as I've ever witnessed."

He wasn't pleased to be the object of Sir Algar's ire, but if it meant people would realize that he wasn't falling in love with Tamsin…. "Forgive me, my lord. I have much on my mind."

"It's not my forgiveness you should be seeking," Sir Algar said with a sniff as he sat. "I expect you to treat Tamsin with courtesy, if not charm. And she is a font of knowledge. I doubt there's much about a noble household or fortress she doesn't know, and you should avail yourself of her expertise while she remains your guest. She could help you with the household accounts, too. You've said before that you find the task tedious. She may be able to suggest ways to make it less troublesome for you."

Rheged regretted upsetting Sir Algar, especially after his recent impulsive acts. "If you think it advisable, my lord, and if the lady will agree."

And provided I can keep my distance.

"You should also avail yourself of the lessons she can teach you regarding what to look for in a wife. She is the very pattern for a noble wife—honorable, dutiful, intelligent, kindhearted, chaste."

Chaste? God help him, chastity was the last thing

he thought of when he was near Tamsin. And Sir Algar was so very complimentary.... "Perhaps you should seek her hand, my lord."

"Have you completely lost your mind, Rheged?" Sir Algar demanded. "Tamsin is young enough to be my daughter!"

"Other men have taken younger brides, my lord. And Blane is older than you."

Rheged had seen Algar upset, but he'd never seen anything quite like the expression that came to his overlord's face as he glared at him now. "Never speak of this again, Rheged, to me or any man. And in the morning, you will ask for Tamsin's help with the accounts, you will learn what she can teach you and you will be polite and grateful."

"Yes, my lord," he dutifully replied.

When Tamsin came down to break the fast the next morning, Rheged rose from his place beside Sir Algar, tugged down his tunic and strode purposefully toward her.

Her heart began to beat faster and her face to flush, despite her determination to keep her demeanor—and her feelings—calm. "Good morning, Sir Rheged."

The knight glanced back at Sir Algar, already chewing on bread and honey, before he spoke, and she wondered if his overlord had sent him to speak to her.

"My lady," he began, his tone wooden, as if he had memorized the words, "Sir Algar believes I have much to learn about how a castle household should be managed, and that you would be a most excellent teacher.

I would be both pleased and grateful if you would assist me with my household accounts."

Out of the corner of her eye, she saw Sir Algar watching expectantly. Still not sure of Rheged's feelings, she would have liked to refuse. She didn't want another quarrel. But she didn't want to disappoint Sir Algar, either, especially when he had been so kind and generous. "Certainly, Sir Rheged. It would be my pleasure."

"He keeps his accounts in the upper chamber, don't you, Rheged?" Sir Algar called out. "I suggest you discuss the accounts there. You should have quiet and privacy for going over such things."

That would mean they would be alone, and although Tamsin was determined not to let Rheged affect her, she didn't want to be alone with him, so she said (and it wasn't exactly a lie), "It's warmer here."

Sir Algar frowned. "Ah. Very well, here, then. After you've eaten, Rheged can fetch the accounts and I'll leave you two alone."

Tamsin ate slowly, but eventually the meal was finished. Sir Algar declared he'd supervise the repairs to the yard and left the hall, while Rheged went to the upper chamber to get the accounts. Meanwhile, Hildie managed to find a large square of parchment, a pot of ink and some quills, which she set out on the table in front of Tamsin.

She wondered where the accounts were. She'd seen nothing like a scroll or a list when Hildie had taken his clothes out of the wooden chest so she could mend them. Maybe there was a secret compartment in the chest, or the wall, perhaps. Under the bed?

Rheged appeared on the steps from the upper chamber, bearing a wooden box Tamsin recognized as the one containing the little slips of discarded bits of parchment that had been on the shelf.

The ones she'd been using to light the rushlight or the brazier. *Those* were his accounts?

Rheged set the box in front of her with much more force than necessary. "Have you meddled with this?" he demanded, his voice low as he glared at her.

"Yes, but I had no idea those scraps were important," she replied truthfully, keeping her voice level.

"Scraps?" Rheged repeated through clenched teeth. "God give me patience! What did you do with those *scraps*?"

She couldn't blame him for his anger this time. If someone had interfered with her accounts at Castle DeLac, she would be furious. "I'm sorry, my lord, but I used them."

"How, on God's green earth?"

"To light the rushlight. And the brazier."

"You *burned* them?"

"I had no idea they were important," she replied, her regret giving way to frustration. "How could I? They looked like mere jumbles of letters and numbers and ink blots. It would take an expert days to make sense of them."

"Or a few moments of my time," he returned indignantly. "But because they made no sense to *you,* you burned them."

She started to stand.

He put his hand on her shoulder. "I have asked for your help, and you have offered it. Forgive my display of temper."

The words seemed to be ground out of him with reluctance, but at least he said them, so she would be magnanimous, too. "As I hope you'll forgive my ignorant destruction of some of your accounts. Fortunately there seems to be enough left to enable us to make a record on this larger parchment. This accounting should be easier to keep safe, no matter who you share your chamber with."

The moment she mentioned sharing his chamber, she blushed and hurried on, hoping he would attach no particular significance to her words. "We should begin, I think, by dividing your…notations…into different types—food, clothing, weapons and so on."

"As you wish." He lifted the box and dumped the contents onto the table.

That wasn't quite what she meant. Nevertheless she said nothing and began picking up the slips of parchment and trying to organize them.

Unfortunately it was as if the notations were written in some kind of code. Rheged, however, had no such trouble, his long, slender fingers sorting the pieces with surprising ease and swiftness.

But then it should be easier for him. He'd written the nearly illegible notes.

Tamsin smoothed out a small piece of parchment before her. "What does '*f* and *p,* ten and twelve *b*' mean?"

Rheged answered without looking at her or pausing in his sorting. "Fish and peas, ten baskets of fish, twelve baskets of peas."

"You seem to have bought a lot of peas."

"Peas are cheap and I like peas porridge."

"I assume the whole household does, too," she remarked, adding the note to the pile for foodstuffs. "The total number of baskets of peas you've paid for this year is—"

"Three hundred and sixty-two," he quickly replied, although his attention was still on his task.

She checked the other notes in the pile and discovered he was right. "Have you a list of totals somewhere else?"

"Here," he said, tapping his forehead.

"You have the totals of all the goods and food you've bought and sold this year in your head?"

"Yes."

Although his expression was serious, he couldn't be.

She picked up the slips of parchment with notations about fleece and swiftly wrote down the totals and quickly tallied them. "How many bales of fleece have you sold?"

"Sixteen hundred and fifty-two."

"I have sixteen hundred and forty-two. Perhaps a slip is missing."

"Check your totals again."

Pursing her lips, she did.

And discovered she was wrong. The correct answer was sixteen hundred and fifty-two.

"I've bought four hundred and seventy-three butts of ale, one hundred and three barrels of wine and ten kegs of mead."

She checked those figures. He was correct, and he knew it, judging by the satisfied smirk lurking in his eyes and the corners of his lips. "Why do you bother to write anything down at all, then?"

That got rid of his smirk. "I thought I should leave a record of some kind in case I died."

Died?

"In a tournament or in battle. It does happen."

Of course he was right to consider his own swift and unforeseen demise, yet it was impossible to imagine him lifeless, all the vitality gone from his muscular body, his eyes dulling with death.

"I realize my writing is crude and difficult to read, but I didn't know how to write until one of the priests who followed the troops taught me during a lull between battles. It amused him, I think, and gave us both something to do. Before that, I had to keep track of everything I owned and how much I was owed in my head because I had no way to record it. So if you'd rather not—"

"No, no, I'm happy to be of service," she said, regretting she'd been so impatient. "Since you can recall everything so clearly and I inadvertently destroyed some of the records, I suggest we give up sorting these bits of parchment. You can tell me the totals, and I'll write them down, and we can begin the new records from there. Unless you'd rather practice writing?"

"God, no. I'd rather run naked in the rain."

Trying not to imagine Rheged naked in the rain, or anywhere else—which proved to be much easier than picturing him dead—she began to gather the bits of parchment. "I suppose I can use these to light the brazier and rushlights now." She thought of something else. "If you had all the totals in your head, why were you so angry that I burned some of them?"

"I wasn't pleased you'd seen how poorly—"

Hildie burst into the hall as if she'd been launched by a catapult.

"My lady! My lady!" she cried, running up to them. "It's my sister, Frida. Her baby's coming and she's asking for you, my lady."

Tamsin's hand went to her chest. "Me? I'm not a midwife. Isn't there a midwife?"

"Aye, my lady, over the ridge. Joseph—Frida's husband, that is—is going to fetch her. But first he come here to get me, and you, too, my lady."

"But what can I—"

"I don't know, my lady, and that's the God's honest truth! Joseph doesn't know, either, except maybe Frida thinks you know everything."

"I wonder how she came to have that impression," Rheged said, his eyes on the rafters above as if addressing the angels.

Hildie ignored him, and so did Tamsin. "Joseph, bless his heart, is near frantic. He come with his wagon to take us. Please, won't you go to her, my lady? Just to say a few words to ease her mind, if there's naught else you can do?"

"Of course," Tamsin said. Although she'd never attended a birth before, if her presence could ease the poor woman's suffering in any way—

"Unfortunately the lady is forbidden to travel," Rheged said. "Her leg—"

"Isn't in such terrible condition that I can't ride a short way in a wagon. I can see the mill from the upper window, so I know it's not far."

Rheged knew better than to protest again when he saw that look in Tamsin's eyes.

Chapter Twelve

"Does it usually take this long for a baby to come?" Rheged asked Sir Algar as they sat by the hearth in the hall much later that night.

The evening meal of eels cooked in ale, leek soup and bread had been served long ago, and the tables cleared and taken down. Several of the soldiers had already bedded down for the night on their straw-stuffed mattresses, snoring and snorting and trying to ignore the hounds snuggling in the rushes beside them.

"I gather it can," Sir Algar replied, refilling Rheged's goblet with more mulled wine.

The Welshman cupped the goblet in his strong, lean fingers. "She said she knew nothing of childbirth, so why hasn't she returned? Surely the miller would have brought her back by now if all was well."

"She's probably staying until the child arrives. She's a woman, after all, and women are always excited when babies come."

"That may be," Rheged said as he got to his feet, too impatient to wait any longer, "but I'm going to the miller's cottage anyway. I want to be sure the journey wasn't too much for her."

"Go, then, if it will set your mind at ease." Sir Algar sighed and shook his head. "Sadly, it won't be long before she must go on a longer journey, back to her uncle and the marriage that awaits her. The more I get to know her, the more I agree with you that that marriage would be a terrible thing. But there's still the matter of the agreement, and the king. And the lady's own wishes, of course. She is as adamant as you would be if you had given your word, even if you later came to regret it."

Rheged didn't want to think about regrets, either now or in the past or in the future. The lady had made up her mind, and there was nothing neither he nor Algar could do.

Whatever the future held, though, he would first make certain she hadn't overtaxed her strength today.

He threw on his cloak and left the keep, crossing the yard with swift strides, no longer having to sidestep holes from missing stones. He had never known his hall to be so comfortable, either. Tamsin had worked miracles in the short time she'd been there. Who could say what she might accomplish if she could…?

But she couldn't and it was pointless to think otherwise.

He ordered the guards at the gate to open the wicket door while, with his free hand, he took the torch from the sconce at the left side of the thick oaken gate.

The flame flickered and flared as he made his way along the dark street of the village, the moon hidden behind the scudding clouds. The wind whipped his cloak about him, and the air smelled heavy with rain.

It wouldn't be long before it started. A lone dog barked somewhere close at hand, and a dim light shone through the shutters in the last cottage where the fishmonger lived.

Soon he heard the mill wheel making its slow circle in the river, and he could see the shape of the mill and the cottage beside it. The window of the cottage facing the road was dark, and no sound broke the stillness, as if all within were dead.

Dead like his parents, the day he'd come home from begging and found their bodies in the hovel that had been their home, too hungry and weak to ward off the ravages of the coughing sickness.

Dead like so many who'd fought beside him battle.

Rheged quickened his pace.

Dead like that poor family of peasants he'd found murdered by outlaws on his way to a tournament three years ago.

He broke into a run, covering the distance as fast as his long legs could take him until he drew near the miller's house.

There was a light inside. The shutters had been tightly closed and the light shone through only the narrowest of cracks in the door, but it was light nonetheless. Then he remembered that the house had two rooms, one at the front and one at the back where the miller and his wife slept, and where no doubt their baby would be born.

He pushed open the door and stepped into an oven, or so it seemed. The place was as hot as the smith's forge in high summer. Steaming pots and pans of water stood near the hearth in the extremely clean and tidy cottage. The furnishings were plain, but well made, and Frida's loom stood in the corner, a length of weaving half completed on the frame. Two cloaks hung on pegs beside the door, a plain one that was likely Hildie's and a darker one with a fox fur collar.

Hildie was pouring a bucket of water into another pot, perspiration dripping from her glowing face, while Tamsin sat near the door leading to the back room, her leg propped up on a cushion, her expression like that of a general waiting for word of enemy forces. She looked exhausted as well as anxious, as if she were the one giving birth.

He was about to speak when Hildie saw him standing there. "My lord!" she gasped.

Tamsin started and looked at him with surprise. "What are you doing here?" she demanded while a low moan issued from the back room.

Now that he knew Tamsin was all right, he wished he'd stayed in his hall. "I came to see why you hadn't returned."

He walked closer and doused the torch in one of the buckets of water.

"Don't!" she cried, too late. "We might need that water!"

"You have plenty and Hildie can fetch more if it's needed. Can I get you something to drink? Is there wine? Have you had anything to eat?"

Another terrible groan filled the air. Hildie sat heavily on a nearby stool.

"I just want it to be over," Tamsin replied tensely, her eyes full of dread, "and well over!"

"The midwife is here?"

"Yes, and Sarah seems to know what she's doing."

"Then surely there's no need for you both to stay."

"I can't leave now, not until I know the baby's arrived safely," Tamsin protested. "I'd never be able to sleep a wink anyway."

Another loud cry, more like a scream than a groan, came from the back room. They all stared at the closed door until a baby's cry, loud and hearty, filled the silence.

"Oh, thank God, thank God!" Tamsin murmured.

She looked more beautiful in her relief and joy than any woman Rheged had ever seen.

Hildie rose with her hands clasped like a woman beholding visions. "I knew she'd be all right!"

"Aye, thank God," Rheged said as he marched to the shuttered window, thinking they could all use some fresher air.

Tamsin got up swiftly and started toward him with barely a limp. "No, you can't! The night air—"

"Has never been harmful to me," he interrupted, both happy and sad to see her move so easily. "I've slept under the stars many a time and, as you can see, haven't suffered for it. And you've been out and about after dark, too."

In your uncle's courtyard, where we kissed.

"We're grown. I won't take a chance with a baby."

Again Rheged saw that stubborn look in her eyes. He was closing the shutters when Joseph, usually a dour fellow, came bounding out of the back room. "Hildie! My lady! Did you hear him?" the thin man exclaimed. "He's a healthy one and no mistake! And a son! God save me,

I'm the happiest man in England—a fine healthy boy and Frida come through fine, too."

He saw Rheged, stumbled and righted himself. "Oh, my lord! What brings you? You can't have heard so soon."

"I came to escort the lady home," he replied. "I congratulate you on the birth of your son."

"Thank you, my lord, thank you!" Joseph spun around like some sort of entertainer. "Where's the wine?"

Smiling broadly, Hildie handed him the wineskin and patted him on the shoulder.

He grinned at her, then handed the wineskin to Rheged. "You'll have a drink with me, my lord, won't you? To celebrate? What a baby! What a boy! He's got a full head of hair, too—black as his mother's. Frida came through it like a veteran, the midwife says. Going to be fine and likely to have ten more as easy as jumping a log! By God, it's hot in here!" he finished as he crossed to the window and threw open the shutters before Tamsin or Hildie could stop him.

The midwife, a plump woman of late middle years, gray-haired and wrinkled around her eyes, appeared at the door of the back room, a bundle in her arms and a smile on her pink-tinged face. "I thought the lady'd like to see him, seeing as she waited so long." Sarah checked her steps when she saw Rheged. "My lord?"

"I'd like to see the child, too, if I may."

With a nod and a smile, the midwife came forward. Instead of just folding back the blanket to show the child's face, though, she shoved the baby at an obviously startled Tamsin and rushed toward the open window.

"By the Blessed Virgin, who opened the shutters?" she demanded as she pulled them closed. "We'll all catch our deaths!"

Rheged heard the words, but his attention wasn't on the angry midwife closing the shutters, or Hildie standing nearby, or Joseph taking a long pull at the wineskin. He was looking at Tamsin's face as she held the babe, her expression one of joyful amazement, as if the child with the tuft of dark hair had magically appeared in her arms.

Rheged had never really thought about having children, except as something vaguely desirable when he got his castle and a wife. But now, when he saw Tamsin holding a baby, a powerful yearning took hold of him—a yearning not just for a child of his own, but for a child with Tamsin. A boy like him, or a girl like her, it didn't matter, as long as it was theirs.

The baby's bow-shaped mouth opened like a bird's, and then he scrunched up his face and started to wail.

"What did I tell you?" the miller cried with delight. "Healthy as a horse—a herd of horses!"

"Aye, he's a healthy one," the midwife agreed with a smile. "And now it's back to his mother to eat," she said, lifting the child from Tamsin, who held him a moment longer than necessary before she gave the baby up to Sarah and watched her carry him away.

Rheged recognized that expression on her face, for he knew the feeling: longing for something feared unattainable, the desire for a future that might not come to pass.

"Here, my lady, have a drink to my son's health!"

Joseph cried, his eyes glowing both with joy and the effects of the wine as he shoved the wineskin at Tamsin.

She accepted and took a sip, then passed it back to the miller, who thrust it at Rheged. "And you, too, my lord! Have a drink to my son!"

Rheged took a gulp of the thin wine before handing the wineskin back to the excited father. "I think it's time the lady returned to the castle."

"First I'd like to take my leave of Frida, if I may, my lord," Tamsin said.

The miller's face fell and he flushed. "She's asleep, my lady, and the chamber…well, it's not put back to rights yet."

"Then please pass on my good wishes to her. Hildie may stay here tonight, and tomorrow, too, to help you."

"Thank you, my lady!" the miller and Hildie cried in enthusiastic unison.

Rheged put Tamsin's cloak about her, then held out his arm to escort her to the door. She hesitated a moment before she laid her hand on his forearm, her touch as light as goose down but thrilling nonetheless.

"Thank you for coming, my lady," Joseph said, following them to the door. "It helped Frida, knowing you were here."

Tamsin gave him a smile as Rheged closed the door.

"I'm glad I could be of some use," she said. They made their way to the horse and wagon now in a small byre by the mill. "Although I really did nothing. Hildie and Sarah did all the work. And Frida, too, of course."

Despite her cloak, she was shivering, no doubt the result of coming out of that overheated cottage into the cooler night air. Rheged took off his cloak and, before she could protest, wrapped it about her as well, enveloping her in its warmth. Then he swept her up in his arms.

It seemed Tamsin wasn't so very tired after all. "Put me down!" she demanded, struggling. "I can walk!"

"You're exhausted."

"But—"

"Oh, for the love of God, woman, can't you just accept my help and be thankful?"

He waited for her to answer, then felt her relax. "Oh, as you will," she conceded, her arms slipping around his neck. "If you're going to be stubborn about it—but I'm fully capable of walking."

"I don't doubt you're capable of nearly anything, my lady," he replied truthfully.

He thought he felt her smile as she laid her head against his shoulder. "So long as you understand that I'm not helpless," she said before she yawned.

"You are the least helpless woman I've ever met."

When she didn't answer, he glanced down to see that her eyes were closed and her mouth was ever so slightly open as her breasts slowly rose and fell.

A wave of tenderness swept over him, inexpressibly sweet and yet awe-inspiring, too. For in that moment, he knew that he could never give her up to Blane, or any other undeserving man.

Even if he could never be worthy of her himself.

With a sigh, Tamsin stretched and opened her eyes, realizing at once she was in the big bed in the upper chamber of Cwm Bron. She couldn't tell whether it was day or night, though, because the only light was the feeble flame of a rushlight, and the shutters were closed.

Wondering how long she'd slept, she rolled onto her side—to see Rheged seated on a stool on the far side of the room, his back against the wall, his legs straight out in front of him, his arms crossed and his chin on his chest. It looked like he was deep in thought or… sleeping?

She glanced at the closed door. How long had he been there?

The last thing she remembered was Sir Algar helping her up the steps while she told him about the baby. One of the other maidservants—Elvina, the quiet one—had helped her get into the bed warmed with a heated stone wrapped in linen.

She also remembered Rheged carrying her to the wagon at the mill. She should have kept insisting he put her down. She shouldn't have given in to the impulse to relax in his strong arms, no matter how safe and protected she'd felt.

Nor was it wise to recall how he looked when he appeared in the doorway of the miller's house holding that torch, like Prometheus bringing fire—tall and strong and powerful.

Or when he watched her holding the miller's baby, a look of such longing in his eyes. She *must* forget those things, or she would never be able to leave here.

She sat up and discovered she wore only her shift beneath the covers. She grabbed the blanket and pulled it up to her chin as Rheged, with something that sounded rather like a snort, abruptly raised his head. "You're awake," he said.

"How long have you been there?"

He rolled his shoulders, uncrossed his arms and

stretched them over his head, his movements as smooth and sinuous as a big cat's. If he had been trying to make her aware of his strength and athletic grace, he couldn't have done so in any better way.

"Awhile. How do you feel?" he asked, getting to his feet.

"Quite well, thank you. Why are you here?"

"To make sure you haven't taken ill."

"What o'clock is it?"

He walked to the window and opened the shutters. "I make it barely past dawn."

Since his back was to her, she grabbed the blanket to wrap around herself and got out of bed. Ignoring the chill of the stone floor on her bare feet, she hurried to close the shutters, lest people see him there.

"Since it's morning, there's no need to fear the night air," he said as she backed away.

"It's not that," she said, feeling the heat of a blush. "My reputation has already been seriously damaged, and I would rather not compound the harm by having all and sundry know that we're alone in your chamber and that you've been here for at least a part of the night."

Rheged's dark eyebrows rose, and unless she was mistaken, a smile lurked at the corners of his lips. "If it's your reputation that concerns you, perhaps you shouldn't have gone to the window dressed in little more than a blanket."

"I don't like to be mocked, my lord."

The amusement left his features. "Nor do I," he admitted. "And that is poor recompense for your kindness to the miller and his wife, so I hope that you'll forgive me, my lady."

He sounded so sincere…and she shouldn't have been so harsh. After all, he'd been there—and sleeping on a stool—because he was worried about her health. And she, of all people, knew how ingratitude could sting.

She gave him a smile that she hoped would show that she regretted replying with annoyance. "I wonder how Joseph is feeling this morning."

She was relieved to see the hint of a grin return, as well as the sparkle of laughter to his brown eyes. "No doubt his head aches, at the very least."

"Frida is an excellent weaver, my lord. You should buy whatever she can make and sell it at Shrewsbury, or even London. I'm sure you'd turn a good profit."

"If you're sure, I will. You're a very shrewd and clever woman."

The blanket slipped and she tugged it back in place as she took a step back. "Thank you, my lord."

"And beautiful, too."

He thought her beautiful? She could count the number of compliments she'd received on the fingers of one hand. All had been dutifully spoken, without a single ounce of sincerity—until Rheged had arrived at Castle DeLac. The warmth of a blush flooded through her.

"Forgive me if I've upset you," he said softly.

Upset? Sweet Mother Mary, he'd done considerably more than upset her since she'd met him. He'd turned her whole world on its head. "I'm not used to compliments."

He came closer. "You should be."

"Mavis is a beauty, my lord. I'm not."

"Your cousin is lovely, I grant you, but…" He fell silent when he remembered how she'd bristled the last time he said something less than flattering about her cousin. Her beautiful cousin, who surely would have been that old lecher Blane's first choice for bride.

Tamsin knew the man, knew how his wife would surely suffer, and yet she insisted on fulfilling the marriage contract—because if she did not...*another might have to take her place?*

He cupped Tamsin's shoulders, and his gaze searched her face. "The betrothal—if you don't return...?"

Elvina entered the chamber without so much as a tap on the door.

"Oh, I—I'm sorry, my lady," the startled Elvina stammered, looking from Tamsin to Rheged. "I came to help the lady dress."

Tamsin stepped free of his grasp, her heart racing like a hare being pursued. "Rheged is leaving."

"I bid you adieu, my lady," Rheged said, walking to the door.

Tamsin told herself she was glad he was leaving before...before things went too far. It didn't matter what he'd been about to say, the question that was in his eyes.

Elvina sidled into the chamber. "I really didn't mean any harm, my lady. We all thought he'd be gone by now."

They *all?*

If everyone in the castle knew that Rheged had been there, alone, with her, it would be more cause for scandal and a ruined reputation and servants' disrespect— except that judging by the remorseful expression on Elvina's face, she really was sorry for intruding. Indeed, it was as if she wasn't surprised because Rheged was there, but because he hadn't yet left.

As if everyone assumed they were already lovers and had been for days.

If that was so, she should be appalled. Angry. Indignant. Fearful for the future.

Instead, she felt…free. Liberated.

As though she no longer had a secret that was becoming more and more difficult to keep.

Chapter Thirteen

In the huge kitchen of Castle DeLac, well aware of the other servants watching, Mavis faced an angry cook and a sobbing spit boy who'd let a pot of porridge burn.

Tamsin would know exactly what to do and what to say at such a time. Tamsin would be able to handle this situation with calm dispatch, while *she* felt as if she were drowning.

Poor Tamsin! Please, God, let her be all right! Mavis silently prayed, as she had so many times since that Welshman had taken her away for his own selfish purpose.

Armond the cook cleared his throat loudly, bringing her back to the present, although her fears for Tamsin were always with her, an ache in her heart that wouldn't go away.

Momentarily ignoring the irate Armond, Mavis spoke to the crying boy. "No need for tears, Ben. I'm sure you'll take more care next time, and it would be much worse if you'd been burned."

The lad sniffled and wiped his nose on his sleeve, then hiccupped and nodded.

"As for your behavior, Armond," she said, turning to the cook, "there was no need to strike the boy, and you'll never do it again. My dear cousin gave you a warning about such behavior that you have apparently chosen to ignore. Therefore, you will pack your things and leave Castle DeLac today."

"But…but my lady!" the big man stammered, his ruddy visage growing even redder. "Your father—"

"Has more important things to do than deal with kitchen matters," Mavis said sternly, wishing that were indeed so. Unfortunately, ever since Tamsin had been taken from them, it seemed her father considered drinking wine his major duty.

Oh, Tamsin, I pray God you're safe and not suffering!

"Go, Armond. Vila, you will be in charge of the kitchen," Mavis said to the most experienced of the kitchen servants.

As Armond departed with a sniff and a scowl, the stick-thin Vila stared at Mavis with stunned disbelief. "But, my lady, I'm a woman!"

"Who's been serving and helping the cooks of Castle DeLac for years. I'm sure you'll be able to manage." She addressed the equally shocked servants. "You will obey Vila as you would Armond, or me, or Lady Thomasina."

The servants exchanged glances, obviously as concerned yet as hopeful as Mavis, before she left the kitchen.

The moment she crossed the courtyard toward the washhouse, the gates opened to admit a large party of armed and mounted men. No alarm had been sounded, so they must be friends or guests. She stood back to watch as they filled the yard. The obvious leader of the cortege wore chain mail covered by a gray surcoat bearing the crest of a boar being strangled by a snake. Behind the soldiers came a wagon covered with canvas pulled by an ox.

She had no idea who these visitors could be. Her father entertained so many lords and knights, always seeking to increase his power and influence. Unless it was... *Oh, please, God! Not Sir Blane!*

The man in chain mail looked her way, then raised the visor of his helmet.

He was not Sir Blane, and her heart began to beat again.

"Greetings, my lady," the stranger said in what she supposed was meant to be a charming manner, although he sounded more like a charlatan at a fair. A leer of the sort Mavis was all too familiar with came to his fleshy face. "You are the Lady Mavis, are you not? I can't believe there are two women of such unsurpassed beauty in Castle DeLac."

"Greetings, Sir Knight," she replied, resisting the urge to wrap her arms around herself to hide her body from this man's lascivious gaze. "I am indeed Lady Mavis, and I welcome you to Castle DeLac."

The man dismounted and bowed. "I am Sir Broderick of Dunborough."

Not Sir Blane, but a son. What would this man and his father make of Tamsin's absence, and the reason for it?

Perhaps he would insist on rescuing her cousin, at least. That would be the only reason she could be pleased by their arrival, Mavis thought as she collected herself. "You've come in advance of your father?"

"My father is in the wagon. He can stay there for the present while I speak to Lord DeLac."

Sir Blane must be unwell, and she wondered if that was good or bad. "Your men are welcome to the hospitality of our hall, and if you will come with me, I shall take you to my father," she replied, hoping he would not be completely insensible from too much wine, although it was not yet noon.

Acutely aware of the man strolling behind her, she led him to the solar. It wasn't just the clink and rattle of his mail and the hard sound of his boots striking the flagstones that told her he was close behind. She could feel those leering eyes following the sway of her hips and swing of her braid.

She pushed open the solar door, to see her father resting his head on the table. "Father, Sir Blane and Sir Broderick have arrived," she announced, hurrying ahead of Broderick and more than willing to break her vow not to speak to her father again, given the circumstances.

"Eh?" he muttered, sitting up when Broderick entered the room.

"This is Sir Broderick, Sir Blane's son," she said when the younger man, with an expression of arrogant scorn, came to a halt and regarded Lord DeLac. Then he surveyed the solar with its fine furnishings before his gaze finally came to rest on the silver goblet and carafe by her father's elbow. "Perhaps I should speak with your father another time, my lady."

"Nonsense!" her father cried, as wide-awake as he

ever got these days. "I was just resting my eyes. Sit, my lord, sit. Where is your good father?"

"My father is still in the wagon in the courtyard." Broderick's thick lips curved up into a smile that made Mavis feel as cold as ice. "He, too, is resting."

"Well, then, let's let him rest, eh? Mavis, my dear, pour our guest some wine. And me, too."

She went to the carafe and noted it was empty. "I shall have to get more, Father. If you will both excuse me—"

Broderick reached out and took the carafe from her hands. "Surely a servant can do that. I would rather you remain." Again those fat lips curved up into a smile. "It isn't often I get to see such loveliness."

Although she yearned to flee, she stayed for Tamsin's sake. She had made a promise, and she would keep it.

She went to stand beside her father as Broderick went to the door and bellowed for a servant.

"Where the bloody hell is Tamsin?" her father muttered.

"Don't you remember?" Mavis whispered anxiously. He must have had even more wine than she thought.

Sally appeared and, her eyes lowered, hastily took the carafe from Broderick. Since Sally had been here the last time Sir Blane was in Castle DeLac, Mavis wasn't surprised Sally would seek to pass unnoticed now.

When the nobleman came forward again, Mavis instinctively moved back behind her father's chair.

"Perhaps we should also summon Lady Thomasina," Broderick suggested.

Mavis looked sharply at her father, who pulled at his beard before speaking—a sure sign he was about to lie.

Except that he didn't. "She isn't here," he said. "Please sit down, Sir Broderick, and I shall explain."

Broderick laughed as he pulled a chair in front of her father's table. It was a horrible laugh, full of mockery and scorn rather than good humor. "You did well not to lie to me, DeLac. I know the lady is not here."

He must have heard the news from someone who'd been here for the tournament and gone. One of the guests, perhaps, or the minstrel.

Who had told him was unimportant.

What was important was the way this man revealed his knowledge—a sly, deceitful way, intending to trick or shame them.

Broderick glanced at Mavis, then turned his attention back to her father. "I'm sure you've done all you can to get her back from that Welsh ruffian."

"I've offered a considerable ransom," her father lied, "and she will be returned shortly."

If he lied about the ransom, he could be lying about Tamsin's safe return, too. Anything her father said could be suspect.

"She's no longer a virgin, I assume," Sir Broderick asked with unexpected calm.

Mavis couldn't see her father's face, but she noticed the back of his neck reddening. "Sir Rheged assures me that she is as she left here."

If only she had some way of knowing if that was the truth, or another lie, but she would likely only hear the truth from Tamsin herself.

Broderick laughed again, a mocking, scoffing sound. "You believe that lout? And if she is intact, why the delay?"

"She was injured the day he rode off with her. An arrow in the leg."

"She is hurt?" Mavis gripped the back of her father's chair, her knuckles whitening. "You never—"

She fell silent when she felt Broderick's eyes on her again, her heart sinking. Tamsin might even be dead, for all she could believe her father.

"You didn't tell your daughter about her cousin's injury?" Sir Broderick demanded.

"No, he did not," she confirmed.

Her father twisted to glare at her with bloodshot eyes. "It matters not, my dear, since you've agreed to take her place as bride."

"Is that so, my lady?" Broderick inquired coolly, as if her father had made a remark about the weather or the state of the crops.

Loathing both her father and this knight but determined to do what she must if she could ensure Tamsin's safe return, Mavis regarded Broderick with defiance and pride. "Yes, it is. And I will honor that pledge, as long as my cousin returns before the wedding."

"There, you see? All is well," Lord DeLac said, rising. "Let's tell your father the good news."

"Not yet," Broderick said, holding up his hand to stop him. "We haven't agreed to any changes to the betrothal agreement."

"But Mavis is surely the better bargain. Thomasina is plain, and a shrew. Mavis is neither."

Again Broderick ran his coldly measuring gaze over Mavis, and she wanted to slap his impudent, lascivious face. "I agree that your daughter is beautiful, and spirited, too. However, the agreement was for Lady Thomasina, and we will accept no other."

Her father sank slowly back into his chair. "I see. How much more do you want for Thomasina's dowry, then?"

"Five hundred marks."

"Five hundred!" her father spluttered. When Broderick stayed silent, he cleared his throat and swallowed. "That is a considerable sum."

"Are you forgetting her reputation has been soiled?"

Mavis knew what she had to do. Stepping forward again, she said, "I will take my cousin's place as bride and my father will supply a larger dowry."

Her father slapped the table and hoisted himself to his feet. "You are in no position to change the contract!"

"I am the bride," she reminded him.

"No, you're not," Broderick declared. "We will have Thomasina or no one."

Mavis stared at him with disbelief. "You'll have the same alliance for considerably more money if I am the bride."

"We will have the woman Rheged wanted in our household and then we'll see the Welshman hanged for his crimes."

"But Rheged didn't take her because he wanted Thomasina in particular," Mavis protested. "He wanted to get back at my father and she was just the means to do it."

Broderick regarded Mavis with outright scorn. "Are you truly that stupid, my lady? Or perhaps it's only that you don't know the man. If Rheged merely wanted to be revenged upon your father, he would have done so in some other way, never through a woman. He's uncouth and a Welshman, but he does have that much honor. I assure you, he took your cousin because he wanted her, and this nonsense about a wound is likely just that." His fat lips curved up again. "And whether or not she's a virgin doesn't matter, as long as Rheged knows she's in Dunborough while he waits to die."

Mavis had met cruel men before, but never had she met one so happily evil.

And since anger and defiance only made him worse, she must try another tack.

"My lord," she said, using her most persuasive tone of voice and in spite of the roiling in her stomach, "surely your father would rather have a beautiful virgin bride and a thousand marks—"

Her father started to speak, until she silenced him with a look. "And one thousand marks," she repeated.

"It is not my father's decision to make," Broderick returned. He went to the window and shouted down to his men below to uncover the wagon. "If you'll please join me at the window, my lord, my lady," he said with great politeness, although it was an order nonetheless.

Her father rose at once. Mavis would have liked to refuse, but she also wanted to know what Broderick was about, so she reluctantly went to the window, standing on the other side of her father and as far away from Broderick as possible.

The men rolled back the canvas covering to reveal a shrouded, slender body. "That is my father," Broderick said evenly. "He died last night."

"Then the betrothal contract is broken!" Mavis exclaimed, so weak with relief, she had to hold on to the windowsill.

"Unless Lord DeLac still wishes an alliance in the north, for I am quite willing to abide by the *original* contract in my father's place."

"Father!" Mavis cried. "Surely you can't—you won't make Tamsin marry him, not when I'm willing to take her place!"

Her father turned to her with a look of cold satisfaction. "Is someone speaking to me?"

"Father, please!"

"I look forward to a long alliance, Sir Broderick," Lord DeLac said, turning toward the door.

Mavis ran in front of him, determined to stop him and prevent her cousin's marriage.

Her father pushed past her. She went to follow him, to try to make him change his mind, until Broderick grabbed her arm.

"I would speak with you, my lady," he growled, his voice low and harsh, his grip painful.

Gone was the placid negotiator, replaced by a furious brute as he forced her to face him. "It's not your place, woman, to interfere in the plans of men."

Staring into Broderick's angry face, Mavis thought of the one thing she could do that might save Tamsin. "While you apparently know little of the plans of women, my lord," she replied, making herself smile, "I had hoped I would make my father angry enough that he would leave us alone."

Broderick's eyes narrowed.

"I fear I've played my part too well." She demurely lowered her eyes. "I have a confession, Sir Broderick.

The moment I saw you in the yard, I felt…" She raised her eyes and lowered them again, feigning bashful dismay. "I have never felt such stirring in my heart for any man, my lord. I thought at once that if I could take Tamsin's place…even as your father's bride…he was old and you would be in the same household…it would have been a sin, but even so…and then when you offered to take your father's place as long as Tamsin was the bride…I was filled with jealousy, my lord. I don't want Tamsin to have you."

Broderick put his knuckle under her chin and raised her head so she had to look at him. "Indeed, my lady? You played your part well," he murmured before pulling her into his arms and smothering her lips with his.

Unwilling though she was, she submitted to his kiss, endured it when his tongue thrust into her mouth and wailed in silence as his hands pawed her body.

She even forced herself to put her arms around him and smile when he drew back with a look of triumph that swiftly turned to scorn. "No woman can play a part that well," he said, his lip curling with disdain, "but if you should be telling the truth, take heart, my lady. Perhaps your cousin will share."

With that, he sauntered from the room, while Mavis scrubbed her lips with the cuff of her gown and silently vowed that neither she nor Tamsin would ever be that man's bride.

"Well, my lady, your wound has healed even better than I'd hoped," Gilbert said with a smile as he examined her leg two days after Frida had her baby. "There will, of course, be a scar, but otherwise nothing more to trouble you."

Except returning to Castle DeLac.

"Thank you for your help," she said, trying to sound pleased. "I suppose I can begin the journey back to my home today?"

To the home that was no home, to marry a man she would never love, certainly never desire and whom she could easily come to hate.

Gilbert finished tying the clean bandage around her leg. "Yes, my lady. In a wagon, though, not riding."

"I never ride. My uncle didn't allow me to learn."

What he had really said was that it would be a waste of time and a horse.

"I hope to see you again, although not for my medicinal skill. If I do not, I wish you continued good health, my lady," Gilbert said as he picked up his medicinal chest.

"Thank you, Gilbert, and I wish the same for you, too," she replied. The physician smiled, nodded a farewell and left the room.

After he was gone, she got to her feet, walked slowly to the window and looked out over the courtyard, now fully repaired. She spotted Hildie and some of the other women gossiping at the well, laughing and smiling in the way only the safe and secure can do. The guards at the gate stood relaxed and easy, too, because they feared no danger.

If she stayed, not only would Mavis be in danger, their lives would be disrupted, their safety and security put at risk. And for what? Her selfish need and longing.

Her love, for a man who could never be hers. Who should never be hers.

There he was now, striding purposefully across the yard to intercept the physician. Tamsin drew back when Rheged glanced at the window. Gilbert would tell him she was well enough to travel, that she could leave Cwm Bron as she had so forcefully, deceitfully declared was her desire.

She looked around Rheged's chamber, still barren, still Spartan, more like a soldier's quarters than a lord's, yet she would miss it nonetheless. Her gaze lit on the little wooden box, now empty. Lifting it down from the shelf, she smiled wistfully, remembering Rheged's nearly indecipherable notations. How hard it must have been for him to admit his ignorance! How difficult to learn to read and write when he could have been drinking or gambling or wenching with his companions.

If she had been one of those camp followers, she would have tried with all her might to persuade him to leave the ink and quills and parchment and sport with her instead.

But she was not a camp follower. She was a lady, bound by contract and her given word to marry Blane of Dunborough.

She started to put the box back, then hesitated. A small knife for cutting thread rested on the dressing table, near the spool of thread she'd used for mending.

Why not? she asked herself. What harm could it do? He might not even find it. Nor care by the time he did. She did it anyway, cutting a small lock of her hair, tying it with a bit of ribbon, then placing it in the box and putting it back on the shelf before she went below.

To find Sir Algar and Rheged waiting.

Sir Algar approached, his hands outstretched to take hers in his soft lean ones. "My lady," he said with a smile, while Rheged, grim as death, stood motionless behind him.

Despite the smile on his lips, Sir Algar's eyes were just as grave. "Gilbert tells us you are fit to travel."

"Yes, my lord," she answered, not looking at Rheged, "and since the day is fine, I would ask that I be taken back to Castle DeLac at once, as I was promised."

"Of course, if that is what you truly wish," Sir Algar said, gripping her hands more tightly. "If it is not, however, if you would rather not return to marry Blane—"

"I must, my lord," she interrupted. "I have given my word, and you know even better than I what my uncle might do if I do not."

Only then did she glance at Rheged, still stone-faced, still motionless. "I won't bring trouble to you or your liegeman or your people."

Sir Algar led her to the chair and gestured for her to sit. He sat on the bench beside her and motioned for Rheged to come closer. "I appreciate your concern and your great kindness, as well as the sacrifice you're prepared to make. I also understand that you're a woman of honor and duty. But, my dear, Blane is not worthy of such a sacrifice. If you fear for Rheged's safety if you stay in Cwm Bron, then come with me to my castle. I am prepared to offer you sanctuary and I shall try to persuade your uncle to set you free."

Sanctuary, not marriage. But even so, she could not accept. "I thank you with all my heart, my lord, but I won't put you or anyone else in jeopardy, and I have given my word."

Only then did Rheged come forward, regarding her steadily with his piercing dark eyes. "Your cousin," he said, the words calm but firm. "Your uncle will give her to Blane if you don't return."

As Tamsin stared at him, Rheged knew he'd found the true reason she would marry Blane, along with the explanation for the desperation that came to her eyes every time he gave her reasons she should not. Yes, she had given her word and honor demanded she adhere to it, but he had always sensed there was more to her reasoning than that.

Now he knew it was love, and now he knew love's power, as he never had before. He also knew Tamsin's determination and the strength of her resolve. She would do what she felt right, even at the sacrifice of her own happiness. She would not be Tamsin otherwise. Nor would she ever be content.

"Is that true, my dear?" Sir Algar asked quietly. "He would give even his own daughter to that villain?"

"A marriage must be made," Tamsin replied, "and if my marriage will prevent a host of suffering, how can I refuse? I cannot and will not be so heartless and so selfish."

She waited for Rheged or Algar to protest. To explain again that Blane was evil and would make her life a misery. But they did not.

Instead, Sir Algar sighed and took her hand in his. "As much as I wish it could be otherwise, I can't, in good conscience, deny what you say, or refuse you the chance to do what you so clearly wish to do, regardless of the price you'll pay. I admired and respected your mother, and I was glad when she escaped the prison her father and brother made for her. I admire and respect you all the more, my dear, for walking into the prison your uncle has created." He looked at Rheged, standing stiffly in front of them. "You must take her back, Rheged."

The knight she loved said nothing, revealed nothing, except to nod his acquiescence. But she knew he could not do less. If she could be so strong, he must be, too, and accept what had to be.

"It will take a little time to pack your things and prepare the wagon," Sir Algar said.

"I have nothing to pack."

"You must keep the clothes and comb I gave you," he insisted. "They are gifts."

She didn't have the heart to refuse again. "Thank you, my lord."

Sir Algar rose. "Hildie and I shall see to that," he said. "In the meantime, Rheged, perhaps the lady could give you her opinion of the site of your new castle."

Tamsin could not resist what seemed to her a final gift, the chance to have a little more time with Rheged, however painful it made their parting. And yet… "I'd be happy to, but I can't ride," she said, for the first time truly regretting that she couldn't.

"You can see it from the wall walk," Sir Algar said. "Rheged?"

"I would be delighted to hear the lady's opinions," he said, his expression still revealing nothing as he held out his arm to escort her from the hall.

Tamsin placed her hand on his arm and let him lead

her out into the yard. If only she could stay! If only Mavis, Rheged, Sir Algar and so many others weren't at risk! If only she were free!

They reached the bottom of the stone stairs leading to the wall walk, and again she hesitated.

"If your leg is too sore to climb the stairs..." Rheged began.

"No, it isn't that. I'm afraid to be up high," she admitted. "I'm always afraid I may fall, even if there is a railing."

He smiled then, not in mockery or derision, but the comforting smile of one who knows, and understands. "I'll take the outside," he said, moving so that she was on the inside of the steps, nearest the solid wall.

She found it easy to start up the stairs then.

"The very thought of venturing out across open water in a boat fills me with terror," he confessed as they walked up the steps together.

"Yet you went to France."

"I was paid to fight in France, so it was cross the water or starve."

"If you hadn't sailed for France, you might not be a knight. Sir Algar told me how you earned your title. I think I would have died of fright."

"It's easier when you have nothing to lose."

"Except your life."

"When you're poor and a peasant, that doesn't seem like such a risk."

Once they were on the walk, she stood in the shadow of the tower with the rough stone wall behind her.

"There," Rheged said, pointing to the western edge of the ridge where the ground had fallen away to make a cliff. "We'll have to cut down more of the wood, but a fortress there will overlook the entire valley and the road."

"In clear weather like today," she replied, trying to concentrate on the site and not the man beside her whom she might never see again after today. "Since part of the ridge has fallen away, I trust you've looked for caves or fissures that could cause problems with the foundations."

"I haven't yet hired a mason to do such things."

"What about the fox you hunted and killed? If foxes or wolves have dens there, that could mean the rock is prone to cracking."

"We caught the fox miles from here."

"It could have been leading you away from its den." She thought of something else vital to a fortress. "What about a source for water? High ground is always drier. If the castle is besieged and water becomes scarce, the inhabitants won't be able to hold out for very long. You could dig a well, I suppose, but that will take time and more money." She paused, then added, "You might have to find an extremely wealthy bride."

"If I marry."

"You should marry. You should have a wife who loves you and cares for you. You should have children, Rheged. Strong boys, like you, and daughters—"

"Who look like you," he said, turning to her quickly, his deep voice low and fierce, his eyes full of fire. "I would have my children look like you. Be like you, as strong and clever and honorable as you. As loving and caring, willing to sacrifice all for those they love. I would have you as the mother of my children, Tamsin, or I'll have no one!"

She could only stare at him, hearing the truth in his words and seeing the need and yearning burning in his eyes—a need and yearning that matched what was in her own heart.

He took hold of her shoulders and looked down at her. "There is only one woman I want for my wife, and she's promised to another. Only one woman I want in my life and in my bed, and she has given her word to marry someone else."

"And I must keep it!" she cried, the tears starting as she fought to be strong and remember who would suffer if she was weak and took what she wanted more than anything in this world or the next.

"I know," he said, his hold relaxing. "You would not be the Tamsin I love otherwise." Again his grip tightened. "One kiss, Tamsin," he pleaded, pulling her closer. "One kiss, to remember when we're alone and lonely in all the years to come. One. Only one."

How could she deny him that? Or herself?

She couldn't, and she yielded, for she, too, wanted something to remember when she was alone and lonely, when another man made her his wife. When another man took her to his bed.

Their kiss was all that and more as his lips moved gently, tenderly over hers.

She held him close, this powerful, passionate warrior who loved her, wanting him to take her, wishing that he could, her whole body urging her to pull him deeper into the shadow of the tower where they could not be seen. To let him claim her and make her his, as she would claim him in body, if not in law.

"Riders!" a guard shouted from the gates. "Armed and clad in mail and carrying the banner of DeLac!"

Chapter Fourteen

Rheged rushed to the edge of the walk and looked out at the road leading to the fortress. Tamsin stayed farther back, but she could see the road well enough to realize the guard was right. That was her uncle's banner, and the large man leading the party with an armored knight beside him had to be her uncle.

"Why has my uncle come—and why now?" she asked with anguish.

"No doubt we'll find out soon enough," Rheged replied as he took her hand and led her to the stairs leading down from the wall. Again he took the outer edge to ward off her fear, although that dread was gone, overwhelmed by a greater terror. When they reached the yard, the gates were closed and Gareth was waiting for them, a few of the men with him.

"Let DeLac and his men enter," Rheged said, "but first I want every soldier assembled in the yard, in armor and with weapons."

As Gareth started shouting orders and more men appeared, Rheged turned to Tamsin. "They'll be here very soon. Go to the upper chamber. You'll be safe there."

She shook her head. "No. He's my uncle. I'll stay and hear what he has to say."

"As will I," Sir Algar declared, trotting down the steps from the keep, his expression grave. "I'm as responsible for this as you, Rheged."

"My lord—"

"Do not argue with me," Sir Algar commanded, and Rheged said no more.

As they waited, Tamsin clasped her hands, while Rheged stood with his arms crossed, his feet planted, still as a statue. Sir Algar shifted from foot to foot, his gaze darting from the gates to the men on the walls to the soldiers mustering below.

It seemed as if an age passed before Gareth, now above on the walk near the gates, responded to a hale. After answering, he called to the men below to open the gates, and Simon DeLac, arrayed in a long, thick black cloak over the armor he'd only ever worn for show, rode into the yard of Cwm Bron. Beside him came the unknown knight, and he was followed by a force of twenty men, one of whom carried DeLac's banner.

There were not enough men to give battle, thank God. Not today.

Then Tamsin looked more closely at her uncle. Despite the billowing folds of his ermine-collared cloak, he had obviously grown thinner. His face was pale, too, and there were dark circles under his eyes, as if he hadn't slept in days.

The cloaked and helmeted knight riding beside him wore a gray surcoat bearing a coat of arms featuring a boar and snake. This man's armor, while expensive, was also clearly made for use. Drawing his mount to a halt, he raised his visor to reveal brown eyes hooded by heavy dark eyebrows that loomed over his hawklike nose. Otherwise, his face was fleshy, his lips thick, and his clean-shaven chin thrust forward with pride and arrogance. He regarded her, and all about him, with a sneering, scornful gaze.

Rheged put his hand on the hilt of his sword while Sir Algar muttered an oath.

"What is it?" Tamsin demanded under her breath. "Who's the man beside my uncle?"

"Whoever he is, he wears the crest of Sir Blane's family," Sir Algar replied.

"That is Sir Broderick of Dunborough," Rheged said grimly. "Sir Blane's son and heir."

Tamsin felt sick. Obviously Rheged had been wrong and Blane hadn't tarried on his way to Castle DeLac.

And yet… "Where is Sir Blane?"

No one answered as her uncle slowly dismounted and walked toward her, completely ignoring Rheged and Sir Algar, too.

"Ah, Thomasina, my dear, there you are," he said, smiling like he was truly pleased to see her and she was at Cwm Bron for a friendly visit. "And quite well, I see." He gestured at the man still mounted. "Thomasina, this is Sir Broderick of Dunborough, Sir Blane's eldest son."

"My lady," Broderick said with a nod of his helmeted head, likewise ignoring Rheged and Sir Algar.

"Greetings, Sir Broderick," she replied, glancing warily at Rheged before she came forward. The master of Cwm Bron hadn't moved, nor had his stony expression changed. "May I present Sir Rheged and his overlord, Sir Algar."

"My father spoke well of you, Algar," Broderick said before regarding Rheged with disgust. "As for this Welshman, we're already acquainted."

Tamsin tried to hide her shock. Rheged had said the family were like vipers and he'd recognized Broderick, but she hadn't considered exactly how he'd come by that knowledge. No doubt she should have asked.

"Neither you nor Lord DeLac is welcome here, Broderick," Rheged growled.

"Nor have I any wish to be within ten miles of *you*," the knight replied, dismounting. "But you've stolen something that belongs to me and I've come to get it back." Broderick turned his unwelcome attention back to Tamsin. "A betrothal agreement was made and signed, and I intend to hold your uncle—and you—to it." His lips curved up, more smirk than smile. "Although there must be a slight change, given that my father is dead."

"Dead?" Tamsin mouthed, staring at the man with the cold eyes and thick lips so like a toad's.

"If Blane's dead, there's no more betrothal," Sir Algar said, moving closer and speaking with relieved confidence. "The agreement is null and void."

Broderick's beady dark eyes seemed to glow with satisfaction as he dismounted and smiled the most ugly smile Tamsin had ever seen. "We've made a new agreement, DeLac and I. He has agreed that this lady will now be *my* wife."

Tamsin gasped with horror.

"No, she will not," Rheged said firmly. "Get out of Cwm Bron and take DeLac with you."

His voice was so hard and cold, his manner so commanding, she marveled that Broderick didn't turn tail and run.

Instead, Broderick regarded Rheged as if he were an insect he'd like to crush. "Who do you think you are, Welshman, to disregard the law? An agreement has been made and signed, and will be upheld." He took three steps closer. "And I intend to have you charged and executed for this lady's abduction and rape."

Tamsin stepped forward. "Whatever my uncle has said and signed, *I* have not agreed to marry you, my lord. Nor have I been raped."

"Do you think anyone will believe that, if *I* say otherwise?" Broderick scornfully demanded. "I am my father's heir and have the ear of the king. So you will marry me, and I will have this Welshman tried and convicted.

"What say you, my lord?" he demanded, abruptly addressing Sir Algar. "Are you willing to risk your lands and titles for a liegeman who acts with such selfish arrogance and disrespect for the law? For I assure you, if you interfere, the king will know that you hindered the return of this lady to her uncle."

"I won't let you force Tamsin to do anything against her will," Sir Algar replied. "If you bring charges against Rheged, I will speak on his behalf. As for the king, you may find he's not so great a friend to DeLac as he's led you to believe, or to you, either. John thinks first and foremost of John, and I have influential friends at court, too."

"You would put your entire demesne at risk for this Welshman and my niece?" DeLac scoffed, his vanity and vitality momentarily reviving. "Have you grown a spine, then, after all this time?"

Swaying, her uncle made his way to Tamsin. She could smell the wine on his breath from ten paces away. "Tell me, my dear, has Algar told you how he deserted your mother, a woman he claimed to love, rather than risk losing even a portion of his lands? All it took was a hint from my father that it could be so, and Algar departed DeLac, never to enter our hall again. Didn't you ever wonder, now that he's apparently become such a friend, why he never sought you out when you arrived in my household? He's had years to do so."

Tamsin looked at the man who had been so kind to her and read guilt as well as dismay in his face.

Yet even if her uncle spoke the truth, and no matter what had happened in the past, Sir Algar had been more like a loving relative to her since her arrival here than Simon DeLac had ever been. "There is no need to involve Sir Algar in this dispute, my lords. I'm willing to return to DeLac and marry Sir Broderick."

"I won't let you," Rheged declared.

She turned to him and regarded him with sorrowful determination. "Please don't try to stop me, Rheged. I could never be happy, not even here with you, knowing—"

"What sort of talk is this?" Broderick interrupted. "Perhaps there was no abduction at all. Perhaps the lady planned to come here all along, to live in this hovel and be this Welshman's whore."

With an oath, Rheged drew his sword and marched

up to Broderick until they were nose to nose. "Leave Cwm Bron, Broderick, and take DeLac with you before I kill you. I will not warn you again."

Tamsin rushed to intervene. "Rheged, I will go with them. I *must* go with them."

"Not while I breathe."

When Broderick pulled his broadsword from its sheath, Sir Algar hurried to stand between them. "There is another way, my lords," he said, his tone and expression desperate, yet commanding. "Surely this matter can be settled on the tournament field, by combat. Lord DeLac and I can be the judges."

"Gladly," Rheged instantly agreed.

Broderick straightened his shoulders. "I am willing, on one condition—that it be a fight to the death."

"Agreed," Rheged said just as swiftly, before Tamsin or Sir Algar or anyone else could protest.

"And if you try to cheat, Welshman, as you did before, you will also be considered guilty and put to death at once."

Tamsin had no idea what Broderick was talking about. Nevertheless she was certain of one thing. "Rheged has no need to cheat to win."

"Such a passionate defense!" Broderick said with another smirk. "I trust you'll defend me just as passionately when we are wed."

"That day will never come," Rheged said sternly, "for I'm going to kill you. And as the lady says, I have no need to cheat, since I can win by skill alone. However, I shall agree to those terms as long as the same holds true for you, and that you'll swear before God that when I win, both Tamsin and Mavis will be free of any obligation to your family."

"And the rest of your family will leave us alone, too," Tamsin added. "Will you agree to that, Sir Broderick?"

His dark eyes flared. "Yes."

Sir Algar turned to Lord DeLac. "Simon?"

"Yes, by God. I want this over and done with!"

"As do I," Rheged said. "I'm ready to fight Broderick here and now."

"Of course you are," Broderick retorted. "You have your warhorse here, and all your men-at-arms. I don't."

"Tomorrow, then?" Sir Algar proposed.

"Tomorrow," Broderick agreed. "At Castle DeLac, and the lady will come with us now."

"Here," Rheged retorted. "And the lady stays, unless you feel fighting here gives me an advantage. If so, we'll go to Castle DeLac in the morning."

"I need no advantage of any kind!" Broderick retorted. "Let the combat be here, then—to *your* advantage."

"Stop!" Tamsin cried, sick of the arguing. Sick of the fighting. Sick of men deciding her fate for her, even Rheged. "Rheged fought at Castle DeLac, so you could say he knows that ground, too. Wherever you fight, though, I have no wish to return to Castle DeLac unless and until I must."

"As we are all chivalrous men, we should let the lady have her way in this," Sir Algar interposed. "As for where the combat will be—"

"Oh, for God's sake, let it be here and let her stay!" DeLac declared as he staggered to his horse. "What does it matter if she's here or there, or where the combat is?"

"I am willing to fight here," Broderick declared magnanimously.

"Excellent," Sir Algar said. "The combat that will decide the ladies' fates will be tomorrow, at the noon, in the meadow by the river. Are we all in agreement?"

"Yes," Broderick said with another nasty smile.

"Yes!" DeLac replied impatiently.

"Yes," Rheged said with a brisk nod. "Enjoy this night, my lord, because it's going to be your last."

Broderick flushed even as he scowled. "Tomorrow you die, Welshman, and this woman will be mine. Now come, Lord DeLac. We're leaving."

Broderick grabbed DeLac by the arm and pulled the older man toward his horse. DeLac hoisted himself into the saddle, nearly falling before he managed to get himself balanced and upright.

In the meantime, Broderick got on his horse and regarded Tamsin with another terrible smile. "You need have no fear, my lady. When we're married, I'll forgive you any little…lapses of judgment. After all, I wouldn't want my bride to hate me."

"It is already too late for that," Tamsin replied grimly.

With a curse, Broderick savagely wheeled his horse and led her uncle and his men out of the gates.

When they were gone, Tamsin let out her breath, then turned to Sir Algar. "If you'll excuse us, Sir Algar, I would speak with Rheged alone."

She didn't wait for his answer, or for Rheged to agree, before she started toward the keep.

Of course she would have many questions, and explanations must be made, Rheged thought as he followed her to the hall.

Instead of asking her questions in the hall, however, Tamsin continued to the steps leading to the upper chamber. Once they were alone, Tamsin turned to face him, her hands clasped before her and an anxious and troubled expression on her lovely face. "You didn't tell me you've met and fought Broderick before," she began without preamble.

"I didn't think it mattered, since you would be going back to Castle DeLac. I did tell you the family was a brood of vipers."

"But not exactly how you knew." Tamsin looked at him with a wariness that it hurt him to see. "Why does he claim you cheated the last time you fought?"

"Because he refuses to believe I beat him honestly even though I could hardly stand. On the morning before the melee, I was dizzy and weak like I've never been before or since. I'm sure I was weakened on purpose, with some kind of poison. Not enough to kill, but enough to ensure that I couldn't fight well. I have no doubt Broderick wanted to make certain that his list of triumphs remained unsullied by a loss, especially to a man like me, without noble blood. Unfortunately I had no proof of his perfidy, so I could make no formal charge."

"Couldn't you have simply been ill?"

"I'm never sick."

"You could have bowed out of the fight when you realized you were too weak to win."

"Except that I needed the prize money, or Jevan and I were going to starve."

"Is there anything else you haven't you told me?"

"I would never have guessed that Broderick would want you for himself. But rest assured, my lady, I will beat him tomorrow."

"I wish it hadn't come to this!" she cried, clasping her hands in agitation. "I should have gone back sooner!"

"No, you shouldn't have. You couldn't. You could have lost your limb, or perhaps your life."

"But now you stand to lose your life because of me."

"No, my lady, because of what I did. I took you from Castle DeLac, and whatever happens, I have no regrets. If I had left you there—"

"I would be marrying Broderick, with no hope for freedom." She regarded him with a desperate yearning. "Now I have hope, but at what cost?"

"Don't worry, my lady, I—"

"Tamsin," she whispered.

"Have no fear, Tamsin. I'll beat him," Rheged said softly, taking her hands in his. "And whatever happens, you mustn't blame yourself. He would have found some other reason to fight me one day. He's determined to assuage his wounded pride and have his vengeance. Nor would Algar be safe from his scheming, since I'm his liegeman, especially now that Blane is dead."

"I only wish there was another way!"

"I would fight a hundred men to keep you safe and happy," he replied.

For once his emotions were plain to see upon his face, so visible and vivid she could scarcely draw breath.

He loved her. Loved her as she had always dreamed of being loved. Loved her as she loved him.

"I want to be with you every day and every night," he whispered, his words confirming the evidence in his eyes. "I want to be in your heart the way you're in mine. I want you in my bed, my arms, my life forever. I love you, Tamsin. I need you, as I never thought I'd need or want another living soul. I want you with me always. I want you for my wife."

His expression changed again, and suddenly Sir Rheged of Cwm Bron, champion of tournaments, warrior and knight, looked at her as if she held the power of life or death over him, as if she alone possessed the keys of the kingdom both here and in the life to come. "If you don't want me for a husband, tell me so."

Before she could answer, he stepped back and shook his head. "You *should* refuse me. You deserve more than a peasant raised to knighthood who rules a ramshackle castle and has no money to repair it. You should be a great and respected lady, wed to a husband who realizes what a priceless prize he's won. After I defeat Broderick, you should leave Cwm Bron and find a better man."

She put her finger against his full lips and shook her head, for that look of sorrowful yet resolute decision told her all she needed to know, all she would ever need to know, about the true depth of his feelings for her. Despite the missteps, the mistakes, the errors and arguments, against all odds, she had found the best man in England, and he loved her. As she loved him. As she would always love him. "There is no better man. No braver, finer man. No one else has ever loved me as you do, or thought me a priceless prize. If I could stay here with you, if I could be your wife, I would be the happiest woman in England."

Then doubt brought forth its cruel little fangs. "I only wish I had a dowry worthy—"

"You have wisdom and spirit and goodness and beauty. You have everything and more a man can want. You alone are dowry enough."

"As you alone are enough. I want nothing more than to be your wife, Rheged. I've wanted it since that first night, but I was afraid to even dream that such a thing could be. I love you, Rheged. Knight or peasant, king or servant, I love you. But Broderick—"

"Will die and you will be free." He smiled then, joyfully, wonderfully. "I've never had better cause to fight well. When I win and you're free—"

"I will gladly marry you."

Like an arrow released from a bow, he tugged her into his arms and kissed her with all the passion and heat and longing any woman could ever want or hope for.

Confirmed in her love, keen in her desire, she surrendered to the desire surging within her.

Until he broke the kiss and stepped back. "I should go. I must go. Now."

She stood motionless and silent, her heartbeat throbbing in her ears, her body warm and waiting.

"I must go, Tamsin," he insisted, his voice rough with need. "Tell me to go. Order me to leave."

Still she said nothing.

Before she moved to block the door.

Chapter Fifteen

"Rheged," she whispered, opening her arms to him. "Rheged, my love."

All the reasons he should leave her fled his mind. Nothing existed but her, here with him, as he took her in his arms and kissed her with all the passion and desire she inspired.

Aroused, excited, he brushed his fingers over her bodice, until he encountered the knot of the lacing at the neck of her gown. Swiftly, eagerly, he untied it and slipped his hand inside. Her breasts were perfect, her mouth and tongue amazing, her body made to fit against his. *She* was perfect.

How warm her skin was! How soft, like the finest fleece. And her hair…so long and thick and soft. His lips left hers and he nuzzled her open bodice lower, his mouth gliding across her firm hot flesh lower and lower, until he reached her nipple and drew it into his mouth.

She gasped and arched, her hands clutching him. "Take me to your bed, Rheged," she pleaded softly and without a hint of shame. "Please, Rheged!"

He would have had to be immortal to resist her insistent invitation, and he was not.

He swept her into his arms and carried her to the bed. She pulled him down atop her and captured his lips with hers, a demanding, harsh kiss that spoke of needs that must and would be met. Desire that would permit no refusal. She would have him now, and he would not, could not, deny her, for they were one in passion, one in need, one in desire. One in love.

She shifted to untie the drawstring of his breeches. He held his breath until she succeeded, and he was free. His heartbeat pounding like a blacksmith's hammer on an anvil, he reached down and dragged her skirts up to her hips, his knuckles grazing her stockings, then the bare skin of her thigh.

Primitive need and primal excitement took control. Thoughts ceased, replaced only by the longing to possess her. Hands and fingers and palms grazed and brushed and stroked, explored, discovered as tongues entwined, joined in a sinuous dance.

He touched her where her thighs met. If he had any doubts that she was ready, another eager arch of her body put them swiftly to rest.

He positioned himself, then slowly pushed inside. She was tight, so tight. With renewed need and urgent yearning, he pulled back a bit, then thrust again. Panting, she gripped his shoulders and raised herself as if offering her bared breasts to him. He eagerly licked and teased her pebbled nipples, while her gasps and moans excited him yet more.

Tension built, coiled, waited…until she grabbed his shoulders, levered herself up and cried out like a feral creature, her body throbbing and gripping him. With an answering growl low in his throat, he climaxed, carried away on wave after wave of blissful release.

Panting, sated, he lowered her and laid his head upon her shoulder. He had never felt so wanted, so necessary, to any woman. No other woman had ever seemed so eager to be in his arms or as excited to be there.

He had admired her from afar, wondered what it would be like to make love with her, and now...and now he was as close to heaven as it was likely possible for a mortal man to be.

Sighing, Tamsin reached up to tuck a lock of his long, dark hair behind his ear, for the first time noticing the thin scar there. "How did you get this?"

"I think that was...France. Yes, shortly after I arrived. The padding of my helmet came away and I cut myself trying to get it off when the battle was over. If I hadn't been so parched, I would have had more patience."

"Was that the battle after you scaled the wall?"

"No, another, minor one some years before."

"I want to hear all about your battles, and everything else about you."

He smiled. "That would take some time."

"A lifetime," she agreed. "Oh, Rheged, I pray we have a lifetime!"

Determined to make her forget what awaited the next day, he stroked her hair, marveling at its rich thickness. "When was the last time you cut your hair?"

He felt her lips turn up in a smile. "Mavis tried to trim my hair when I was thirteen. Trying to get it straight at the bottom, she kept cutting and cutting until she was almost at the scalp. A scarecrow had better hair by the time she was done."

"And what about you, Wolf of Wales with the savage hair?" she asked, looking up at him and twisting the end of a lock of his hair around her finger. "When was the last time you cut your hair?"

"When Algar gave me Cwm Bron. I thought I ought to look the part of a landed knight. Instead, I looked like a shorn sheep and swore that never again would I cut my hair like a Norman."

"Looking like a Viking no doubt makes your opponents even more wary."

"Perhaps," he agreed with an unexpectedly mischievous expression, and she knew she'd guessed aright.

"And you call me clever!"

"You are. The cleverest, more intelligent woman I've ever met, as well as the most beautiful," he murmured before he kissed her again.

This time, he was the first to draw back. "I suppose we should return to the hall."

She couldn't disagree. "Yes, lest Sir Algar think I'm upbraiding you again."

Rheged sat up and regarded her with furrowed brow. "Perhaps it would better to let him think you're angry than to have him guess the truth."

She, too, sat up and laid her arm around Rheged's shoulder before kissing him lightly on the cheek. "The servants already think we're lovers and probably have thought so from the day I arrived. I'm sure Elvina was upset the other day because she thought she'd interrupted something rather like…well, what we've just done."

Rheged didn't appear at all surprised.

"You knew?"

"Not exactly, but I should have expected it." He blushed like a naughty little boy. "It seems Gareth told the men about the Welsh custom of abducting the bride and it probably didn't take much imagination to believe we were already lovers. I did tell him that wasn't our plan," he hastened to assure her. "I thought I made it clear that I didn't even like you, so no one would guess how I really felt. God help me, I was even trying to deny my feelings to myself." He ruefully shook his head. "Gareth will be saying he was right and I planned to marry you all along. Maybe my heart was wiser than my head."

She rose and picked up the ivory comb from the table beside the bed. "When you first returned to Cwm Bron," she said, running it through her tumbled locks, "I hoped you had come to save me from my betrothal, in spite of what I'd said, only to realize—much to my dismay—that it was the bogus prize that had caused you to return. That's why I was so angry."

"You weren't angry because I took you?" he asked as he, too, got off the bed and began to tie the drawstring of his breeches.

"Oh, no, I was furious—and justly so, my love. I meant when you were standing in the courtyard shouting for my uncle."

"I think I loved you even then. I think I loved you from the first time I saw you giving the remains of the feast to the poor at the gates. You were so kind and generous, I knew you were different from any other lady I'd ever met."

She flushed as she set down the comb and tied her bodice closed. "I didn't know you saw me."

"Which made your kindness all the more impressive."

Facing him, she held out her arms. "How do I look?"

"Beautiful," he replied, reaching for her.

"Thank you, sir," she said, stepping back, "but I meant, do I look like a woman who's just had a tumble on the sheets?" She smiled. "To think I would ever have to ask that!"

"Nor did I dream, a sennight ago, that I would be in love with the most amazing woman who, incredibly, loves me, too."

She put her arms around him and held him close. "Come to me tonight, Rheged," she whispered as a little thread of fear returned, winding around her heart.

It drew even tighter when they returned to the hall and she saw all the worried, anxious faces among the soldiers and the servants gathered there—a forceful reminder that more than she and Mavis and Sir Algar would suffer if Rheged lost tomorrow.

Rheged's strong hand took hold of hers, and she found hope again, albeit one tempered with the realization that much depended on Rheged's strength and skill.

There was one man missing from the hall. She gestured for Hildie to come closer. "Where is Sir Algar?"

The maidservant didn't meet her gaze as she twisted her apron in her hands. "Gone, my lady. Back to his own castle."

Gareth stepped out from among the soldiers. "He said he would return in time for the contest tomorrow."

Despite his explanation, it didn't take a seer to see

that he was dismayed, too. Once before Algar had fled rather than stand up to the DeLacs.

"He will return," Rheged said firmly, his grip on her hand tightening. "Now let us eat and drink and celebrate my good fortune, for this lady has consented to be my wife."

There was a moment of stunned silence, until Gareth cheered and the hall exploded with the noise of the soldiers also cheering and stamping feet, and the servants, too. Then came the calls for wine and ale to drink to Sir Rheged and the lady, followed by more raucous cheers from the soldiers and a few bawdy jests, too.

"Perhaps I made a mistake announcing our intent," Rheged said, leading Tamsin to the table. "They'll all be drunk tonight and the worse for it tomorrow unless I put an end to it."

He got to his feet and held up his hands for silence. "Men of the garrison of Cwm Bron—and the best men in the land—although I'm happy that you're pleased for me, this is not the time for feasting and celebrating. That will be tomorrow, after I've defeated Sir Broderick."

"And you will!" one man called out.

"With one blow!" shouted another.

"He's as good as dead now!" cried a third.

Again Rheged held up his hands. "Believe me, I have every reason to do my best," he said, glancing at Tamsin. "So let us dine and rest tonight, the better to celebrate tomorrow when my enemy is vanquished. There will be more than enough wine and ale for all, and Foster will prepare a feast worthy of a wedding."

"Aye, my lord, aye!" Gareth cried while the men

cheered with renewed enthusiasm and the servants applauded.

And Tamsin hid her dread behind a happy smile.

"My lady!" Charlie cried as he ran into the hall where Mavis was supervising the laying of cloths on the tables for the evening meal. "They're coming back, your father and Sir Broderick!"

"And Tamsin?" she asked eagerly when Charlie skittered to a halt. "Did you see her?"

Charlie flushed and didn't meet her gaze. "No, I didn't, my lady. Just the men, that's all I saw."

Sweet savior! Surely they wouldn't have left Tamsin behind!

Unless she was dead.

Her heart in her throat, Mavis dashed to the yard, to see her father, Broderick and their men riding beneath the portcullis and into the yard. Men and horses were all clearly exhausted; they must have ridden hard to get back before nightfall.

She anxiously scanned the mounted group for her cousin.

Charlie had been right, Tamsin wasn't there.

Holy Blessed Mother, don't let her be dead! Mavis prayed as she rushed toward her father, who looked half-dead as he hauled his horse to a halt. Clutching the toe of his boot, she cried, "Where is Tamsin? Oh, Father, tell me she isn't dead!"

Her father shook his foot as if she were a fly. "Get off, girl! Of course she isn't dead."

"Then where is she? Is she so badly hurt she can't come home?"

"It seems the lady has decided to remain where she is, for the time being, until I kill Rheged," Broderick answered for her father.

She turned to the knight with both dismay and a revulsion she didn't bother to hide. "She has *chosen* to stay there?"

"Yes, she has, the bi—" Lord Delac caught Broderick's eye and remembered that, incredibly, the man still wanted to marry his whore of a niece. "It appears I may have been right all along about her and that Welshman."

Mavis still could not believe that. Not entirely, although when she'd recalled the times Tamsin had mentioned Sir Rheged, there might have been something in her eyes....

"Here, oaf, help me down!" her father ordered one of the grooms, who hurried to help the nobleman dismount.

Broderick, for all his bulk, swung down easily from the saddle. "I must confess, my lady, I find it difficult to believe that you had no inkling what was afoot with your cousin and that Welshman."

"Whatever *might* have been between them, I'm sure Thomasina has been virtuous," Mavis replied.

Tamsin would never willingly give up her virtue, not to any man. Not unless she was married. Mavis was completely certain about that.

"Well, there's something between them now," her father returned. "Sir Broderick is to be commended for his generous intention to keep the betrothal agreement in spite of your cousin's shameful behavior."

Tamsin was *not* shameful, and as for Broderick's "generous intention," if ever a man was completely lacking in anything that remotely resembled generosity, it was surely Broderick of Dunborough.

"Even to the point of fighting to the death for Thomasina on the morrow," her father continued.

Mavis stared at him, aghast. "They are going to fight to the death over her?"

"Jealous, my lady?" Broderick asked with a mocking look.

She turned on him like an angry hornet. "I'm simply surprised that you would be foolish enough to condemn yourself to death."

"It will be Sir Rheged who dies, my lady, so I suggest you have a care how to speak to me. After all, we are going to be family."

"If you win," Mavis retorted.

"Enough!" her father growled as one of the grooms helped him from his horse and he staggered toward the hall. "I want bread. And honey. And wine. Mulled wine."

Mavis started after him, but Broderick blocked her way and brought his face so close to hers she could smell his unclean breath. "If you value your cousin's life, my lady, you will remember that when I am her husband, her life belongs to me."

Hating him to the depths of her soul, Mavis faced him squarely. "And you had best remember, my lord, that Sir Rheged of Cwm Bron isn't called the Wolf of Wales because he cannot fight."

"If your father's wise, he'll marry you to some Scot and send you far away."

"If you are wise, my lord, you'll get out of my way."

Broderick hesitated for a moment, then stepped aside and let her pass.

He watched her march to the hall, and his expression was not one of admiration.

Mavis didn't join her father or the servants in the hall. She ran up to the chamber she'd shared with Tamsin and reached beneath the bed for the bundle she'd prepared. Clutching it to her chest, she sank down upon the bed.

If Rheged won tomorrow, Tamsin would be safe. She would have to take Tamsin's place as bride to the disgusting Broderick, but surely there would be at least a day before any marriage could take place. If Rheged lost tomorrow and Tamsin came back, there would still be time enough to flee.

Please, God, she prayed as she buried her face in the bundle, *give us a chance to flee!*

After the food had been eaten and the tables cleared, Tamsin leaned close to Rheged. "I believe I shall retire now, my lord."

He kept his eyes straight ahead as he very quietly answered, "But you will be expecting me?"

"Oh, yes." She furtively slid her hand over his powerful thigh. "I'll be waiting. Clad only in my shift."

He looked at her then, his expression a mixture of such surprise and delight she had to smile in return.

"Here, now, you two, what's going on under the table? You're not wed yet and no vows taken!" Gareth jovially called out.

"Can't a man talk to his bride-to-be?"

"Talk, aye, but it's not the talking I'm talking about."

"Have a care, Gareth, and remember you're speaking to your lord," Rheged chastised with such obviously bogus annoyance Gareth winked before he impudently replied, "Oh, aye, Sir Rheged, my lord."

"Perhaps we shouldn't even try to be discreet," Rheged muttered under his breath.

"Perhaps not," Tamsin agreed. "But let me leave first anyway."

His eyebrows rose, but he didn't protest, for he had not forgotten what she'd said about waiting for him clad only in her shift.

Chapter Sixteen

A little while later, Rheged discovered Tamsin was as good as her word. Not only was she naked save for her shift, but her unbound hair was loose and cascading over her body like a lustrous cloak.

As Rheged stood looking at her, a delicious thrill of anticipation ran through her. "Let us to bed, my lord," she whispered.

"Gladly, my lady, gladly," he replied, his lips curving up in a smile so seductively appealing she couldn't say a word even if she wanted to.

She didn't want to. She wanted to make love with him.

Reclining on the bed and feeling like a queen about to be loved by a king—a magnificent, powerful king who was hers to love forever—she watched Rheged tug off his tunic and shirt. His clothes were always plain, unadorned, simple, and he looked marvelous in anything, but he looked even better half-naked. Her gaze roved over his taut belly and broad chest and the scars that marked his torso, the outer evidence of his military battles and survival.

But there had been other battles, too, of a sort that she also had fought.

She loved him, and she always would, no matter what happened on the morrow.

"Do you like what you see, Tamsin?" he asked, his voice low and husky.

"Very much," she replied, watching him tug off his boots and then his breeches, the latter so swiftly she caught barely a glimpse of the rest of his powerful body before he took her in his arms and kissed her fervently.

Despite the passion that fueled their desire, in spite of her yearning anticipation and the speed with which they'd loved before, he took his time now, as if he believed they had hours…days…nights…years to love. She would think so, too. She would pretend that they had the rest of their lives to live and love together. That this was but the beginning, not the alpha and omega both.

Leaning his weight on his elbow, he kissed her tenderly, his free hand gliding lightly over the curves of her body, exploring her with slow deliberation. She responded in kind, letting her hands study him, finding the places that made him sigh and gasp, as she was sighing and gasping, teaching and being taught.

But she could feel the need burning within him as it smoldered within her, ready to burst into eager excitement.

Not quite yet. First there was more kissing and caressing, more delicate stroking and touching, like seafarers who'd landed on a new and lovely shore, one they had years to wander.

Until the discovery grew more heated, with a greater purpose that must be fulfilled, and sooner than the dawn.

More than ready, she reached down to guide him to her, and with a smooth thrust, he was inside. They were together once more, completely and utterly.

One in passion, one in love, joined as man and woman, husband and wife, to be one in all that life had to offer, the good and the bad, joy and sorrow, to celebrate together or comfort each other if the need arose.

And then the passion and need and desire took them, rushing them forward, filling and compelling them onward and over the edge until they cried out together in ecstasy.

After a long moment, as the waves receded and cast Tamsin back upon the shore, she cradled Rheged's head against her breasts and stroked his hair. This was happiness. And contentment. This was joy such as few women would likely ever know. She was so blessed... if only for tonight.

He caught her studying him and when he grinned, she could see the boy he must have been, as well as a glimpse of the children they might have. "You aren't sleepy, Tamsin?" he asked with another seductive smile while he caressed her. "I shall have to think of something to tire you."

But he also stifled a yawn.

"I think we've both sported enough for one day," she said, "and now it's time to rest. You mustn't be too tired tomorrow."

"I could beat Broderick if I'd been awake for a week," he assured her.

Yet in spite of his assertion, Rheged had to admit, if only to himself, that he *was* weary, and Broderick was angry, bitter and determined—the worst kind of opponent to face.

His throat was somewhat scratchy, too, but that, he thought with an inward grin, could be from the way he'd growled in triumph when he reached the height of ecstasy in Tamsin's arms.

"Perhaps it would be better if I slept," he reluctantly agreed.

As Tamsin sighed and snuggled against him, a feeling of tender affection stole over him. How delightful and wondrous it was to think that they could be friends and confidants as well as lovers.

She raised her head to look at him, her expression suddenly serious. "I don't want to marry anyone but you, ever! Whatever happens tomorrow, I never will!"

He pressed a kiss to her forehead, loving her beyond all measure. "Whatever happens tomorrow, you are the only woman I have ever loved, or ever shall." He kissed her lightly on the lips. "Be of good cheer, Tamsin! I beat Broderick before when the stakes were not nearly so high, and I'd been rendered weak. I'll beat him again. Knowing your opponent and the tricks he might play is like having another shield." Another wave of weariness washed over him. "Now close your eyes, Tamsin, and try to sleep, and so shall I."

Although Tamsin doubted sleep would come soon, if at all, she did as he suggested and soon realized he'd dozed off. Clearly he wasn't afraid of Broderick, and if he could sleep so easily, perhaps she could rest, too.

Even so, it was a long time before Tamsin's eyelids finally closed and she fell into a fitful sleep, to dream of Rheged, his long hair flying, half-naked, armed with only a bow and riding into an ambush.

"Then you think it might come to a battle between DeLac's men and us?" Rob asked Gareth in a whisper as they sat together on a bench in the hall of Cwm Bron. It was nigh onto midnight, and the men who weren't on watch were asleep on pallets nearby, along with the hounds. Men and dogs made small noises or grunts as they turned but didn't wake.

Gareth stared at the glowing remains of the fire in the hearth. "It might, if Rheged wins. DeLac might not want to fight over her, but one look at that Broderick tells me he won't take losing lightly, and he's got enough men of his own at Dunborough to give us some trouble if he wants to."

"Well, if he's so foolish, our men'll be up to it," Rob replied stoutly. Then, clasping his hands loosely, resting his elbows on his knees, he sighed and shook his head. "I never thought I'd see Rheged lose his head over a woman, though, or risk everything for one, either."

"I wouldn't have said it likely, either, once upon a time. But she's a rare woman, you have to admit."

"Rare enough I hope I never meet another like her. Give me a woman who knows her place and stays there."

"That might do for you, Rob," Gareth said with a grin, "but never for Rheged. He needs someone to match him strength for strength, and I think he's found her. Now, me, I like a quiet woman."

"You like a woman if she's between eighteen and forty," Rob returned. "But truly, Gareth, do you think Rheged would give up Cwm Bron and his title, even his life, for that woman?"

"Aye, I do."

"Well, then, that's enough for me. I'd still be dragging stones for that lout of a mason if he hadn't offered me a place here. What do we do if that Broderick loses and comes back with more men? What if he wants a fight?"

Gareth's smile was as grim as Rheged's could be. "We give him one."

Tamsin awoke with a start, then lay still. It was only a dream and she was in bed with a living Rheged, warm and safe. The cock crowed beyond the walls, and the dim light of early dawn shone through the crack in the shutters.

A new day, and such a day! Of hope and dread, of triumph if Rheged won, and horrible despair if—

He must win! He would win!

"Rheged, wake up," she said, gently nudging him. "The sun is rising, and so must we."

His only answer was a mumble before he reached out and brought her hand to his chest.

"Rheged," she repeated more firmly and pulling herself free. "Wake up!"

He stirred and began to sit up, then fell back upon the pillows, his breathing raw and rasping. She saw at once that his face was pale and perspiration dotted his forehead and upper lip. Although his eyes were open, they were glassy.

"Rheged!" she cried. "What's wrong? Are you ill?" She put her hand on his forehead. "You're burning!"

Ignoring the slight ache in her leg, she rushed to the washstand to wet a cloth. She wrung it out quickly, then hurried back to put it on his forehead. "Are you in pain? Your stomach? Your head?"

"Throat. Head. Both," he croaked, starting to shiver.

She wrapped him up in the blankets as best she could, then swiftly pulled on a gown. She rushed to the door and down the stairs. Several soldiers and a few of the servants were stirring, and she spotted the groom seated at one of the tables shoving a crust of bread into his mouth. "Dan! Fetch Gilbert!"

The groom sat stunned, staring at her.

"Not for me, for Rheged. He's sick!"

Tossing the bread to one of the ever-present hounds, Dan leapt to his feet and ran from the hall, passing a startled Hildie who was coming in from the kitchen entrance.

"Hildie, bring cold water and more linen—small squares. Quickly!"

She didn't wait to see if her orders were obeyed but immediately went back to the chamber. Rheged had thrown off the covers and managed to sit up, his bare feet on the frigid stone floor.

"What are you doing?" she cried, her fear making her sound shrewish. "You must lie down!"

He tried to stand and nearly fell. "Got…to kill… Broderick," he said, his voice so thick and hoarse it was nearly unrecognizable.

She ran to help him sit again. "You can't even stand, let alone fight! Get back in bed."

He swallowed hard, or tried to. "Water. Parched."

"Get back in bed and I'll bring you some water," she promised.

For a moment, she thought he was going to fight off her helping hands and insist on standing again.

"Water," he rasped, and she hurried to fetch the only water she had—the clean water in the ewer for washing.

He lifted the jug to his lips and some got into his mouth, but more splashed down his chest and he almost dropped the jug. She caught it just before it hit the floor.

"Please, Rheged, lie down," she pleaded, shocked at how weak he'd become. "Gilbert will be here soon."

Rheged wet his lips and then with effort, his voice hoarse, spoke a single word. "Poison."

Poison? He thought he'd been poisoned? By Broderick, no doubt. "How? When?" she whispered as her terror grew. "We were together—"

A knock sounded on the door and she rushed to open it. Hildie stood here, linen in one hand, another ewer of water in the other. Her mouth open, she stared at the bed and the still-naked Rheged.

"Get more water," Tamsin ordered as she took the ewer and linen. "And a goblet. Go! Now!"

Hildie instantly obeyed. Tamsin hurried to dampen another cloth to put on Rheged's forehead. For now, Rheged could stay naked under the blankets.

He began to shiver, his teeth chattering. She tucked the blankets more closely about him and, feeling completely, utterly helpless, fetched another cool, damp cloth.

He struggled to rise again. "Must…get…up," he muttered, sounding as if every word tore his throat. "Must…fight."

"Not today," she said firmly. "Lie down and rest, Rheged. Your opponent has yet to arrive. The combat can't begin until he does, so lie back and rest."

"My armor—"

"Never mind about that now."

"Jevan—"

"Rheged, you *must* rest!"

His protests seemed to have taken what little energy he possessed, and he finally lay back, panting heavily.

And then—thank God!—the physician arrived.

"He's feverish and his head and throat hurt," Tamsin said to Gilbert as he set down his medicinal chest and swiftly examined Rheged. "He's had chills, too. He can barely talk and he's very weak. He thinks he may have been poisoned."

"Poisoned? With what?"

"I don't know! But this illness did come upon him suddenly."

Gilbert glanced at her sharply. "Did you eat the same things he did last night?"

"Yes, I think so."

"What about the wine?"

"I don't know. I can't remember. Isn't there something you can give him to ease his suffering and make him well?"

"I shall do my best, my lady, whatever ails him."

"Never…get…sick," Rheged rasped.

"So you say, my lord," Gilbert replied. He opened Rheged's mouth and peered inside while Tamsin hovered anxiously behind him. "Any trouble swallowing, my lady?"

"Yes, I think so."

Gilbert rose and faced her. "I don't think he's been poisoned. It looks more like an infection in the throat. A serious one, but not from poison."

"What are you going to do?"

Gilbert went to his medicinal chest and drew forth a small clay vessel covered with waxed parchment. "Is there water? Oh, yes, I see it. I'll prepare a potion from willow bark that should lower the fever, dull the pain and help him rest more comfortably." He poured some white powder from the vessel into a goblet, then added a little water.

"You're sure he wasn't poisoned?"

"Not unless someone has created one that infects the throat first and foremost."

"How long will it take for your potion to work?"

"Soon, I hope. He should also gargle with salt water, if he can. Most of all, he should rest."

"No!" Rheged growled, proving he was awake and well enough to understand, "Must...fight...*today!*"

"Impossible, my lord," Gilbert decisively declared. "You're not fit enough to fight, unless you want to lose."

"I...won't!"

"Then rest while you can," Gilbert replied in a more placating tone, yet the look he gave Tamsin told her Rheged simply could not fight that day.

If he did, he would surely lose.

"He will not rise from his bed today," Tamsin said firmly. "The contest must and will be postponed."

Surely a man as proud and vain as Broderick

wouldn't want to claim victory over a sick man, no matter how desperate he was to win.

An anxious Hildie appeared at the threshold of the chamber. "My lady," she announced in a whisper, "Sir Algar is here."

Although nothing could relieve her fear completely until Rheged had recovered and the combat was over, Hildie's news was welcome. "Thank you, Hildie," she said before addressing Gilbert. "I must tell Sir Algar what's happened, and then I shall return."

She left the chamber and hurried down the stairs, to find Sir Algar waiting for her, his expression full of sympathy and worry. "What is this I hear? Rheged is ill?"

"Yes, he's very sick, with an infection in the throat. He's in no condition to fight. There must be no combat today."

"Of course not!" Sir Algar exclaimed. His white eyebrows furrowed. "Perhaps you shouldn't stay where there is sickness. You're welcome to come to my castle until he's better."

"Thank you for the offer, my lord, but I can't accept. My place is here, with Rheged."

She smiled in spite of her worry. "He's asked me to be his wife. Nothing would make me happier, my lord, except to see him well."

"You and Rheged…married!"

"Yes, my lord. As soon as he's better and the threat from my uncle and Broderick no longer exists."

"Nothing would please me more," Sir Algar replied. "And he will win, my dear, whenever this contest takes place."

"With God's help," she answered. "Now you must excuse me, my lord. I need to be with Rheged."

Sir Algar held her back. "I should explain why I left here yesterday."

"Later, my lord," she replied, her worry about Rheged overwhelming any other concerns.

The door to the hall flew open and Gareth charged into the chamber, coming to a halt when he spied Tamsin and Sir Algar. "What's this I hear about Rheged being sick?"

"His head hurts and he can hardly speak, his throat is so painful," Tamsin replied.

Gareth stared at them with dismay. "I can't believe it! I've never seen him sick, not in all the time I've known him. Not even when he's been cold and wet through."

"We've sent for Gilbert," Tamsin said, starting for the stairs.

"It's got to be poison. That oaf's tried it before. By God, I'll kill him myself!" Gareth declared, fury in every word.

"No!" Sir Algar cried so fervently Tamsin halted and turned back.

"No," the older man repeated, his tone more calm but strong nonetheless. "This must be between Rheged and Broderick."

Tamsin knew he was right, and said so. "Otherwise my uncle would be within his rights to attack Cwm Bron," she explained.

"We can beat him—and anyone else they send against us!"

"At what cost?" Tamsin returned. "How many would die? And if the king should become involved, Rheged could lose all even if you win a battle, or hold Cwm Bron against attack."

"The lady speaks the truth, Gareth," Sir Algar said. "We shall speak to Lord DeLac and Sir Broderick and seek a postponement of the combat until Rheged is well again."

"And if he dies?"

"If he dies, the lady will need another champion."

"Rheged isn't going to die!" Tamsin exclaimed, refusing to admit that possibility, even to herself. "My uncle will agree to the postponement and Rheged will recover," she finished as she hurried to the stairs.

As soon as she was out of sight, Gareth looked at Sir Algar, his eyes full of fire and resolve. "If Rheged dies, I'll kill that Norman."

"If Rheged dies, I'll help you."

Chapter Seventeen

When Tamsin reached the bedchamber, she found Gilbert and Hildie trying to hold down a struggling Rheged. A dented metal goblet lay on the floor beside the bed, the contents spilled.

"Must…fight!" Rheged croaked, kicking and twisting.

Tamsin hurried to his side and, taking his perspiring face between her hands, spoke firmly, hiding her own desperation. "Not today, Rheged. You cannot fight today. Lie still and rest, the better to fight tomorrow."

He settled for a moment, his eyes darting about wildly before coming back to her. "For you, I must," he said hoarsely.

"Tomorrow," she repeated, although she had no idea when he would be well enough to face Broderick.

Rheged's eyes closed and his breathing began to slow. Sighing, Tamsin let go and moved back, and Gilbert and Hildie released their hold on his arms.

"By all that's holy, he's a strong man," Gilbert said,

running a shaking hand over his sweating face. "I tried to give him a draught to sleep, but—"

"I know," Tamsin said while Hildie picked up the cup.

As the maidservant was going to get a rag to wipe the floor, the door to the chamber opened and Gareth hurried inside, coming to a halt when he saw Rheged, pale and feverish, in the bed.

But he recovered quickly and looked at Tamsin. "They're coming, my lady."

He didn't have to say who.

"I leave Rheged in your capable hands, Gilbert. And yours, too, Hildie," Tamsin said as she followed Gareth from the room.

Muttering what was either a prayer or a string of Welsh oaths, Rheged's friend led the way down the stairs. "Never seen him sick before, my lady, and that's the truth," he added as they walked swiftly through the empty hall.

"Sir Broderick will agree to a postponement," she said firmly, telling herself it must and would be so.

Gareth put his hand on the latch of the hall doors and paused to regard her with grim eyes. "If it comes to a fight, my lady, we're ready. Every man here will die for Rheged."

Her eyes filled with tears, but she blinked them back. She wouldn't have Broderick or her uncle see her crying. "I trust it won't come to that, Gareth."

Then she pushed open the doors and went into the yard to stand beside Sir Algar, who was shifting from foot to foot. Gareth joined his men ringing the yard. She wished there were more of them, for in truth, she had no faith at all in Broderick's honor, or her uncle's, either.

"Rheged?" Sir Algar asked under his breath as the approaching force announced their arrival and the thick gates began to open.

"Resting better," she said, hoping it was still so.

Her concern did not lessen when the mounted party rode into the yard of Cwm Bron like a conquering army, with Sir Broderick at the head, her uncle beside him and fifty armed soldiers behind.

As befit a man so obviously vain, Broderick's helmet sported a tall scarlet plume and he wore the finest sur-coat she had ever seen, made of scarlet velvet, his crest heavily embroidered in brown and gold. His mail and gauntlet gloves gleamed in the autumn sunlight. His prancing black horse was huge, taller and broader even than Jevan, and it tossed its head like a bare-knuckle brawler looking for a fight.

Her uncle, meanwhile, looked like a jester play-ing at being lord. His cloak was rumpled, his hair un-kempt, his horse's trappings mud-stained and torn near the girth. Even when his horse stood motionless, Lord DeLac swayed in his saddle, suggesting he was already deep in his cups.

"A fine day for combat, is it not?" Broderick said with apparent joviality. He raised his visor and scanned the cloudless sky before dismounting and approaching Tamsin. Her uncle slid off his horse, barely managing not to fall. Broderick's soldiers likewise dismounted and stood in rows, as disciplined as any Tamsin had ever seen.

"Where is your champion, my lady?" Broderick demanded, fixing his scornful gaze on Tamsin. "Fled before the battle?"

"Sir Rheged is ill and cannot fight today," she replied, keeping her voice calm. "The combat must be postponed."

"What's this? Sir Rheged claims to be sick?" Broderick mocked. "How unfortunate, especially since this attempt to delay the combat will avail him nothing. If he cannot fight, he forfeits, and that's the same as losing. He will be judged guilty and have to pay the price."

Tamsin regarded the man before her with disdain. "Are you truly so lacking in honor you would force an unfair fight?"

"Apparently I must remind you that *he* started this when he abducted my father's bride," Broderick replied.

"Sir Broderick, the lady is right," Sir Algar declared. "This contest must be postponed until Sir Rheged is well."

"Of course you'd speak for your pet," Broderick said, sneering. "I'm sure Lord DeLac agrees with me. DeLac!"

Her uncle took a few staggering steps closer. His eyes were red-rimmed and puffy, and his mouth was slack.

"What do you say, DeLac?" Broderick demanded. "Will you let this contest be delayed?"

Her uncle stumbled to a halt and regarded them with stunned disbelief. "Delayed? No! Rheged must fight or be judged guilty."

"Today," Broderick prompted.

"Of course today," her uncle replied peevishly. "This must be settled now, once and for all. I'm weary of riding and it's too bloody cold."

"This is a matter of life and death, Uncle!" Tamsin protested.

DeLac's face reddened. "You should be grateful I agreed to let this matter be decided here at all! By law, you belong to Broderick, as I've already decided—and as your guardian, have every right to do!"

Tamsin straightened her shoulders. "According to the law—"

"The hell with the law or attorneys' tricks! You will do as *I* say! For once you'll be as obedient as a woman ought to be! You will know your place instead of trying to run everything and everyone around you!"

She gasped as if he'd hit her. "If I took charge of your household, Uncle, it was only because I was trying to please you and make things comfortable for you so that you would love me at least a little. Do you think I enjoyed having to give all the orders and see that they were obeyed? That I liked having to watch every ha'penny, only to be chided for spending too much? Or that I was happy to spend my days making sure work was done while you sat in your solar drinking wine and eating sweetmeats, entertaining all your friends while I toiled like a servant? Yet in spite of all my efforts, you would gladly hand me off to a man who'll surely make me miserable, and after he kills one of the finest men in England when he's too weak to defend himself. You're a selfish blackguard, Uncle, and I'm ashamed to be your niece!"

As Lord DeLac spluttered, Broderick shook his head. "Tsk-tsk, my lady! There's no need for such harsh recriminations! Granted, your uncle is not a generous man, but it's not as if he's condemning you to hell.

I am, after all, a wealthy man, and you'll be better off in Dunborough bearing my sons than you would be living in this ruin with a man who barely has enough to pay his garrison. Indeed, to show you how kind and generous I can be, I *am* willing to forgo a trial today or any other day, provided you honor the betrothal contract and marry me."

"I would rather die!" Tamsin declared. At the same time, Gareth and the men of Cwm Bron took a step forward, their hands on their weapons. Broderick's men shifted closer, too, likewise gripping the hilts of their swords, and they watched Broderick as if awaiting his command to attack.

The Norman held up his hand, signaling them to stay where they were. "A useless threat," he said calmly, although she could see the fury in his eyes. "I can always marry your cousin, and take the matter of the broken betrothal and Rheged's part in it to the king. I have no doubt John will rule in my favor, and Sir Rheged will pay a heavy price."

"I could beat that lout on my deathbed," Rheged called out hoarsely.

Tamsin whirled around to see her beloved standing at the bottom of the stairs leading to the keep, Gilbert and Hildie hovering anxiously behind him. His pale face shone with the clammy sheen of feverish perspiration and he held on to the railing so tightly his knuckles were as white as his face. In his other hand he held his broadsword.

Despite his obvious illness, there was a stern resolve in his expression that told her why they hadn't been able to keep him in his bed.

"You're too sick to fight anyone, Rheged," she said, starting to go to him.

"Not *him,*" he rasped in reply, pushing away from the steps and walking forward with a slow, deliberate pace, all but dragging his sword, his glazed eyes fixed on Broderick.

"He's going to lose one way or another, my lady," Broderick said with a sneer, "so if he wants to fight today, I have no objections."

"I do!" Tamsin cried, grabbing Rheged's arm to prevent him from going any farther.

Gareth and his men took another step forward. Broderick's men slid them sidelong glances but didn't move.

"I also object," Sir Algar declared as he went to stand in front of them. "It wouldn't be just and you know it, Broderick. Nor would it be wise. You may have influential friends at court, but so do I. I don't think either you or Lord DeLac should be anxious to find out who holds more sway over the king."

"It wouldn't be you."

Although Broderick's tone was bold and mocking, Tamsin saw a shadow of doubt in his eyes that told her he wasn't as confident of the king's support as he maintained. "Then let us take the matter to the king," she proposed.

"No," Rheged growled. "This ends today. I'll win."

"But you're not well!" she insisted, holding his arms and looking into his feverish eyes. "You *mustn't* fight today!"

"Isn't that touching?" Broderick jeered. "Charming, even, how the lovers cling to each other."

Her whole body alive with righteous indignation,

Tamsin whirled around to face him. "The kind of love we share is something you will *never* know, Broderick. Even if you kill Rheged, I will *never* be your wife. I'd rather join a convent. Or die fighting you myself!"

"You? You would challenge me?"

"If I must."

"Impossible," Sir Algar said firmly. "Broderick, as an honorable—"

"He's not honorable!" Tamsin interrupted. "He's a cheat, an arrogant bully, a little boy in a man's body—"

"How dare you speak to me that way?" Broderick demanded.

"I dare because you're a coward!" Tamsin retorted. "I dare because you sicken me. I dare because you're a disgrace. I dare because you don't deserve to be a knight, let alone any woman's husband."

His cheeks fairly quivering with rage, Broderick drew his sword. "You must be mad—and the world will be well rid of you both!"

"Put up!" Sir Algar ordered, raising his hand as he came to stand between them. "This is no—"

Broderick's sword came down hard and fast. Blood gushed from the huge gash sliced through Sir Algar's cloak and the flesh beneath and he fell, groaning, to the ground. Crying out with dismay, Tamsin knelt beside the fallen nobleman and helplessly tried to stanch the flow of blood from his shoulder with her bare hands. Behind her she could hear the movement of men and the jingling of their mail, and the sound of swords being pulled from their scabbards.

And then Rheged's voice, harsh and raw. "Stay back, all of you!" he ordered. "I'm going to kill this dog."

Still trying to stop the bleeding, Tamsin started to stand. Rheged could not fight. Must not fight. Yet already a pale and sweating Rheged, hunched over so that the tip of his blade nearly touched the ground, was circling Broderick like a wolf sizing up its prey.

Gareth and his men moved to form a circle around them, blocking Broderick's soldiers as the two knights faced each other.

Someone lifted her hand from Sir Algar's bloody shoulder.

It was Gilbert, kneeling on the other side of the injured knight. He pressed his hand over the long, terrible wound. "I'll tend to him, my lady," he said softly.

Tamsin straightened just as Broderick lunged at Rheged with his broadsword. But even sick, Rheged was too fast for his opponent. He dodged the blade and lashed out with his own, trying to strike Broderick's legs below the edge of his chain mail.

He missed the man's shin, and when Broderick spun away, Rheged followed him, his sword dipping as if it was too heavy for him to hold.

She must stop this!

Before she could intervene, Rheged raised his sword and brought it down, missing Broderick again. He tried to raise his sword, but it was stuck fast in the space between two cobblestones. As Rheged tried to work it free, Broderick kicked him in the jaw, sending Rheged sprawling.

"For shame!" Tamsin cried as she hurried to help her lover.

Gareth was beside her in an instant, and the rest of

the men Cwm Bron surged forward, muttering with anger and disgust.

Rheged waved them all back. "No!" he hoarsely shouted. "This is my battle to win."

Gareth and his men stayed where they were, although every face made it plain that they wanted to disobey.

Kneeling, Rheged tried once more to free his sword.

"It's your battle to lose," Broderick snarled like the beast he was.

Ignoring him, Tamsin didn't take her eyes from Rheged. "This is my battle, too, Rheged, and I won't let you die."

"Out of the way, bitch!" Broderick ordered before pushing her aside. He kicked Rheged hard on the shoulder, knocking him sideways to the ground. Then he raised his sword, ready to bring it down on Rheged's neck.

With a cry of rage, Tamsin threw herself at Broderick, tackling him and landing so that he was flat on his back and she was atop him. His sword flew from his hands and clattered on the cobblestones. He tried to push her off with one hand while he went for a dagger hidden in his wide sword belt with the other. Tamsin grabbed the wrist of his hand holding the dagger, squeezing and twisting as hard as she could, trying to make him drop the blade or at least push the weapon lower. Grimacing, Broderick tried to shove her arm away. He was strong, but she was desperate, and with the strength of desperation and a cry to heaven to help her, she gave his arm another mighty push.

His mail had bunched higher on his legs, and the dagger plunged into his groin.

With a screech, Broderick bucked her off. Staggering to his feet, he yanked the dagger from his thigh. "You bitch! You damn, stinking bitch!" he cried as blood poured from the wound onto the ground below.

Broderick fell to his knees while Tamsin, panting, struggled to her feet. Broderick's men broke through the barrier the men of Cwm Bron had made and surrounded their fallen leader. Meanwhile Gareth and several of his soldiers hurried to help Rheged stand, and to support her, too.

In all the commotion, her uncle managed to climb onto his horse and turn it toward the gates.

"The judgment is for Rheged," Tamsin called out. "You will bring no charge against him, and Mavis and I are free of any marriage agreement you've made!"

"Be free, then, and be damned, you and that Welshman!" her uncle shouted as his horse snorted and pranced beneath him. "But Mavis is still my daughter and that you cannot change!" he cried, then punched his heels into his horse's side and galloped out of the gate.

Tamsin hurried to the exhausted Rheged being supported by Gareth and Rob. Some of Broderick's men had lifted the nobleman onto their shoulders and were carrying him to his horse.

"Broderick lost," she assured her beloved, for Rheged looked too tired and sick to comprehend all that had happened.

He proved her wrong. "Take me to Algar."

Taking Rob's place, she put her shoulder under Rheged's arm to help him, and with Gareth's help, they made their way to the fallen man. Out of the corner of her eye, Tamsin saw Broderick's men put him down and stand back, as if they feared contagion.

The man's face was pale, his eyes closed, his mouth slack, his chest unmoving and given that great red trail of blood... he was dead. By her hand. She had killed a man. An evil, cruel man, but a man nonetheless.

She turned away. She would deal with her guilt later. For now, her attention must be on Rheged, and Sir Algar lying so gravely wounded where he'd fallen. The physician's medicine chest sat open nearby, and Gilbert had covered the wound with a thick bandage. Still the blood seeped through, and more blood had puddled around Sir Algar's neck and head.

Gilbert didn't have to tell them that time was fast running out for the wounded man.

Kneeling beside Sir Algar, Tamsin took his hand and pressed a kiss upon it. She could feel the pulse in his wrist, faint and very slow.

Algar opened his eyes and turned his head toward her. "I—I loved her," he gasped. "Your mother."

"I know," she whispered.

He shook his head and swallowed. "But I was a coward...not brave enough to fight for her."

"It doesn't matter now," Tamsin assured him.

"That's...not...all. She was with...*my* child...when she fled. You."

Tamsin stared at him in stunned disbelief. It couldn't be true. Even if her parents hadn't told her, surely she would have known...felt...

He nodded and grimaced with pain. "You're mine. My daughter. My heiress. She loved him, too...the man you think...your father. But not as she loved me. My priest…and attorney…they know. They'll swear to it. I went home to get…I brought my will…so you would see…and believe."

He turned his head toward Rheged. "You deserve her. You are…the son I never…so you both have my blessing and…now I die…content."

Whether or not he was her father, Tamsin knew there was one gift she could give the dying man, one that only she could give. "I love you, Father," she whispered, bending to kiss his cheek.

Algar's lips trembled with a smile as his eyes clouded over. Then, with a sigh, he died.

"Oh, Rheged!" Tamsin murmured, turning to him.

To find him lying unconscious in Gareth's arms.

Despite the morning's chill, Mavis paced the wall walk of Castle DeLac, seeking any sign of her father and his escort on the road. Whatever had happened yesterday, whether Broderick had triumphed or Rheged, the men from Castle DeLac would have had to overnight at an inn or tavern somewhere along the road home, so she had spent a sleepless night and come to look for them at the first light of dawn.

Wrapping her cloak more tightly about her, she remembered standing in this very place with Tamsin the day of the tournament, in spite of Tamsin's fear of high places. She recalled how they had watched for the returning knights and squires, and Tamsin's curiosity about Sir Rheged. And what she'd said about cutting his hair. She'd thought of that conversation many times in the past few days, and every time came more and more to believe that perhaps Tamsin had admired the Welsh knight. Maybe it was even possible that she wanted—

A rider came into view.

She leaned out in the crenel between the merlons, trying to see who it was. It looked like her father's horse. Yes, that had to be him—she recognized his cloak. But he was alone, save for two soldiers riding behind him. Tamsin wasn't with him, nor Sir Broderick and all his men.

Did that mean Broderick had lost? Or won?

As the cry went up to open the gates, Mavis ran down the steps, her heart pounding.

Nor was she the only one anxious to find out what had happened. The faces of servants were visible at several windows, and more of the soldiers were in the yard than was usual for that time of day.

She reached the gates just as her father rode through them, nearly knocking her down.

"Father!" she cried as he pulled his horse to a halt. "What happened? Where is Tamsin? And Broderick?"

"Wine! I want wine!" he shouted, all but falling from his horse, his hair disheveled, his clothes little better.

"Father, please! What—"

He glared at her, the fleshy folds of his cheeks quivering with rage. "Broderick is dead. Your damned slut of a cousin killed him.

"That's right, my girl," he snarled, his breath already wine-soaked. "The man's dead, and by your cousin's hand. He was just about to finish the Welshman when she attacked him."

Tamsin had attacked Broderick and killed him? It seemed unbelievable, and yet, if she were desperate…

"They claimed Rheged was too sick to fight. And they call me a cheat!"

"But Rheged's very skilled. He would have no need to cheat. No doubt he—"

Her father gave her a backhanded blow that sent her sprawling to the cobblestones. Out of the corner of her eye, she saw Denly and some of the other servants coming toward her as if they meant to interfere. She waved them back. Her cheek aching, her knees and palms painful, she began to stand.

Her father hauled her upright and glared at her as if he hated her. "I'll wager you think this is the end of it, eh? No more alliance for me in the north. Well, you're wrong. No woman thwarts me! Not you and not Tamsin! Broderick has brothers, and by God, one of them will have you.

"The rest of Broderick's men are on their way back to Dunborough to tell them what's happened. I don't doubt Broderick's brothers will be here soon, and whichever one wants you can have you, by God!"

He shoved her away and started for the hall. "Bring me some wine!" he shouted, his words ringing through the yard.

Mavis watched him go and promised herself that she would be gone before any more men of Dunborough came to Castle DeLac.

Chapter Eighteen

Scattered images came and went in Rheged's mind. Tamsin, her hands red with blood. Broderick threatening. DeLac reeling like a sot in the saddle. Tamsin beside him, murmuring words of love. Heat, then cold, then burning. Tamsin helping him to drink. Broderick on the ground. Tamsin with a bloody dagger. Pain as he tried to swallow. Tamsin urging him to drink. Algar... Broderick...DeLac...Tamsin...

Whoever else came and went, Tamsin was always there, like an angel, clear and visible, worried and gentle. Tamsin. His lover. Beloved.

He opened his eyes and there she was still, a smile on her face and her eyes full of love.

"He's coming round," she said to someone behind her waiting in the shadows of the dim chamber. She cupped his cheek, her touch tender and light. "How do you feel, Rheged?"

He tried to swallow and discovered that while it wasn't easy, it wasn't painful, either, and when he spoke, he didn't feel as if the words were ripping the flesh of his throat. "Better."

Gilbert appeared and gave Rheged a sympathetic smile, his gaze studious as he regarded the Welshman. In his long, slender fingers, he held a metal cup.

"No more talking now, Sir Rheged," he said, his voice like his mien—compassionate, but with iron behind it. "Drink this."

Rheged sat up and raised the cup to his lips. The medicine tasted so vile he nearly spit it out at the first swallow. Yet because Tamsin watched so worriedly, he did as he was told and downed it all.

"Very good, my lord," Gilbert said. "Now if you'll open your mouth, I'll examine your throat."

Rheged submitted as the man produced a twig scraped free of bark, placed it on his tongue and peered inside his mouth.

"Excellent!" Gilbert declared, straightening. "You've made a remarkable recovery. I'm never seen a man so sick get well so quickly!"

"I'm never sick." Rheged started to sit up and found that more difficult than he expected. "I was poisoned."

"No, Rheged, you weren't," Tamsin said.

She glanced at Gilbert, who came forward again. "My lord, you were ill with an infection of the throat, a serious one. The signs and symptoms were unmistakable." He spoke with such confidence, Rheged had to believe he was telling the truth. And yet...

"But I don't get—"

"Yes, you do," Tamsin interrupted with a little smile. "You're mortal after all, my love, and it's no shame to get sick. Now eat some bread and soup. You need to regain your strength."

Hildie appeared at the foot of the bed with a tray bearing beef soup thick with peas and lentils, and a soft bread. It smelled wonderful and Rheged discovered his appetite had returned with a vengeance. Meanwhile, Gilbert packed up his medicinal chest. "I'll leave you now," he said softly. "Remember, my lady, he still needs to rest."

"I'll remember," she replied, and then Hildie, too, left the chamber.

Tamsin sat on the bed to watch Rheged eat. After the first few mouthfuls had taken the edge from his hunger, he asked, "How long was I asleep?"

"It's been two days since you fought Broderick."

"Two days!"

"After the battle, you swooned. Thankfully Gareth was behind you and caught you as you fell. He and some of the others carried you here. Your fever didn't break until dawn this morning. You rested more comfortably after that."

"While you, I think, haven't rested at all."

"I dozed a little this morning."

He tore the loaf in two, set one part down and took a bite of the other. "You should sleep, Tamsin." He gave her a grin. "Beside me, I think."

"You heard Gilbert. You need to rest. I'll sleep later…if I can," she finished in a whisper, with a look in her eyes that told him she was troubled by more than his illness.

"What's wrong? Has your uncle—"

"He hasn't come back, and I doubt he ever will. I think he's had enough of both of us."

She looked down at her clasped hands. "I don't know if you remember, Sir Algar—"

"Is dead," he said solemnly, remembering all too well. "And so is the vicious brute who struck him down, thanks to you."

"Even so, I wish I hadn't killed him."

Rheged gently took her hand. "It is never easy to know a man died at your hands. But if you hadn't killed Broderick, think of the harm he could have done. By your act, you've given all the other women he's wronged in the past a measure of justice, too."

She nodded, his words bringing comfort, and yet... "You called his brothers vipers. Might they not come here seeking vengeance, the same way as Broderick did?"

Rheged toyed with the spoon in his soup as he considered. "It's possible." He set the spoon down. "But I have hope we needn't fear that they'll be overly upset by Broderick's death. It was fairly clear that they hated him, and with good cause."

"I pray you're right!"

"If they try to make trouble, there is still the matter of Sir Algar's murder, for that's what it was."

She rose and walked to the window before she faced him again. "Sir Algar said I was his daughter, yet my mother never once implied that another man might be my father. Granted I was young when she and my—her husband—died, but still! Do you think Sir Algar was right? Or could he have been trying to make amends for abandoning my mother?"

"You never knew about Sir Algar's relationship with your mother?"

Tamsin shook her head. "No. After I met him, it was obvious that he'd cared for her, but I had no idea he wanted to marry her, or that he'd given her up."

"He wasn't the man I thought he was," Rheged murmured with regret.

"Yet I think he paid a heavy price for his cowardice. He's never married another. And whatever he did in his youth, he was a good and kind friend to us."

She covered Rheged's hand with hers. "There is more, Rheged. He brought back his will when he returned the day of the contest, and he names me his daughter and heir to his estate."

"If he's made you his heir, you're rich," Rheged said, happy for her until the full import of what Sir Algar had done hit him like an avalanche. Now that she was wealthy, men would flock to marry her. Men with large estates. Handsome men, powerful men. Men with more to offer. "That makes me your liegeman, my lady."

She frowned. "Liegeman? Are you not going to be my husband?"

"You accepted my offer when you were poor and without family. You're rich now, Tamsin. You can have any man for the choosing."

Her smile lit the chamber and made him feel like singing. "Then I choose Sir Rheged of Cwm Bron, who is rich in goodness, rich in honor, rich in all the ways that truly matter. Indeed I think I am the pauper here."

"You were rich the first day I met you," he replied. "Rich in spirit, rich in intelligence, rich in compassion."

"Rich in desire."

He put the tray on the table beside the bed and reached for her. "Rich in love."

She pulled back and shook her head, although with obvious reluctance. "You're supposed to rest, Rheged."

"Then get in bed and rest with me, for tomorrow, we must wed."

"Tomorrow?"

"You have some reason to wait, my lady?"

"You've been very ill."

"I'm getting better by the minute," he murmured, his actions giving some evidence that he was indeed much better.

"It's very tempting, my lord, my love, especially since I found this in your belt." With love glowing in her eyes, she reached into the cuff of her sleeve and pulled out the lock of hair she had left in the box on the shelf.

"I've never had a talisman before, but I thought I should have one when I fought Broderick, and what better?"

"I didn't know you'd found it."

He smiled, embarrassed, yet unrepentant. "I didn't. Hildie gave it to me and told me what it was when she was trying to get me to stay in bed. Apparently she thought if I had a reminder of you, I would be less inclined to risk dying. The poor woman didn't realize I would have no life worth living without you."

"Nor I without you," she replied, lifting the blanket and laying down beside him.

"You're still dressed," he noted with disappointment as he put his arm around her.

She nestled closer and laid her head on his shoulder. "It's rest you need, Rheged, and it's rest you're going to have," she replied, yawning, and gently removing his hand from her breast.

He didn't feel tired, but she obviously was, so he kissed the top of her head and said no more.

Hildie looked down at the sleeping couple and nudged Elvina. "What did I tell you? Lovers for days. I knew it the moment I saw the way he looked at her."

"And she at him," Elvina said with a sigh.

There was a rap at the door and both maidservants turned to see Gareth standing on the threshold.

Hildie ran up to him and pushed him out of the chamber. "They're asleep and they both need their rest, you great ox."

"Then what are you two doing here?" he demanded, hands on his hips.

"Leaving!" Hildie retorted, pulling the door closed after Elvina joined her and giving him another shove that made him back down a step. "And you're not to bother them again."

"I need the watchword for tonight," he protested.

"Are you that stupid you can't make one up yourself?" Hildie retorted before, giving him another little push.

"Watch it, woman, or you're going to break my neck."

"Then get out of our way."

Gareth pressed himself back against the curved wall to let Hildie and Elvina pass. When Elvina went to go by, he smiled at the shy, quiet young woman.

Blushing very prettily, Elvina lowered her head and hurried on her way.

A frown creased Gareth's forehead as he watched her go. "Might as well celebrate two weddings with one feast, if she'll have me," he murmured.

Then, being Gareth, he grinned.

Mavis pulled the hood of her black woollen cloak over her head and clutched the small bundle to her chest as she cautiously made her way down the servants' stairs and into the yard. In the east, the sky was just beginning to lighten. If she were a better rider, she would have risked fleeing Castle DeLac in the darkest hours, but she had to take a fast horse, and had not the skill to risk speed without sunlight. She'd already lost one night because of the weather; she couldn't risk waiting for another chance.

Fortunately she had never been one to rise early, not even after Tamsin had been taken, so she could hope that she wouldn't be missed until terce. By then, if she took her father's best horse, she could be far away.

She must be far away.

She waited in the shadows until she saw the guard pass, then scurried across the space between the family apartments and the woolshed. She had to wait another few moments while another guard passed on the wall walk above before she dashed across the alley and slipped into the stable.

It took a few moments for her eyes to adjust, her heart and thoughts racing while she waited, holding tight to her bundle.

She had only another shift and pair of shoes, a flint, some jewelry and a few coins in the bundle. She prayed God that would be enough to keep her until she could find sanctuary at a convent or other religious house. Not one close by where her father could find her, and perhaps force the sisters to return her, though.

She'd considered heading for Cwm Bron. Her cousin would surely take her in and protect her as best she could, but Mavis didn't want to risk involving her cousin in her escape. Let Tamsin be safe and perhaps even happy with—

A horse shifted restlessly in the stable closest to her. Perhaps she'd startled it. She looked up at the hatch to the loft overhead where the stable boys and grooms slept.

Nothing. Only silence. She started to breathe again, until the horse whinnied and straw rustled and a deep voice said, "Steady, Hephaestus!"

Who was *that*? She didn't recognize the voice, so it couldn't be one of the grooms or soldiers. And the accent was that of a Yorkshireman. Whoever it was, she mustn't be seen, so she pressed herself farther back in the doorway. She didn't dare open the door and slip out, lest she be heard and her plan thwarted.

"What's disturbed you, eh?" the man continued, his voice low and gentle. "Strange stable, is that it? And ridden too hard and too fast for too long? Well, I shall make it up to you, any road. I'll see if there's an apple in the kitchen to spare."

Able to see better now, Mavis could make out the shape of a man near the head of the horse in the stable. He was tall and broad-shouldered and fairly young, to judge by his voice, although certainly no lad.

She watched as he came out of the stable and went to the trough, where he splashed water on his face and neck. Straightening, he shook himself like a dog and then raked his hair back with his fingers.

By the saints, it was nearly as long as Sir Rheged's!

The stranger straightened his tunic, which seemed to be fairly plain, then reached back into the stable for a sword belt that he buckled around his narrow waist. His nose was straight and his jaw strong, his lips unexpectedly full. His eyes were large and as dark as the eyebrows above them.

"I'll see about that apple now," he said to the horse. "But you must be patient, Heffy. I am a very important fellow, you know, and I cannot appear to be begging."

He said the last with a wry, self-mocking tone that made Mavis even more curious.

The man went to the door leading to the yard, but before he opened it, he rotated his head and rolled his shoulders, then tugged down his tunic and took a deep breath. It was like watching one of the entertainers at a feast prepare for his performance.

"Is there something you need, my lady?"

With a gasp, she looked up to see at the round, middle-aged and bearded face of the head groom peering down at her from the open hatch above, and her plans to flee evaporated. "Oh, Allen, there you are!" she cried, making it sound like she'd come to speak to him on purpose.

"You heard that Sir Roland arrived in the night, then?"

Sir Roland? It was a not-uncommon name, but no specific Roland came to mind.

"Charlie told you, I suppose," Allen continued. "I hope he didn't disturb you, my lady. Sir Roland said you wasn't to be disturbed or any fuss made. He said he'd sleep in the stable with his horse. Fine animal, that, I must say!"

She was tempted to agree, and she didn't mean the horse. "Did he ride far yesterday?" she asked as Allen came down the ladder that creaked beneath his weight.

"I don't think he stopped more'n twice all the way from Dunborough."

Mavis's throat suddenly went dry. She swallowed hard, then tried to sound calm. "Dunborough?"

"That's what he said. He's related to that Broderick, I take it."

"He might be his brother."

Allen frowned. "Hope he's not going to make trouble for you and your father, my lady."

"I hope so, too." She turned to go.

"Need that taken somewhere, do you?"

She paused and turned around, eyeing the groom quizzically. He nodded at the bundle in her hands.

"No, no, it's just some things for the poor," she lied. "I was on my way to take it to the chapel for Father Bryan when I thought I heard someone in the stable. It must have been Sir Roland. Now I had best get to the chapel, and then I must see to the accommodation for our guest." She gave the groom a smile. "I still don't know how Tamsin managed to do all that she did."

"You're doing fine, my lady," Allen assured her. "Everybody says so, especially since your father… That is, His Lordship's not…"

"No, he's not," Mavis agreed before she left the stable and cautiously started back the way she'd come, doing her best to avoid being seen by any of the servants who were stirring.

Her escape would have to wait one more day. It was unfortunate, but there was nothing she could do, so she went back to her chamber with her bundle.

Once there, she hid the bundle beneath her bed again before changing her gown from the simple, coarse traveling gown of heavy wool she'd been wearing to a more expensive, prettier one of a delicate green, like leaves in the spring. After all, it would look suspicious if she wore that brown gown, and if the green one was a little fine for daily wear, well, it was the first one she'd seen in her clothes chest.

She had barely finished tying the front laces of the bodice when there was a quick knock on the door. She opened it to find Charlie standing there, hopping from foot to foot as if the soles of his shoes were on fire. "If you please, my lady, you're to go to the solar. Right away."

"But surely my father—"

"He's awake, my lady, and shouting for you. He's in a right foul temper, my lady."

Perhaps Sir Roland had insisted on speaking with him at once.

Although there was no one nearby, Charlie dropped his voice to a whisper. "Denly's in the hall and he says you're to call him if you need him."

If her father struck her again, or tried to hurt her, he meant. She was grateful for the offer, but her father was rarely sober enough to harm anyone these days. Nevertheless she said, "Thank you, Charlie, and tell Denly

I'll remember," before she gathered up her skirts and hurried past him.

Once at the solar door, she took a moment to calm herself, then entered.

A broad-shouldered man with hair to his shoulders was standing with his back to the door, his arms crossed over his chest as he faced her father. He was seated behind the vast table and looked worse than usual, his face mottled, his nose red, his eyes overly moist, his clothes stained and soiled. He hadn't even bothered to change since he returned from Cwn Bron, and he hadn't stopped drinking, either.

She didn't have to see the features of the man standing in front of him to know it was Sir Roland of Dunborough. She could tell by his broad shoulders, long legs and hair to his shoulders.

"Sir Roland," her father slurred with a wave of his hand, "my daughter, Mavis."

The younger man turned, and his deep brown eyes widened. "You are more beautiful than they told me," he said with obvious surprise. Then it was as if a door had closed, for his expression became as grave as a bishop's.

"I am delighted to meet you, my lady," he continued, his tone as formal as his bow.

"And I, you, my lord," she replied with equal formality.

Her father reached for the wine goblet at his elbow. "She's yours if you want her, Sir Roland. Same terms, same dowry, as your father agreed to for Tamsin."

Still looking gravely at Mavis, Sir Roland didn't so much as glance at her father as he replied. "I shall be honored to have this lady for my wife." Then, for just a moment, the gentle man in the stable returned as he lowered his voice and said, "If she will be pleased to accept me."

"Of course she will," her father exclaimed. "It's that or a convent."

When Mavis answered, she spoke not to her father, but to Roland of Dunborough. "I accept, my lord."

Chapter Nineteen

Some time had passed before Rheged and Tamsin finally left the bedchamber and made their way to the hall below. Servants and soldiers greeted their arrivals with clapping, stamping and cheers, much to Tamsin's blushing delight and, she could tell, Rheged's pleasure. He held up his hands for silence, and when the noise had mostly died down, he said, "I'm glad to see you all, and so is my lady, who will become my wife on the morrow."

There were more cheers and clapping after that announcement, as well as calls for wine to toast Sir Rheged and his bride. Hildie, Elvina and a few other servants hurried to fill the goblets, including those on the table where Rheged and Tamsin would sit.

Tamsin thought of one man who should be there, and sighed.

Rheged squeezed her hand. "He's pleased, I'm sure," he said quietly, giving her a little smile.

"I'm sure he is, too," she replied.

The soldiers and those servants not serving had

likewise taken their places, except for Gareth, who remained on his feet. "We wish you joy, my lord, my lady, and plenty of children to come!"

Again Tamsin felt the heat of a blush and the squeeze of Rheged's hand before he rose and gravely said, "I shall do my best."

The hall filled with laughter and the general cacophony of several people talking at once, while the bread and trenchers and thick stew began to arrive. The meal was a long and lively one, yet all the while Tamsin was mindful of Rheged beside her, his apparent good health and what that might mean when they retired.

She was just about to suggest they do when Gareth, somewhat the worse for wine, made his way toward the table. He leaned over, close to Rheged. "My friend, I have something to tell you."

Her husband-to-be raised an eyebrow.

"I took a wife today."

Although she, too, was startled, Rheged almost fell off the stool. "You...what?" he demanded as if Gareth had announced he was starting his own crusade.

Gareth turned and called out to Elvina. Blushing bright red, the young woman drew closer. "Have no fear, my love, he won't bite," Gareth said with a laugh. "I thought I'd follow your example, Rheged. Elvina agreed to be my wife and we said the vows, so...I'm married."

The silent Rheged still looked stunned.

"I'm so happy for you both!" Tamsin cried, rising and hurrying to embrace the shy maidservant and Gareth, too. She faced her husband. "We have even more reason to have a feast tomorrow!"

"Aye, yes, aye!" Rheged said like a man waking from

a long sleep. Rising, he said something in Welsh and didn't even take the time to go around the table, but climbed right over it to clap his friend on the shoulder. Then he laughed and said, "For once you beat me, eh, Gareth?"

The two men laughed, and embraced, and soon were drinking to each other's health and good fortune while the women who loved them looked on indulgently and smiled.

And Hildie moved a little closer to the oblivious Rob.

The next day Rheged and Tamsin, dressed in their finest, stood on the newly built dais in the hall of Cwm Bron. As they faced each other, Father Godwin, who'd come from a nearby monastery at their request, blessed their union as well as the ring Rheged placed on Tamsin's finger. It was a plain band made of gold, yet to her, it was more beautiful and worth far more than if it had been made of diamonds, and when they kissed, it was to seal a union she knew would last till death.

Below the dais, the tables were spread with clean linen, the torches and new candles burned brightly, a fire crackled in the scrubbed hearth, and loaves of bread and fruit in baskets had already been put out. The table where Rheged and Tamsin were to sit was decorated with bunches of evergreen boughs, the scent adding to the various delicious smells emanating from the kitchen.

"I should have known you could prepare for a wedding feast at a moment's notice," Rheged said after the ceremony was over and they took their places for the wedding feast.

"I didn't do this," she protested. "I haven't had the

time." She nodded at Hildie, grinning like a fiend at the kitchen entrance. Other servants were in the hall, and while all were happy, only Hildie bore a look of proud satisfaction. "I think this must be Hildie's doing."

"However it happened, I'm grateful," Rheged said before the priest began to bless the meal.

Rheged felt nearly completely well. He might have felt even better if he'd stopped celebrating Gareth's marriage and gone to sleep sooner, but that would have meant ignoring Tamsin, or trying to, when they went up to the bedchamber. Trying not to touch her had been difficult before; once she slipped into bed beside him, it had been impossible. Nor did she even try to talk him out of making love, perhaps because she was just as eager and full of desire as he.

Gareth and Elvina sat together nearby. Gareth didn't appear to be suffering any ill effects from the night before, and Elvina looked radiant with happiness.

Rob led another rousing cheer for both the grooms and their brides, and then the feasting and drinking and celebrating began in earnest. The soldiers toasted their leader so many times it seemed Rheged could barely get a bite to eat. Tamsin laughed at their jokes, and more when Rheged blushed at some of them.

"I'll speak to them tomorrow about the respect due to their lord and his wife," he muttered under his breath after Dan made one particularly bawdy jest.

"Fear not, my lord," she replied, lightly resting her hand on his thigh. "I've been dealing with merchants, servants and soldiers for years. While they often curbed their tongue when I was near, they weren't successful every time. I daresay I could tell you a few worldly tales that would make theirs seem fit for a nursery."

Rheged regarded her with a mixture of awe and dismay. "You could?" Then his eyes grew bright with amusement, and something more besides that made her blood warm. "You must share them with me later," he whispered, leaning closer, "when we're alone."

"I hope that will be soon, my lord."

"As do I, beloved, as do I. I suppose we shouldn't alarm the priest, though."

"I suppose not." Tamsin nodded down the hall, where Hildie was now sitting on Rob's lap and laughing. "I think there might be another bride and groom before long."

"Perhaps marriage is catching. I certainly never thought Gareth would tie himself to one woman."

"Are you comparing marriage to bondage, my lord?" she asked with bogus dismay.

"If it is, I'm happily bound to you and never want to be free again."

As they smiled at each other, one of the guards from the gate entered the hall and trotted toward the dais.

Tamsin sat up straighter and glanced at Rheged with genuine concern. "Do you suppose something's wrong? Perhaps my uncle—"

"I'm sure it's nothing," Rheged replied. "Indeed I realize now I forgot to give the guards the watchword for the night." His grin took away her fear, and his next words made her smile. "For some reason, I seem to have had other things on my mind. I believe it will be…joyous happiness."

"That seems a rather lighthearted password," she replied with apparent solemnity.

"Perhaps you're right," he mused, likewise apparently serious. "It will be..." He hesitated a long moment. "I can't seem to think of anything suitably serious."

By then the guard had reached the dais. He leaned over the table so that only Rheged and Tamsin could hear. "There's a fellow seeking entrance at the gate, my lord, says he's Roland of Dunborough."

Tamsin's stomach knotted, her happiness overcome by dread.

"How many men does he have with him?" Rheged demanded, getting to his feet, his hand moving instinctively to his hip where the hilt of his sword should be.

"None, my lord. It's just him—but he's a tough-looking sort!"

Rheged's shoulders relaxed a little. "Let him through the gate. I'll speak with him in the yard." He noticed Gareth, who had risen, too, and gestured for him to sit. "Another guest, that's all, and one I should greet," he explained loudly, then spoke more quietly to Tamsin. She, too, had gotten to her feet. "If he's come alone, there's no need for you—"

"I'm your wife, Rheged," she gently, but firmly, interrupted. "Anything that concerns you concerns me."

"You won't stay here even if I command it, will you?"

"You should know the answer to that by now."

With a sound that was a cross between a snort and a laugh, he took her hand and led her from the hall, but not before she saw him slip his eating knife into his belt. Nevertheless he acted as if nothing was amiss as they passed Gareth.

"What's happened?" he asked, frowning and nodding at the guard who was downing a mug of ale.

"I never gave the men a watchword for the night, and Tamsin wants to—"

"Look at the stars," she finished for him.

"Oh, watchwords and stargazing, is it?" Gareth said with a wry expression. "Well, if you say so."

"I do," Rheged replied gravely, taking Tamsin's hand.

"What *is* the watchword? Love and marriage? Babies to come?"

"Old dog, new tricks," Rheged replied.

Gareth's roar of amusement followed them from the hall.

Tamsin and Rheged warily approached the man standing in the center of the courtyard beside a magnificent black stallion. The fellow's gaze wandered over the keep and the walls until he saw them. After that Sir Roland waited as motionless as one of the statues in a churchyard, and his horse was just as still.

As they drew nearer, the man's features became clearer. Tamsin had thought Rheged's visage grim and hard, but it was only because she hadn't met Roland of Dunborough. Tall as Rheged, broad-shouldered, narrow-hipped, his hair dark, as were his hooded eyes, Roland looked as if he had never smiled in his life and never would.

Which was a pity, she thought, for otherwise he was a handsome man who looked nothing like his older brother.

"Greetings, Sir Roland," Rheged said when they

reached him. "My lady, this is Sir Roland of Dunborough. Sir Roland, this is Lady Thomasina, my wife."

He spoke the last word fiercely, as if challenging the man to refute it.

Roland did not. He ran a gaze over Tamsin that was so lacking any emotion or expression Tamsin shivered.

"My lady, a pleasure. My lord, we meet again," Roland said, his voice deep and just as lacking in emotion. "I received word of my brother's death from Lord DeLac. He implied there was some…irregularity… during a trial by combat."

"Your brother was trying to kill my wife until she stopped him with a dagger he'd concealed in his sword belt," Rheged replied bluntly.

"He was about to kill Sir Rheged, who was in no condition to fight that day, as your brother well knew, and I tried to stop him," Tamsin added.

Roland sniffed with disdain and for a terrible moment, Tamsin feared he was going to accuse them both of murder, until Roland said, "I could expect no better from that blackguard."

Rheged had obviously been right—there was no love lost between Sir Blane's sons.

"He also brutally attacked my overlord, Sir Algar, without warning or just cause. The wound was mortal," Rheged said.

"Ah, yes. I was sorry to hear of that. As to my brother's end…" He turned to Tamsin and regarded her steadily. "For that, my lady, I thank you."

Because he was now the lord of their father's demesne, if he was the elder twin after all? Or because he hadn't loved his brother?

She would well believe Roland of Dunborough did not, and never could, love anybody.

"So, are you the next in line, or is it Gerrard?" Rheged asked.

"According to my father's will, I entered the world first. Is Broderick's grave marked?"

Tamsin and Rheged exchanged looks. "We'll have a stone carved."

"Spare yourself the expense. Let him lie unmarked."

Given that vengeance for his brother's death was obviously not Roland's reason for coming to Cwm Bron, and although she would rather not see much more of the man, courtesy demanded that she offer any nobleman the hospitality of the household. "Would you care to join us in the hall, my lord?"

Even as she asked the question, the door of the kitchen opened and Foster, covered in flour, came reeling out wielding a loaf of bread like a weapon. He paused, stared at them a moment, then went reeling back inside.

One corner of Roland's mouth lifted in what might have been the beginning of a smile. "I think not." His grim expression returned. "I came here to assure myself that my brother's body would be treated as it deserved, and to thank you for ridding the world of him. He was a villain from the time he could talk. I won't mourn Broderick, and neither should anyone else."

A great weight seemed to lift from Tamsin, and she could see that Rheged was relieved, too.

"Thank you, my lord," she said, "for easing my mind."

"I gather there has also been some animosity between Lord DeLac and you both over the matter of your betrothal to my father, and then my brother, my lady," Roland continued. "That has also been…" Again his lip lifted ever so slightly. "Dealt with."

Another chill that had nothing to do with the air seemed to blow over Tamsin. "How?"

The man raised an eyebrow.

She swallowed and forced herself to speak with more courtesy. "I beg your pardon for my blunt question, but may we know how the matter has been resolved to your satisfaction? After all, it has caused us a great deal of trouble."

"Lady Mavis and I are to marry."

Mavis—merry, laughing, pretty Mavis—wed to this…this effigy? "Has she given her consent?"

A little furrow of puzzlement appeared between Roland's dark eyebrows.

"My lord, I hope you'll make sure she's willing before you consider the betrothal certain. If she's not, I pray you'll do the honorable thing and allow her to refuse."

"I have no wish to force a marriage," Roland replied, much to Tamsin's relief. "I was there when her father told her of the betrothal and she made no objection."

Tamsin imagined Mavis standing in her father's solar, with her father and especially this Roland, with those cold, dark eyes, looking at her. Mavis had no doubt been too intimidated to speak freely. Fortunately the marriage hadn't happened yet, so there was still time for Mavis to object.

"But if you discover she doesn't want to be your

bride," Tamsin persisted despite his unfriendly mien, "you will release her?"

The man drew himself up even straighter, although she would have thought that impossible. "My lady, while I appreciate your concern for your cousin's feelings, I believe that whatever happens between that lady and me is our business, not yours. Now, since I've obtained the information I sought, I shall go." He bowed stiffly. "Farewell, my lord, my lady. I hope you will do us the honor of attending the wedding when the time comes."

"Of course, my lord," Tamsin replied, silently adding, *If it ever does.*

Roland didn't wait for them to respond before he mounted his midnight-black stallion and rode out the gates.

As the sound of his horse's hoofbeats disappeared in the distance, Tamsin turned to Rheged and regarded him with dismay. "Mavis betrothed to that man! We must stop it!"

To her even greater dismay, Rheged didn't seem as convinced of this as he should be.

"I'm not certain it's our place to interfere."

"You interfered in my betrothal," she reminded him.

"Because, my lady, I was already in love with you."

She smiled, but only for a moment. "I love Mavis like a sister. We must help her!"

"You heard him. She's given her consent."

"She was probably forced, as I was forced. Or too frightened to refuse with that…that *gargoyle* glaring at her. And he's from that brood of vipers."

"I shouldn't have included Roland in that description. Of all Blane's sons, he was the only one who was never cruel. Stern, I grant you, and cold, but not vicious or a wastrel, like Gerrard, and compared to Broderick, he's a saint. And it should also be a comfort to know that from what I've heard about Roland, although he's had a mistress or two, your cousin need not fear he'll have a slew of lovers and illegitimate children."

"But to think of her married to that man!"

"Since we're to go to the wedding, you can surely arrange a few moments alone with her before the ceremony to assure yourself she truly wants to marry him, or to offer her sanctuary if she does not. After all, she's my cousin, too, now. And," he added with a smile, "since my wife has brought me a considerable dowry, I should have some influence at court, as well."

"I hadn't thought of that!" She sighed as he embraced her and held her close. "I have another reason to bless Algar." She smiled up at him. "And you. Indeed I feel so blessed, it seems greedy to want more, and yet I do."

"What is it you'd like, Tamsin?" he asked as he kissed her lightly on the cheek. "Tell me, and I'll do my best to get it for your wedding present."

"I hope you will do your utmost, husband, because what I want is a child. *Our* child."

He laughed softly. "Now, that is a request I'll be most happy to attempt to fulfill." Then he drew back and she was surprised to see how serious he'd become. "I do foresee one difficulty, love of my heart. Once our child is born, you'll be so busy tending it and running the household, I'll hardly ever see you."

"Is that all?" she chided with a look full of love before giving him another tender kiss. "I promise you, my lord, my love, that I'll always have time for you. And we'll always be alone in bed."

Laughing softly, arm in arm, they took a moment to look up at the stars before they returned to the hall and all the household of Cwm Bron celebrating there.

* * * * *

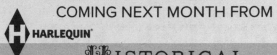
Available July 15, 2014

SALVATION IN THE RANCHER'S ARMS
by Kelly Boyce
(Western)

Rachel Sutter's world is turned upside down when enigmatic drifter Caleb Beckett rides into Salvation Falls. There's something about him that she's instinctively drawn to, but is he someone she can trust?

THE RAKE'S RUINED LADY
by Mary Brendan
(Regency)

Beatrice Dewey keeps falling for unsuitable men, and Hugh Kendrick, trailing rumors of illicit love affairs in his wake, is no exception! Will Bea give in to his skillful seduction?

BEGUILED BY HER BETRAYER
by Louise Allen
(Regency)

Lord Quintus Bredon Deverall has arrived in Egypt intending to escort Cleo Valsac back to England. But soon the passion between them begins to burn under the heat of the desert sun!

NEVER FORGET ME
by Marguerite Kaye
(First World War)

Three emotionally powerful stories set against the backdrop of the First World War. As war blazes across Europe, three couples find a love that is powerful enough to overcome all the odds....

REQUEST YOUR FREE BOOKS!

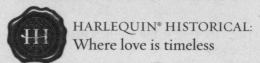

HARLEQUIN® HISTORICAL:
Where love is timeless

2 FREE NOVELS PLUS 2 **FREE GIFTS!**

YES! Please send me 2 FREE Harlequin® Historical novels and my 2 FREE gifts (gifts are worth about $10). After receiving them, if I don't wish to receive any more books, I can return the shipping statement marked "cancel." If I don't cancel, I will receive 6 brand-new novels every month and be billed just $5.44 per book in the U.S. or $5.74 per book in Canada. That's a savings of at least 16% off the cover price! It's quite a bargain! Shipping and handling is just 50¢ per book in the U.S. and 75¢ per book in Canada.* I understand that accepting the 2 free books and gifts places me under no obligation to buy anything. I can always return a shipment and cancel at any time. Even if I never buy another book, the two free books and gifts are mine to keep forever.

246/349 HDN F4ZY

Name	(PLEASE PRINT)

Address	Apt. #

City	State/Prov.	Zip/Postal Code

Signature (if under 18, a parent or guardian must sign)

Mail to the **Harlequin® Reader Service:**
IN U.S.A.: P.O. Box 1867, Buffalo, NY 14240-1867
IN CANADA: P.O. Box 609, Fort Erie, Ontario L2A 5X3

Want to try two free books from another line?
Call 1-800-873-8635 or visit www.ReaderService.com.

* Terms and prices subject to change without notice. Prices do not include applicable taxes. Sales tax applicable in N.Y. Canadian residents will be charged applicable taxes. Offer not valid in Quebec. This offer is limited to one order per household. Not valid for current subscribers to Harlequin Historical books. All orders subject to credit approval. Credit or debit balances in a customer's account(s) may be offset by any other outstanding balance owed by or to the customer. Please allow 4 to 6 weeks for delivery. Offer available while quantities last.

Your Privacy—The Harlequin® Reader Service is committed to protecting your privacy. Our Privacy Policy is available online at www.ReaderService.com or upon request from the Harlequin Reader Service.

We make a portion of our mailing list available to reputable third parties that offer products we believe may interest you. If you prefer that we not exchange your name with third parties, or if you wish to clarify or modify your communication preferences, please visit us at www.ReaderService.com/consumerchoice or write to us at Harlequin Reader Service Preference Service, P.O. Box 9062, Buffalo, NY 14269. Include your complete name and address.

HH13R

*Next month, don't miss Marguerite Kaye's
heart-wrenchingly emotional new anthology,
NEVER FORGET ME. Set against a backdrop of
the First World War, these three linked novellas explore
desire, loss and love that's worth risking everything for.*

It had been a mistake, asking him to dance. It made it impossible for her to ignore the fact that she was attracted to him. She liked the soft burr of his accent, which made her think of misty Scottish glens and rugged Highland scenery. She liked the combination of auburn hair and grey-blue eyes and the latent strength she could feel in that lean, hard body. She liked the hint of sensuality in his unsmiling mouth. For once, she saw not the soldier but the man.

And she so desperately wanted to be held. Not to think. Just to be held. Sylvie relaxed a little, allowing him to draw her closer. He smelled of expensive soap, unlike most of the soldiers, and also a little of that dank, muddy smell that clung to all of them. But mostly he smelled intoxicatingly male.

She closed her eyes. She forgot she was in the club. She forgot the guilt at being alive that dogged her every waking moment. She forgot everything save for the delightful heat in her blood caused by this man's arms around her, this man's body sheltering her, waking the desire that had long lain dormant, making her want to lose herself in passion.

The music stopped. They stood still, two figures frozen in time. And then the music started again and they moved in rhythm, unspeaking, eyes closed, not dancing but holding, touching. His fingers played on her spine. Hers slid down to cup the taut slope of his buttocks beneath his tunic. His lips fluttered over her temple. She put her mouth to the rough skin of his throat. He was aroused. It had been so long since she had experienced the delicious frisson of such intimacy. So very, very long since she had even thought about it.

He was thinking about it, too. He could have stopped dancing at the last song, at the one before or the one before that, but each time the music started up again he pulled her closer. Then the music stopped for the last time, and they were left alone on the dance floor.

"I don't want to let you go," Robbie said, "not just yet."

"Then walk me back to my apartment," Sylvie said, without even considering the dangers of being alone with this stranger, a stranger who had been trained to kill without compunction. A man who represented all she hated and all that had damaged her life irrevocably. A soldier. A warmonger. But tonight, she found that she didn't want to be alone either.

Don't miss
NEVER FORGET ME,
available from Harlequin® Historical
August 2014.

COMING IN AUGUST 2014

Beguiled by Her Betrayer
by Louise Allen

WHAT USE ARE DRAWING-ROOM MANNERS
IN THE MIDDLE OF THE DESERT?

Falling unconscious in the Egyptian sand at Cleo Valsac's feet is *not* part of Lord Quintus Bredon Deverall's plan. He's *supposed* to be whisking this young widow away from her father's dusty camp and back to England—to her aristocratic grandfather and a respectable husband.

Despite her strong-willed nature, Cleo can't help but feel comforted by Quin's protective presence. But she has no idea of this wounded stranger's true identity—or of the passion that will begin to burn between them under the heat of the desert sun!

Available wherever books and ebooks are sold.

HARLEQUIN®

ℋISTORICAL

Where love is timeless

COMING IN AUGUST 2014
Salvation in the Rancher's Arms
by Kelly Boyce

HE HAD MORE THE EDGE OF AN OUTLAW THAN A SHINING KNIGHT.

Rachel Sutter's world is turned upside down when Caleb Beckett rides into Salvation Falls. He brings news of a poker game gone disastrously wrong—not only has her wastrel husband been killed, he's also gambled away Rachel's home!

Suddenly, Rachel is left with nothing but an unpaid debt, and Caleb is holding all the cards—not to mention the deed to her land. There's something about the enigmatic drifter that she is instinctively drawn to, but how can she begin to trust him when so much of his past is shrouded in mystery?

Available wherever books and ebooks are sold.

www.Harlequin.com

HH29795